Praise for *Sub*

"A cheerfully campy take on the usual concerns—conformity, boredom, demonic possession."　　　　　*—Chicago Tribune*

"This delightful fiction debut is the hell-arious *Desperate Housewives*–esque novel that dreams are made of."　　　*—BuzzFeed*

"A delightful, fun, spooky, scary story. At its core it's about friendship and the bonds of love for these four women. Maureen has hit a home run with her first novel."　　　*—Red Carpet Crash*

"This novel about the horrors of suburbia—both supernatural and terrestrial in origin—has plenty of genuinely funny moments. . . . A good fit for fans of Grady Hendrix's *My Best Friend's Exorcism*, Rachel Harrison's *The Return*, or Junji Ito's horror manga *Uzumaki*."　　　　　　　　　*—Booklist*

"A savvy, wildly relatable horror-comedy about suburban angst and the bonds of friendship that serves chilling scares and genuine laughs. Massively entertaining and fun as hell!"
　　　　　　—Rachel Harrison, author of *Such Sharp Teeth*

"Maureen Kilmer strikes the perfect balance in *Suburban Hell*. This is a scary, thrilling, and funny ride through a neighborhood nightmare. The pages turn themselves, you can't stop reading this one."　　　—Samantha Downing, author of *For Your Own Good*

Hex
Education

Hex Education

A NOVEL

Maureen Kilmer

G. P. PUTNAM'S SONS
NEW YORK

PUTNAM
— EST. 1838 —

G. P. Putnam's Sons
Publishers Since 1838
An imprint of Penguin Random House LLC
penguinrandomhouse.com

Library of Congress Cataloging-in-Publication Data

Names: Kilmer, Maureen, author.
Title: Hex education : a novel / Maureen Kilmer.
Description: New York : G. P. Putnam's Sons, 2023. |
Identifiers: LCCN 2023028524 (print) | LCCN 2023028525 (ebook) |
ISBN 9780593422397 (trade paperback) | ISBN 9780593422403 (ebook)
Subjects: LCGFT: Witch fiction. | Novels.
Classification: LCC PS3612.I635 H49 2023 (print) | LCC PS3612.I635 (ebook) |
DDC 813/.6—dc23/eng/20230622
LC record available at https://lccn.loc.gov/2023028524
LC ebook record available at https://lccn.loc.gov/2023028525

Printed in the United States of America
1st Printing

Title page illustration by Sensvector/Shutterstock.com

For Ryan, Paige, and Jake.
May you always believe in magic.

Hex
Education

BEFORE

No one is going to believe we're a juggling club."

I looked over at my friend Alicia. Her face was illuminated by the flames that climbed high above Hawthorne Hall, our dorm, as we stood out on the quad in the chilly autumn night wearing Adidas shower sandals and fluffy slippers. Fire trucks wailed in the distance as they rushed to contain the blaze.

"We just need to keep quiet," Katrina said from my left. "We didn't see anything. We don't know anything."

We were innocent. That was the story we would tell for the next two decades. Just three freshmen who had formed a juggling club, having their usual weekly Saturday night meeting, when a totally unrelated fire broke out.

Juggling club.

Not casting spells.

Not practicing witchcraft.

Definitely not a coven.

As the firefighters sprayed the blaze with water, windows burst, glass rained down onto the sidewalk, and brick crumbled.

EMTs with stretchers raced into the charred building, looking to rescue victims.

"How could this have happened?" I whispered, but neither of my friends answered. "No one was supposed to get hurt." I looked down at my arm, at where I had been burned when the fire started, not really comprehending how badly I was injured.

We thought the magic was harmless, that our coven was a hobby—basically, just an extracurricular activity. Except what we were actually juggling—at least at first—was candles purchased at Walmart, lit with a pack of matches swiped from Hole in the Wall, a bar that served $1 beers and played Dr. Dre, and words that we twisted from books and movies about witches.

The three of us clasped hands as we silently watched the fire that we had started, the magic still coursing between us, begging to be released.

Chapter 1

TWENTY YEARS LATER

A truly magical living space . . .

My computer cursor blinked at me, taunting me with a blank page. Daring me to write the perfect description for my newest real estate listing.

On the outside, the house was beautiful. It was a sage-green American Foursquare with a dormer window sprouting out of the center of the roof and a black front door encased by a large porch. I flipped through the information packet, glancing at each picture.

I had chosen not to include any images of the inside in the listing. The property had sat empty for three years, the house beginning its slow decline without anyone who loved it, someone to take care of it. It would require a lot of renovations, if not a total gut rehab.

There was nothing "magical" about the space, unless the Wicked Witch of the West herself had taken up residence there among the crumbling plaster and hidden critters in the corners.

I flexed my fingers and began to type.

Location, location, location . . .

They were the magic words in real estate, much like *recently rehabbed, move-in ready,* and *motivated sellers.*

And I knew all about magic words.

I typed out the description, nodding in satisfaction. I spun around once in my chair before I hit the Send button to turn in the final MLS listing, ready to go live.

I shut my laptop and peered out the large picture window in my home office that overlooked the front yard, with tall maple trees flanking the driveway and a hedge of pink roses that lined the sidewalk. I frowned as I saw movement near the garbage cans we'd placed on the street for pickup day. I leaned forward and squinted, and it was just as I'd suspected—two small gray bodies were scurrying around in between the cans.

Damn raccoons.

If I had a suburban nemesis, it was the neighborhood raccoons. They were of the craftiest kind, always getting into the garbage cans on the side of the house no matter what we placed on top. We sometimes woke to garbage scattered on the driveway after a particularly hearty meal. One evening, I nearly had a heart attack as I opened one of the cans outside to toss a bag inside and one peeked its head out and locked eyes with me. I screamed and ran, bag of garbage abandoned on the driveway, until my husband, Travis, agreed to venture into the fray. They usually only appeared at night, but on garbage day it was an all-day trash extravaganza.

Other neighbors had been through rounds of exterminators and deterrents, to no avail. But I didn't need any of those things. I had a secret weapon.

I scurried from my desk—looking very much like my neighborhood nemeses—and leaned out the door of my home office, listening to make sure that I was alone in the house. When it was confirmed, I raced back to the window, knowing I only had a few minutes before my twins arrived home from school.

I closed my eyes and felt the magic deep inside of me, where I kept it under lock and key. I focused my intention on the raccoons, imagining a magical barrier around our trash cans, preventing them from wreaking havoc.

I whispered a few improvised words, as I wasn't aware of any known spell to deter raccoons, and then opened my eyes.

I smiled with satisfaction as the raccoons halted in front of our trash cans, looking bewildered as to why they wanted to stop, before they ran across the street and disappeared under our neighbor's car.

Sorry, guys. Go feast elsewhere.

I leaned over and slid open the window that framed my desk, letting a breeze blow through the large, vaulted space. It was September, and still warm, but there was an edge to the air, the faintest warning of fall knocking on the meteorological door. Soon the maple trees would sigh, releasing their foliage, and an earthy scent would waft up from the ground. Our neighborhood would fill with the sound of leaves crunching under the feet of kids as they got off at the bus stop. With pumpkins and fall garlands. With expensive, designer harvest-themed planters standing guard in front of stately front doors in our suburb of Forest Hills, Illinois.

But it was still summer for now.

My white desk vibrated as the back door slammed. Two sets of footsteps creaked against the oak floors, a tumble of arguments and teasing coming from my twin teenagers. I sighed and stood, ready to make my way downstairs and referee whatever fight was brewing. Yet I stopped as I caught a whiff of smoke in the air.

Sarah, the smoke seemed to whisper. *Think of what else you could do.*

It was just for a moment, and then it was gone, replaced by the light, sweet fragrance from the Annabelle hydrangea hedge in my yard.

"Nope," I said, and shook my head as I made my way to the door.

Yes, twenty years later, I still had magic. But I had it contained, made it my superpowered personal assistant for backyard rodents and stains on the couch. A secret household helper at my disposal. It was a part of me that needed to remain hidden for a multitude of reasons, mostly to protect everyone else.

The Kardashians had hourglass figures and paid personal assistants, while I had magic and spells and a body shaped like a shelf-stable milk carton.

I leaned out of my office door. "Hey, guys! I'll be right there," I called down the stairs.

I brushed my hair back into a ponytail, looping it with the elastic around my wrist, and gave one final, satisfied glance at the pest-free garbage cans before I walked downstairs to greet my children.

"Mom, I need money for the cheer fundraiser." My sixteen-year-old daughter, Harper, stood in the kitchen, a bottle of water in her hand, leaning against the quartz countertop. Her long blond hair was twisted in a bun on top of her head, giving her the look of a Lego character. With one hand, she hoisted herself up onto the countertop.

"How about: 'Hi, Mom. How was your day?'" I said with a laugh as I walked into the room.

"Your cheer squad needs more than money." My son, Hunter, her twin, with an equally impressive mop of blond hair, was hidden in the stainless steel fridge. "Like an ethics code."

Harper rolled her eyes and took a swig from her water bottle. "Oh yeah? Well, half of your lacrosse team needs to be sent to one of those *Scared Straight!* prison experiences."

"I wouldn't put it past some of those parents," I said as I pulled out one of the chairs from the kitchen island. Forest Hills wasn't exactly known for being progressive or tolerant. Therapy was for hippies, and only troubled teens wore black nail polish.

Harper and Hunter continued to trade barbs back and forth, and I shook my head with a smile. My husband, Travis, and I always said they came out of the womb hugging and arguing at the same time, ever each other's best friend, fiercest protector, and most worthy opponent.

Hunter appeared from the fridge, holding half of a white-paper-wrapped sandwich left over from the night before, and took a huge bite. He had the appetite of a German shepherd who had been living on the streets for a month. "I brought the mail in," he said, his mouth full. He jerked an elbow toward the pile on the counter.

"Ohhhh, the new Lululemon catalog," Harper said as she plucked the magazine from the stack, causing the rest to spill onto the floor.

"No one needs two-hundred-dollar leggings," I said as I bent down to retrieve the mail. My hand paused and my body tensed when I saw what was on top.

It was an envelope, addressed to Travis and me, from the North Valley University Alumni Center. Still crouching, I tore it open. Inside was a letter and a flyer. The front of the flyer showed a redbrick building with a white clock tower rising high behind it. A large manicured lawn filled with impatiens and begonias opened in front of the building, overlaid with the words: *Homecoming and Alumni Weekend Events*.

I scanned the letter as I slowly stood.

You are cordially invited . . .

"What's that?" Harper said, but her words barely registered. In my peripheral vision, I saw her crane her neck around and peer down at the paper.

. . . to the unveiling of a plaque commemorating the twentieth anniversary of the Hawthorne Hall fire.

"Ew. That's weird. Won't the 'unveiling of a plaque' put a damper on homecoming weekend?" she said. "Homecoming is supposed to be parades and football games." Her face held a far-away expression; no doubt she was thinking of her high school's homecoming festivities, all Spirit Week and themed dress-up days. Forest Hills High School did not mess around when it came to rallying the community and drumming up support from alumni.

I slowly stood and placed the flyer on the island, pushing it away with one finger, before I looked at my kids.

"Probably just want money from alumni," Hunter said, his sub sandwich paused in the air. He frowned as he considered it. "Do we have to go?"

I looked down again at the picture and didn't answer. They knew what I would say. I had to go—we all had to go. Travis, the kids, me.

Because of who had been hurt in the fire.

((

"It might not be that bad. Enjoyable, even. Maybe. Possibly." Travis poured two glasses of red wine from a bottle he had brought up from the basement. The rack was next to the second fridge, where I often "found" extra sliced turkey for school lunches or the ingredient I needed for a particular recipe.

Oh, we're out? Let me just check the basement fridge. I'm sure there's some in there.

Like I said, a magical personal assistant.

I had resisted the magic for years after the fire, afraid of what might happen again. But one night, when the twins were six weeks old, I gave in. They would only sleep in their swings, and around two in the morning one night, Hunter's swing ran out of batteries. Travis was at the hospital, after being called into emergency surgery. So I was alone in the house, the night closing in around me. Not that the distinctions of "night" and "day" mattered with two newborns who nursed every three hours. Time was nebulous, and I was barely surviving.

After the swing halted, I began to panic, looking around the house for a spare set—I was sure we had some—with no luck. He began to scream, and out of sleep-fueled desperation, I whispered an incantation to charge the batteries. Just to give them enough juice to last through the night.

And it worked. So I began to use it for small, low-stakes things, only when necessary, to make life a little easier. Only for good things, white light. Magic needed to be practiced with the best intentions, light and love for all, with the Rule of Three looming in the background. The Rule of Three stated that anything a witch put into the world would come back threefold, good or bad. And I most definitely only wanted the good to boomerang back to me.

Travis slid one of the wineglasses over to me, and I arched an eyebrow at him as I took the glass and brought it to my lips. I took a slow sip, closing my eyes, pretending I was savoring the wine. Really, I was trying to figure out what to say.

I had spent the early evening driving the twins to their practices and then cooking a dinner of gnocchi with Italian sausage and spinach, even though I knew Travis wouldn't be home from the hospital until late since he was on call. He was a pediatric surgeon at Forest Hills Hospital, which meant many mornings I woke up to find his side of the bed empty.

As I stirred the vodka sauce into the pasta dish, portioning a plate for Travis, I tried to think of an excuse not to attend. But short of faking a back injury on the day of the event, I hadn't come up with anything plausible.

He never knew what Alicia, Katrina, and I had done, the things that we had caused. I had vowed to keep it that way, to keep him and the kids far away from my magic. Even though I still practiced in secret, I reasoned it was for small things, just to help out. Nothing like what we'd tried to do in college. So he was in the dark.

For fuck's sake, he still thought we'd been learning how to juggle.

"Sarah, I don't think we can get out of this one," he said. He looked at his wineglass, his dark hair falling over his forehead. It was unfair—I had more streaks of gray at thirty-eight (covered every three weeks religiously in the privacy of my bathroom, after whispering a few careful words)—than he did at forty-two.

I could hear the gentle hesitation in his voice as he carefully trod around the land mines of my past. He always knew where to step, and this time was no different. "My parents already texted me that they're going, and Nancy, of course. They want it to be a Nelson family thing, I guess."

Growing up, a "family thing" was all that I had ever wanted. To be a part of something, to feel loved, wanted, included. Travis, and by extension, his parents, had given me that. Sure, they were quirky and offbeat, and deliriously out-of-touch at times, but they were mine. And as a Nelson, I would need to attend.

I swallowed, the red wine burning my throat, and nodded slightly. "Of course. We should go."

His shoulders sagged in relief as he gave me a grateful smile and put an arm around my shoulder. "Thank you. It might be good to go back, remember some of the good times. And—hey, you might get a chance to reconnect with your juggling club."

Chapter 2

I never thought I would be the kind of person who owned a pool. Growing up, I had a small plastic wading pool, which my mom would fill up with freezing hose water on the spotty patch of grass that served as the lawn behind our town house. She would sit on a faded folding lawn chair next to me, shaded by the shadow of the town house's ugly brick exterior, eyes glazed over as she fixed her gaze on something in the distance. Probably an image of what she'd thought her life would be.

She did her best, but it had always been just the two of us. My birth father had never been involved, and I had never met him. Our lives were fueled by coupons and boxed mac and cheese— the generic store kind, not the fancy stuff from the blue box. She died of a heart attack in her sleep right before I met Travis and missed out on the opportunity to see my life truly begin, missing the good part of the movie.

When Travis showed me this house ten years ago, I saw the pool in the yard and was transported back to those hazy summers in the plastic pool with a crack down the side, even though we were worlds away. I knew my mom would have loved the house.

After Travis had headed upstairs to bed, I took my wineglass outside. I sat down on the edge of the pool and stuck my feet in the lukewarm water, feeling a sense of calm hum through me, as I always did when I was near the element of water.

Our orange tabby cat, Katy Purry, sauntered out of the boxwood hedge that lined the pool area, her ample stomach waving softly as she walked toward me.

"Hey there. Terrorize any chipmunks?" I said as I lifted a hand and put it on her back when she curled up next to me.

Her eyes closed and a loud purr rumbled from her body.

No. Too fast. I need to do more cardio.

I laughed. "You're perfect the way you are."

Yes, my cat talked to me. Well, not "talked." More like telepathically communicated. She may have technically been my familiar, but Katy Purry was far from a sleek black cat perched on the edge of a broom. She was more like an opinionated feline furniture pouf.

I scratched behind her ears, feeling for any knots, and she responded by purring louder.

She had come into my life five years prior, when I went into the local PetSmart to buy food for the goldfish Hunter had won at the school carnival. A local rescue was holding an adoption event, with pets on display. I froze, holding the fish flakes in the air, as I spotted a tiny orange kitten playing with a feathered toy mouse.

She spotted me and turned her head. *Hi.*

I almost dropped the fish flakes when I heard her voice in my head, high and squeaky.

I adopted her and brought her home in a daze, almost unaware of what I was doing. She was so very excited to see our house, it was like having a chatty toddler again.

Do you do spells? Can I see your broom? Do you have a pointy hat?
Yes, in secret. No. Definitely not.

Throughout the years, her voice had grown deeper, calmer. And she'd thankfully stopped trying to sharpen her claws on my throw rugs. Her waist size hadn't stopped increasing, though, as none of us could resist feeding her treats. Of course, I was the only one who literally heard her outbursts of joy when I walked in the door with the tuna-flavored Temptations packets, but the purring was clear enough to the whole family.

Katy Purry rolled over and sighed. As I scratched her orange swath of stomach, I spotted a swatch of hot pink in the corner of the patio. I leaned forward and squinted. It was a wet bathing suit, and not one of Harper's. It must have belonged to one of Hunter's many female admirers. Even from my vantage point across the pool area, I could tell that the bathing suit barely covered the square footage of a Band-Aid.

I figured the unidentified female guest had brought something to change into, as I hadn't gotten a call from Lois Green-glass next door, letting me know a half-naked teenager had just left my house. And that they'd played music with offensive lyrics. Lois didn't miss a thing, the self-appointed town crier. Her preferred form of news reporting was to send out mass texts to everyone on Sunset Lane, signed at the bottom with her name, as though she were communicating via telegram.

Neighbors. Stop.

I wanted to make sure you are all aware. Stop.

A blue Ford Taurus drove down the street at approximately 1:03 pm today. Stop.

It was going over the posted speed limit. Stop.

The only appropriate punishment is a public stoning.
Stop.

—Mrs. Lois Greenglass

I took a sip of my wine and closed my eyes, feet swirling in the soothing pool water, thinking about going back to North Valley.

"Nancy will be happy to have our support there," Travis had added in the kitchen.

He couldn't have been more wrong.

Twenty years ago, Nancy had been horrified at the attention from local news channels, who wanted to interview the "brave student" injured in the fire. She turned down every request, despite my mother-in-law's love of cameras and the spotlight. She wanted to be left alone, and the rest of us wanted to forget.

I looked down at my arm and slowly pushed the cuff of my burgundy sweatshirt up to my elbow. Holding my arm up to the moonlight and the hidden landscaping lights of the backyard, I studied the skin. The scars had faded over two decades. The burn on my arm used to be red, thick, the skin knotted together, like tentacles turned to stone. Thanks to a plastic surgeon and very expensive laser treatments, it had faded into something delicate and shell pink.

I probably could have used the magic to heal my arm, found a spell that would work, but that would have fallen outside of my self-imposed rules. Small things, magical personal assistant, yes. Scar erasing, no. I didn't want something like that to be a witchy gateway drug. The scar was a reminder, a warning, of how quickly the magic could spiral out of control if I wasn't careful. My powers needed to be kept on the shortest of leashes, tightly muzzled.

Any Temptations left? I'm starving, Katy Purry asked, and then looked up at me and squinted.

I laughed and nodded. "Follow me."

I pulled my sleeve down and stood, shaking the water from my feet. I stepped back inside the kitchen, fed the cat, then opened the pantry and rummaged around, sticking my hand into the far back recess.

I pulled out a blue box of Kraft mac and cheese that I kept hidden. I had learned to hide the good stuff from Hunter and Harper, after the great SpaghettiOs incident last year. Other moms had to mark their liquor bottles (which only taught the kids to fill them back up with water—such a rookie mistake), but I had to hide good old Kraft in my house like drugs in a false-bottom dresser drawer.

I gave the box a little shake of satisfaction and filled up a soup pot with water. Stirring in the noodles after it came to a boil, my thoughts whispered, *Double, double toil and trouble.* I shook my head and reached back to the kitchen island, one hand still holding the wooden spoon, and took a long gulp of wine.

Katy Purry jumped on the counter and knocked the box of mac and cheese onto the floor.

Don't skimp on the butter this time.

Chapter 3

Are you sure we aren't lost? I feel like we're in one of those horror movies where the nice family goes down the wrong road and then has to use chain saws to fend off the murderous locals." Harper's voice, barely audible, floated from under her breath in the backseat. She sighed heavily, but I didn't turn around, my eyes fixed on the narrow country road ahead of us.

"It's been like a half hour since we've even seen a house," Hunter said. "Mom?"

I turned around, and he pulled one of his AirPods out of his ear, palming it. "Not too much longer." I forced a smile and then turned back around, my lips pressed together.

Travis moved a hand from the steering wheel and placed it on my knee. I tensed under the weight of it. "Almost there," he said. He gave me a sympathetic smile before returning his hand to the black leather steering wheel.

I nodded and looked out the passenger window, searching for any sign of familiarity. We had left our house two hours prior, the twins mildly grumbling about spending so much time in the car, before Travis turned around and mouthed something that halted the complaints. I don't know if it was a bribe or a plea for empathy, but I was grateful regardless.

Our car ambled on from our quiet suburban enclave, onto the highway and toll roads, until we exited on Route 173, toward North Valley University. When I first saw the white letters on the green background of the highway sign, my throat began to close.

I hadn't been back to campus in two decades, since the night that cleaved my life into two: Before and After.

In my daily life, it was easy to ignore what had happened. Between Travis, the kids, and my career, I tried not to think about the fire too often. But when I thought of Nancy, it brought all the memories rushing back.

My phone vibrated in my lap, and I rolled my eyes when I saw the name on the screen. It was April Scavuzzo, who had just put in an offer on a lakefront condo the day before. I'd told her that it would be at least twenty-four hours before we heard back from the sellers. It had been less than twelve.

"Hi there," I said, my voice rising three octaves. I heard Harper snicker behind me. Having a teenage daughter sometimes felt like having the human equivalent of a lie detector test, a bullshit meter that I lived with and that nothing escaped. Luckily, Hunter wasn't as perceptive, just fueled by energy drinks, protein bars, and Netflix.

I murmured along as April began to fret, worrying about why we hadn't heard anything back yet. "I'm sure it's fine. They've barely had any time at all to consider it. It's a strong offer, above asking. I'm confident they'll accept."

April finally hung up after I tossed out a few more encouraging notes. I turned to Travis and twisted my mouth, slowly shaking my head. "Doubtful."

"Who cares? Doesn't that lady own like five houses already?" Hunter said.

I nodded. "This one's for her au pair, though."

"Sounds tough," he said with a laugh.

I turned around and smiled. "Make fun all you want, but she's been one of my best clients." I pointed to his AirPods. "You can thank her for those."

"Thanks, April," he said in a high falsetto.

I'd become a Realtor eleven years ago, around when the twins started school full-time. I had suddenly found myself with hours alone every day in an empty house. At first, it felt glorious, luxurious, almost like I was doing something wrong and needed to keep it secret. Yet after six months, I found my anxiety growing. There were only so many times I could mop the wood floors—either myself or using a little "help." The day I found myself debating whether or not to use a fabric shaver on the couch and realized that was my only task, I knew I needed to do something. Most of the other women in Forest Hills became obsessed with working out or volunteering at school and for various charities. But I had never been very good at any of that. And I was terrible at gardening. The only plants that seemed to flourish in my garden were those I ignored or forgot I had planted.

I fell into real estate when I ran into our former Realtor at the grocery store and she talked about setting her own hours, having the flexibility to serve her clients. I remember she'd seemed so glamorous when she showed us our house, and she just looked like a normal person in Whole Foods.

Six months later, I had my license and joined a local office, picking up a few clients, mostly Travis's colleagues from the hospital. My business grew quickly, and I moved from town houses and starter homes to larger estates with in-ground pools. Two years ago, the newspaper had done a profile on me, dubbing me "Rumpelstiltskin," the Realtor able to spin 1980s wallpaper into real estate gold.

And I didn't even have a college degree. I was about to revisit the place I'd dropped out of. The alumni mail was always addressed to "Dr. and Mrs. Travis Nelson." I was an odd footnote in North Valley University's history. A former student involved in a significant event on campus, but one who didn't actually graduate. It seemed they wanted to claim me as their own only when convenient.

I turned back around, holding a bag of SkinnyPop. "Anyone hung—" The words stopped in my throat when I saw a beige sign with white lettering, surrounded by stately red brick. *Welcome to North Valley University* was proudly displayed in white lettering. The sign looked like it had been power washed that morning, without a hint of dirt or road dust.

At the top of the hill that held the campus, the pointed spike of the clock tower was like a lookout, both welcoming and warning visitors with black roman numerals against a white face.

"Ah, the old clock tower," Travis said. His voice oozed warmth and nostalgia.

I knew he was looking forward to seeing campus again, despite all that had happened. Travis had graduated and was in his first year of medical school by the time I was a freshman. Thus, his time on campus had been gift wrapped and neatly packaged into memories of all-nighters, raucous Sigma Chi fraternity parties, and late-night pizza deliveries. He got to experience the college life that I had planned, hoped for, before the fire.

Being back on campus stirred no such warm memories for me. Anxiety and fear coursed through my body as I took in the familiar landmarks that held none of the wonderful recollections Travis had. My time on campus was forever marked by what I—we—had done.

We turned right as the road dead-ended at the clock tower, heading toward the convocation center, where the ceremony would be held. A swath of grass just off the street made me freeze.

"Travis. Stop," I whispered as I put a hand on his arm.

"What?" he said as he glanced at me.

I repeated it, and he pulled the car over to the side. It took him a moment to realize what I was staring at.

This empty space was where Hawthorne Hall had once stood. Where before there had been a redbrick building with white porticos and a Juliet balcony, there was now an empty, browning patch of grass, dotted with fallen leaves and a few sticks from the surrounding oak trees.

I opened my car door and slowly stood, half in, half out of the car, eyes fixed on the bare spot. It was obvious where the building had been—the grass around the space was much greener and fuller. A perfect rectangle of brown, scraggly grass marked the ghost of Hawthorne Hall.

It was one of the reasons why there was still interest in the site. After they'd cleared the rubble and tried to rebuild, strange accidents happened. Workers quit because they got sick or were freaked out by the eerie feelings.

The university finally gave up and planted grass there, but it never quite took despite proper landscaping care. That nothing would grow there became something of a whispered ghost story on campus.

Even before the fire, there had been stories that the dorm had been built on some powerful, unexplained magic site, maybe an old burial ground.

We knew that, and we knew that it had amplified our spells and given them a boost. We had brought the underground magic to the surface with our rituals, and even now, it wouldn't totally dissipate.

"Mom?" Hunter said from inside the car.

I shook my head and sat back down. "Let's go," I said, eyes fixed forward.

"There's Mimi and Grandpa," Harper said as we pulled into the parking lot for the convocation center.

My in-laws stopped in front of the entrance as they spotted our car; my mother-in-law, Marcy, furiously waved. I smiled and waved back as we parked.

Marcy tottered over to us on four-inch strappy gold heels, despite the forty-degree temperature. She wore a bright pink skirt suit with a low-cut white blouse underneath. And diamonds, so many blinding diamonds. It was like looking straight at a solar eclipse.

She'd chosen the grandparent moniker *Mimi* herself, as *Grandma* sounded too old, too much like someone who knitted and told stories about the Great War.

"There you are!" she said in her breathy voice, hugging me before I had a chance to stand. She pulled me out of the car—she had the strength of an Eastern European Olympic bodybuilder. As she released me, she frowned. "I'm sure it's difficult to be back here." She hugged me again, and I briefly closed my eyes, accepting it. Marcy was beyond intense, but once you got past the cleavage and the sequins, she loved harder than anyone I had ever met.

I nodded and gave a half smile as I looked over to my father-in-law, Thomas. Travis hugged him, his father only coming up to his shoulder. Thomas was shaped like a hobbit, a wonderful, kind, very wealthy hobbit.

"Did Nancy come with you guys?" I asked Marcy, who nodded. I peered around her pink shoulder to wave at my sister-in-law.

"Nancy, hi. How are you?" I said as brightly as I could. I took a step toward her as she leaned against her parents' car. She wore black capri pants with black ballet flats and a sleeveless purple blouse. The scars on her arms crisscrossed her skin, the sun illuminating the knots and grooves. I swallowed hard when I saw them, the guilt welling up, as it always did.

Nancy frowned when she saw me. Unlike her mother's Botoxed forehead, hers moved. Her brows knitted together, deepening the line between them that had been there since before I met her, my freshman year.

Nancy, my now-sister-in-law, had been our resident advisor at Hawthorne Hall.

During our first dorm meeting, I was a scared eighteen-year-old on her first night away from her mother, listening to Nancy lecture us on the rules of the dormitory. After thirty minutes of her speech, I began to wonder what we were supposed to do for fun, since the speech was only concerned with must-not-do rules. The biggest rule of all was "No open flames."

It was a rule that everyone acknowledged but no one followed. We all understood why it existed—closed space, immature humans, potential for disaster. But nearly everyone on our floor had a scented candle in their room. We just had to keep them away from the smoke alarms and carefully blow them out with a window open. Plus, we figured, they weren't designated as Really Bad. That was reserved for alcohol infractions, overnight guests, and smuggled pets.

I leaned forward and gave Nancy a quick hug, her shoulders stiffening under my gesture, as they always did, which never stopped me from trying.

"How was your drive here? Gosh, isn't it strange to be back?" I said, too quickly. I had moved into Nancy Mode, as my kids called it. Whenever I was around her, I was like a record being played too fast—quick, staccato speech and flittery hand gestures, a manic version of myself that I was well aware of but had no ability to moderate or control.

"Yes. Strange. Also, this whole thing is bullshit," she said as she glanced at the entrance to the convocation hall. "Let's get it over with."

We stepped toward the entrance, and Marcy grabbed my upper arm.

"We have an announcement for everyone!" she whispered in my ear.

Alarm bells went off. The last time Marcy had had an "announcement," it was that she'd found someone to clone her pet Pomeranian, Bubbles. Money was no object in this quest—not that it ever was with Marcy. She paid a healthy five figures for the process, which resulted in two cloned puppies: Double and Trouble, who peed in the house even more than their prototype, something I hadn't thought was possible.

Travis held open the door to the convocation hall for our group. Before I could step through it, a gleaming black town car caught my eye in my peripheral vision. The windows were tinted, and I couldn't see inside, but I instinctually knew who it was. It was more than just a hunch or gut feeling.

A "juggling club" member had arrived.

Inside would be a woman whom I hadn't seen in twenty years but Googled more frequently than I would ever admit. She had long curly hair that fell perfectly around her shoulders after a blow-out, wide-set brown eyes, and a booming volume to her voice, one that she used on potential investors for her biotech startup, Obsidian, which was developing a new kind of surgical knife. It wasn't a surprise that she'd wound up dealing in sharp objects.

The car stopped in the middle of the parking lot, blocking in a landscaping truck filled with workers, who swore at the car. I held my arms perfectly still against my body as I saw the door open and a red-bottomed black stiletto emerge, followed by a trim figure in a black shift dress. She wore large black sunglasses yet shielded her face with a hand as she scanned the crowd.

She was looking for me.

"Is that . . ." Travis trailed off, but I barely heard him.

I lifted a shaking hand in response, my heart thundering in my chest so hard I saw my white blouse moving to the beat.

Despite the distance, the air between us crackled, and my ears filled with static. Twenty years of repressed emotion moved through my body with the force of a fire hose spraying water. She took a step toward me, her stride confident against the black pavement.

I hadn't seen Katrina Andrews in nearly two decades, since I was a scared eighteen-year-old grappling with her new powers and what she had done. Even though I had twenty years of experience under my life's belt—a mortgage, career, health insurance deductibles, gas bills, a favorite bed pillow, and occasional lower-back pain—as I watched Katrina walk toward me, I felt young again.

And it felt so good.

Chapter 4

Katrina." Her name came out like the sound of dried tree branches breaking in the wind. I could feel my lips vibrating with emotion as she walked closer, gliding evenly in her high heels across the parking lot. The past two decades had been good to her. She had a presence about her, an aura. A glow, even.

She'd always had that. An innate sense of power, control even, had emanated from her at eighteen years old, as though she knew the world was hers and she just had to decide what to take. The magic only amplified it.

Freshman year, Katrina lived in the dorm room next to me, and we ran into each other on move-in day in mid-August. A literal run-in—her as she delicately balanced a plastic laundry basket of folded sweaters, and me as I lugged a trash bag full of my clothes.

Her mother watched from the edge of the hallway, and I saw her roll her eyes as I dropped my trash bag, spilling my clothes all over the worn gray carpeting. A guy with short blond curly hair, wearing a blue Nike T-shirt, didn't pause as he walked over them toward his room at the end of the hallway, a PlayStation in his hands with a tower of games resting on it. I spotted *NFL Madden* at the very top.

"Justin Timberlake–looking asshole," Katrina muttered as she bent down to help me pick them up. Her mother gasped at the profanity, and I laughed.

An innocuous moment, yet one that began the bricklaying of my college path.

After the night of the fire, Katrina transferred to Cornell, Alicia went to study at the Chicago School of Magic, and I went home, to work and try to figure out my life. Scattering to the wind like ashes. We couldn't have remained close after all that we had seen and done. That much I knew. Yet I never experienced a closeness in friendship again like I had with them. The fire destroyed so much, including our bond, and I mourned that loss along with so many other things.

As she walked up the steps to the convocation hall, Katrina extended her arms in greeting. I smiled and took a step toward her, ready for the embrace. She was one of two other people who truly understood, and I hadn't realized until that moment how much I needed to feel that again.

But before she could embrace me, Marcy's head popped back out of the front door.

"Sarah, shake a tail feather. They're about to start the program and want everyone inside." She furiously waved a pink-manicured hand, gesturing for me to follow her.

Katrina dropped her arms and looked at me. "Wouldn't want to disappoint anyone," she said with a twisted smile, her dark eyes twinkling as she raised an eyebrow and nudged me with her elbow.

I smirked and we walked into the looming building, side by side, and made our way down the hallway, following the click-clack of Marcy's heels as she scurried toward the room. I paused before we entered, craning my neck around for any sign of our missing piece, Alicia.

Nothing.

"Thank you for that wonderful introduction, Dr. Robertson. And thank you all so much for coming today." Thomas nodded to North Valley's chancellor, who stood off to the side.

The crowd had politely clapped as they wheeled out the plaque, the reason we were here. It had a gold face mounted on an oak frame, engraved with platitudes about remembering the tragic fire. I didn't even read what it said; I was too busy scanning the room for Alicia and stealing glances at Katrina.

Then it was time for my in-laws' "announcement." I suspected it wasn't about more cloned, unhousebroken pets.

Thomas stood at the podium with Marcy to one side, barely containing her excitement, bouncing slightly on her toes. I glanced over at Nancy in the audience and saw her check her watch, ready to be released from familial prison. I then looked over at Katrina, who was surrounded by a conglomeration of important-looking university-affiliated people, flies drawn to honey.

Even though she, like Alicia and me, had left after that September night our freshman year, the university had decided to claim her as their own. It wasn't as though NVU had very many other notable alumni, although I did read that a former student had opened up a sports bar in Milwaukee that invented a new mixed drink involving beer and Bloody Mary mix.

Katrina looked up at me and raised her eyebrows in amusement at my in-laws' scene.

As Thomas began, Harper leaned over and whispered, "How much longer? I have plans tonight." I silenced her with a stare, and I saw Hunter try to hide his phone in his hand while he pecked at a text.

". . . In honor of the wonderful actions of the community after the fire, we wanted to give back. A lasting legacy of hope and triumph." Thomas smiled warmly at Marcy and then at Nancy,

I glanced over at Travis and saw his face was full of surprise.

"And that's why we are proud to announce the Nelson Family Scholarship Fund, benefiting three students at North Valley University." He beamed.

Marcy gave a small pip and looked over at Nancy, who nodded slightly. I could see beads of sweat beginning to appear on Nancy's forehead.

Travis squeezed my hand and then clapped along with everyone else. Nancy kept her eyes trained on the distance, despite my silently begging her to look at me, acknowledge our shared history here.

Dr. Robertson stepped forward to the mic. "On September twentieth, 2003, North Valley University was forever changed by the fire at Hawthorne Hall. Due to the quick response and heroic actions of the first responders, many lives were saved."

I shifted uncomfortably in my chair. Yes, many lives were saved, but Nancy still suffered. While other students were treated for minor burns and smoke inhalation, she endured skin grafts and bandages, pain and physical therapy.

He continued. "The fire helped bring our community together, a shared tragic event," he said. He paused with a serious look on his face, and I was certain his notes read "meaningful look here." "But it is through difficult times that we find ourselves, and—" His speech faltered, and I heard a rustling behind me.

"*Lo siento!*" came a voice through the room, a high, tinkling tone like wind chimes on a breezy summer day. "We took a wrong turn on those twisty county roads!"

I didn't have to turn around to know who it was who had profaned the stuffy ceremony, causing Dr. Robertson's face to turn to stone.

Alicia wore a long blue caftan and gold bracelets up to her elbows. Her bright red hair was piled on top of her head like soft-serve ice cream, and her eyes were carefully outlined with small pink rhinestones glued around them. She was like Amy Adams in *Enchanted*, with fewer ball gowns and musical numbers. She might have had servant mice, though, for all I knew. I wasn't one to judge.

She strode through the room, her arm linked with her wife, Cressida's. I knew her wife's name from when I had Googled her a few years back. On her left was her daughter, Joelle, I guessed around five years old, wearing a light blue silk dress with silver threads running through it. The little girl wore French braids and a sour expression as she took in the crowd, no doubt wondering why she had been dragged to some boring adult event.

"Hey there, girls!" Alicia waved first to Katrina, then to me, the gold bracelets clinking together. She and Cressida slid into two open seats on the perimeter, completely aware of the disruption—that was likely the point of her entrance.

Alicia Lipschitz had arrived, in a way only she could.

The coven was complete again.

Chapter 5

Alicia made quite the entrance," Travis said as we stood to gather our things after the presentation and announcement were over. They had been filled with drawn-out speeches containing exaggerated sympathy for those injured. Other than Nancy, Alicia, Katrina, and me, I had spotted a few other residents of Hawthorne Hall from that year, but I couldn't place their names.

After it happened, I actively avoided any newspaper articles or coverage. The memories of that night were seared into my brain enough, like silhouettes against a building after a nuclear attack. I didn't need to read the articles with interviews from locals or hear what the firefighters had seen when their trucks arrived at the blaze.

The Wikipedia page for the fire read:

> On Saturday, September 20, Hawthorne Hall residence dorm at North Valley University caught fire at approximately 10:56 p.m. The fire began in the basement and quickly spread through the building. The smoke alarms and sprinkler systems never activated due to a battery and mechanical failure across all devices, a mistake due

to a mix-up at the servicing company. By the time students were roused from their sleep by the smoke, many had to jump out of their windows to escape. Thankfully, the building was only three stories, so most were able to drop to safety. The dorm was also mostly empty, many students still out for the evening. The exact cause was never officially determined.

The north third-floor corridor had extensive damage—the corridor where Katrina, Alicia, and I lived. The fire spread quickly on that side of the building, and the rooms in that section were destroyed, turned to ash and rubble. That floor's room for the resident advisor was the most unfortunately placed—almost ground zero for the flames and the black smoke.

That was Nancy's room.

Over 30 percent of her body had been burned by the time they rescued her; she spent months in the hospital and rehab facilities after.

I suffered the burn on my arm, and Katrina and Alicia escaped with only smoke inhalation, skirting any permanent or long-lasting damage. Physically, anyway.

We were lucky. We had time to escape and save ourselves. We didn't have to wait to hear the smoke alarms, which never went off or feel the intense heat of a fire kicking into gear. We didn't need alarms, because when it started, we were in the basement.

There wasn't much left in the rubble after the fire was finally extinguished. Except for a few notable items that were mostly ignored aside from by some Redditors who kept the information alive on the occasional Unresolved Mysteries board.

What they were most interested in was this: under the protection of a metal cabinet that had fallen as the walls collapsed during the blaze, investigators found a collection of candles with strange symbols carved into them, half-burned tarot cards, and pieces of obsidian.

Our casting circle.

Not much was made of it by officials, and it became a footnote in the fire's history.

And the cause, never resolved.

Before I could respond to Travis, Alicia walked toward me, sashaying her hips as Cressida and her daughter trailed behind. On my right, Katrina approached. It felt like a triangle collapsing upon itself, points coming together at the center.

"Roughly seven thousand three hundred and five moons," Alicia said with a smile as we all stopped. I guess she finally learned how to do math.

"Numbers don't make sense to me. I'm an idiot," she had said to me as she sat on her bed in her dorm room, her eyes filling with tears. She nudged her statistics book off her bed and watched it spill onto the floor.

"You're not an idiot," I said gently, and tapped her hand. "This stuff is impossible to understand, and we'll never use it again anyway. It's not worth your tears."

She smiled gratefully and lunged toward me, wrapping me in a bear hug that made me squeak. The first of many hugs from her, out of gratitude or happiness, and then out of fear and worry.

In the present, the crystals glued to Alicia's face twinkled in the fluorescent lighting, nearly blinding me. It was all part of her illusion, her façade. Based on an article that I'd read in the *Chicago Tribune* a year ago, she was a semifamous magician and illusionist—Abracadabra Alicia. She worked primarily in sleight of hand and card tricks while wearing brightly colored caftans. Was it cynical of me to assume she wasn't truly following the rules of stage magic?

I'd met Alicia the second week of school. Everyone else in our dorm had been out at parties, invited to fraternity and sorority events in the hopes of becoming a recruit. The three of us happened upon each other in the bathroom after everyone else had left. Katrina was just coming out of the shower, wrapped in an expensive monogrammed pink towel, as I walked in to wash my face, feeling very sorry for myself that I was the pathetic girl alone on a Saturday night. Alicia was at the sink, rinsing out a goldfish bowl that was the home of her betta fish named Franco.

We all startled at each other's presence, each probably thinking she was the only loser not invited to parties. After a few wary moments, we decided to gather in the basement to watch a movie, friends by default. At least at first.

We spent a few nights together like that, huddled around the big-screen television in the basement of our dorm, one night watching an airing of *The Wizard of Oz*.

"Glinda needs to be punched in the face," Katrina muttered under her cashmere throw blanket. "The Wicked Witch was minding her own business and then they dropped a house on her sister. Assholes."

Alicia tucked her feet underneath her and reached for the bowl of popcorn, shoving a handful into her mouth. "Yes, but she has the most beautiful pink dress," she said over a mouthful. "That's how you know she's a good witch."

"So you would be a good witch just for the fashion, Alicia?" I had laughed and looked at Katrina. "We know which one you would be." I again laughed, but both of them stared at me, an idea born. But it wasn't until a few weeks later, when we watched an episode of *Charmed* together, that we got serious. Apparently, Shannen Doherty was the final push we needed.

"Good math, Alicia. Yes, it's been quite a long time," Katrina said with a wide smile. She glanced over her shoulder at one of her assistants hovering behind and nodded slightly, her lips pressed together in annoyance. Her gaze went to my in-laws and then back again to the assistant.

Ah, startup money. She was here to find investors, to ingratiate herself with any wealthy alumni in attendance. The assistants hurried off, scattering like teenagers after the cops show up at a party.

"Sarah, you look simply wonderful." Alicia clasped her hands in prayer form in front of her chest as I noticed a group of media behind her, reporters. She saw me looking and laughed. "They're doing a piece on me for the alumni magazine. I have a national tour coming up. Can you believe it? Praise be. It's like it all came true."

It all. My head swam as I remembered the words from long ago:

> *As it burns*
> *So shall it be*

The spell we'd cast that night. Black candles, lit one at a time by the three of us, as we whispered our deepest desires. It was our most ambitious spell, the one we hoped would shape our futures.

I swallowed hard, pushing away the memories that clouded my vision as my legs began to feel unsteady. "Congratulations." My voice was barely a whisper. "To you both."

"This is just fantastic. You know—why don't we have lunch? We can catch up on what we're all up to these days." Katrina glanced over her shoulder at the assistant who remained, and she stepped forward. I noticed beads of sweat at the assistant's hairline, and her mascara was smudged. Katrina Andrews was clearly her Miranda Priestly.

The assistant looked down at the phone in her hand. "Of course. I'm on it. I'll make a reservation somewhere?"

I laughed and the assistant turned to me, phone poised in the air. When we were in college, the town of North Valley only had one restaurant that could pass a health inspection—Boca, where everyone took their parents when they visited, which was basically only open during visitation weekends. The rest of the restaurants, if they could even qualify as such, were disgusting taverns and sticky sports bars with signature well drinks with names like "Ultimate Mind Probe." Never mind that the only mind manipulation happening was erasing memories.

Before I could remind her of that, Alicia spoke. "That sounds like such a delight, but I promised the editor of the *North Valley Chronicle* I would join her after the ceremony for a little photo shoot." She brushed a Crayola-red strand of curly hair from her cheek, carefully extracting it from the jewels on her face. "Next time. Or! I will reserve some tickets for you both to one of my shows in the city, and we can have a girls' night after."

Katrina's expression suggested she'd rather eat out of a dumpster than attend Alicia's show, and then she turned to me.

I wanted more than anything to ask if they were still using magic, too. If they were able to hide it as I had, or if they had turned away from it, ignored the power we'd awoken so long ago.

I glanced over at Travis, my in-laws, and the kids, who were standing off to the side of the stage, staring at us. Marcy took a step forward, no doubt ready to move into our circle. It was decidedly not the right time to raise the subject.

"I have to get back to my family. Good to see you ladies. Let's catch up soon," I said.

Katrina nodded, and glanced over at Travis and my kids before her gaze moved to Nancy and then Marcy and Thomas. Her jaw tightened for the briefest of moments before she turned back to me and smiled.

"Of course." She looked warmly at Alicia and me. "So wonderful to catch up with you both. As I said, it's been far too long."

"Well, I should scoot off to that little shoot," Alicia said. "Yay! I'm so glad I got to see my girls!" She clasped her hands again.

Time seemed to slow down, like the turning of a record player going into half speed, as she opened her arms and reached forward, putting one arm around Katrina and the other around me. She leaned forward into us, embracing us like sunlight hugging two mountains at daybreak.

At her touch, I heard my heartbeat rush through my ears, the whooshing sound moving from the center of my body. A burning sensation in my core woke, spreading to my limbs like a vine overtaking a brick wall. It moved down to my fingertips and to the crown of my head. The smell of smoke curled through my nose, and my vision went dark and then light as I stood still in the embrace. My skin tingled with small firecrackers of energy that rushed out of my fingertips.

While I had been using magic in small ways, nearly every day, it never felt like this. It *never* felt like anything close to this.

The magic I had used since after the twins were born was like a whisper. This was a primal scream.

The last time I had coursed with this much strength was twenty years ago.

I felt Katrina and Alicia stiffen next to me as the energy moved through them, encircling the three of us, completing the circuit. A cloud seemed to hover in the space between us, before dissipating into each of us.

With great effort, I jerked back, holding up my palms and looking at them. "What the hell was that?" I whispered, mostly to myself.

Katrina's eyes were wide as she turned her palms over, examining her hands in surprise.

Alicia's face was bright with awe, her mouth open. Her eyes sparkled like the jewels glued to her face. "I haven't felt that in—" She cut off as her gaze moved behind me.

"Mom! Hello? I've been calling you," Harper said as she jogged over to us, her hands thrown up in abject teenage frustration. She stopped when she saw our expressions, confusion and suspicion moving across her face. "What happened? You guys look super weird."

The sight of my daughter broke the moment. I quickly stepped back, shaking my head. It was like I had turned my car on and a radio station had blasted through the speakers, but now I grabbed the knob and turned it down.

"It's nothing. What's wrong?"

"Mimi and Grandpa said they're throwing a big party, like a fancy ball, to fundraise for the scholarship. Can we go shopping for a dress?" she said, eyes aglow with thoughts of a Cinderella ball gown and strappy shoes.

Of course they were planning a formal, splashy event. If there was anything Marcy loved more than swans and diamonds, it was a gala.

"We can talk," I said to Harper as I stepped toward her, putting an arm around her shoulders.

"Ow!" She jumped back, rubbing her arm. "You shocked me."

I looked at my hand, my nails glinting gold for a moment before returning to normal. Fear bubbled up to the surface like a tea bag floating to the top of a mug of boiled water.

"Sorry. Must be a lot of static electricity around here. Power lines or something. We should go," I said to her. I was careful not to touch her again as I stepped toward the exit. I looked back at Katrina and Alicia, still silently rooted in place, staring at me with the same incredulity I felt.

Last summer, Travis had found a dead possum in our backyard, near the privacy fence around the pool. The landscapers were already gone, and we didn't want to wait for them to return the next day while the corpse rotted and decayed in the July heat. So he retrieved a shovel from the garage, after a particularly sitcom-worthy scene of crashing lawn tools and landscaping buckets, and hoisted the shovel under the animal, as Harper and Hunter moaned and screamed in horror.

The second the metal shovel touched the possum, it jumped up, scared, and scurried off under the fence line. Turns out, possums can play dead to fool predators. It thought we were the predators. It was all an illusion. A trick of nature.

As my fingertips tingled with turbocharged energy, I realized the magic was as powerful as it'd ever been. The touch between us was all it had taken for a magical resurrection, a boost.

It hadn't been softened and domesticated.

It had been lying in wait.

Chapter 6

I hoped that the turbocharged sparks of magic were limited to the moment between Alicia, Katrina, and me. The tingle of magic thankfully faded as I walked out of the convocation hall. Harper trotted ahead of me, chattering about potential hairstyles for the gala.

Which was extremely fortunate, since before I could reach our car, a petite twentysomething woman with ombré brunette barrel curls and a camel trench coach stepped in front of me.

"Sarah Nelson? I thought that was you. I recognized you from your real estate profile online." She spoke in an aggressive staccato, a peppery cadence that popped like firecrackers. Before I could answer her, she continued. "My name is Madisyn Parks, and I was hoping I could interview you."

I glanced at my family, and Harper stopped talking, hairstyle apparently silently decided. She lifted her palms in an exaggerated pose. *What gives? Who is that?* Hunter pointed to the car with both hands. Travis made a motion for them to calm down, be patient. His parents were already pulling out of the parking lot in their white Porsche Carrera, Nancy in tow.

"Interview me? For what?" The explosion of magic was slowly

receding, draining back into the earth. I could feel it leaving the soles of my feet and folding itself back up into a manageable size in my core.

"I'm starting a podcast about the events of the night of the fire. I'm calling it *Afterburn*, and I'm picturing an oral history of that night and what happened after. And, of course, hopefully, finally solving the mystery of how the fire started." She smiled and pulled out her phone, ready to hit Record. So many assumptions in that sentence and gesture.

Not to mention, what an awful title for the podcast.

Before I could respond, she added, "You may have heard of me. Last year I wrapped the *Morgantown Murders* podcast, which was number one in subscribers in Apple podcasts."

Without meaning to, I rolled my eyes. Marcy was a fan of that particular podcast, describing each weekly episode to all of us in great detail, without asking. *Never* asking. It concerned a wealthy Texas family and a string of murders and corruption tied to their businesses. The host, this Madisyn Parks, was a green reporter who dedicated her postcollege years to investigating the family, culminating in a podcast sensationalizing the tragedies, peppered with personal rants against fellow journalists. Yet the story was apparently compelling enough to achieve record subscriber numbers.

Delicious, was how Marcy described it, ignoring the fact that people had been brutally murdered in cold blood.

"Sounds very admirable, but I don't think so. I—I don't really have any information you would find interesting." I took a step to walk around her.

She smiled, undeterred. "You were a resident of Hawthorne

Hall twenty years ago, correct?" Before I could answer, she pecked at her phone, swiping to the Notes app. "Sarah Domansky, room three fifteen."

My silence confirmed her ID.

"I know you're busy, but I was hoping you would be interested in giving me a few quick statements now—maybe a few pull quotes—and then setting up an interview for a later time. Lunch or coffee close to your house maybe? My treat," she said. Her finger hovered over the Record button on her phone. She looked up at me and smiled, full of confidence after her recent success. A naïve belief that the world would always acquiesce to her requests, as long as she delivered them with a smile. It seemed it had so far.

I another took a side step toward my family to buy a few more seconds. "I really don't have anything to say, I'm afraid."

"But you were there that night, right?" She leaned in, her voice lowering to a whisper. "Listen, I chose the fire as my next topic because I grew up around here. My father was one of the firefighters on the scene that night. The way he talked about the fire, and how it was almost otherworldly, always intrigued me."

Otherworldly was an interesting word choice.

"Especially after they found those occult items in the rubble," she added, watching my reaction closely.

Even though most had forgotten about the fire, I had gotten a few requests for interviews about it over the years. They mostly came in the form of emails that I could quickly delete and try to forget, or voicemails with which I did the same. I learned never to answer an unknown number on my phone, because I never knew if it was a spam call about my car's expired warranty or a citizen detective asking about the fire. There was also the instance I answered an unknown FaceTime from someone's Tinder date holding a birthday cake, wearing only a birthday suit.

I took another step toward my family. "I'm sorry, but I can't." I moved to the side and my heel caught in an uneven part of the grass, causing me to wobble.

She stepped forward, arm outstretched, to steady me, but I jerked my body away, afraid of the invigorated magic.

I turned and quickly hurried toward my family, who were watching me with a mix of curiosity and exasperation.

"Another time, then," she called across the grass.

"Your title is offensive," I shouted over my shoulder as I walked to the car.

As I reached for the door, I looked back and saw she was lightly jogging in the direction of where Katrina was animatedly talking to a group of people in business suits, and a twinge of worry tweaked my insides for the second time that day.

☾

"Sarah, would you toss me the laptop charger from behind you?" Travis sat at the kitchen island, his computer open in front of him, scheduling a speaking appearance at a medical conference for next month, as I made dinner, browning ground beef for tacos.

I handed him the cord, studying his face. He wore his glasses, black hipster frames that would have looked ridiculous on any other man his age but only served to make him look even more handsome and approachable. The good, patient doctor who set his pediatric patients and their parents immediately at ease.

He looked up and smiled, and I lifted an arm to put around his shoulders, but before it could rest on his body, I felt the strong magic flow through it, like a million tiny explosions. Small invisible golden strands reaching out for Travis's body, the tentacles of an anemone, wanting to pulse magic from my body into his.

I snapped my hand back to my side, afraid to touch him.

"What?" he said with a laugh when he saw my expression.

I shook my head and turned back to the stove, stepping toward the taco meat. "Nothing. Thought I smelled this burning."

I closed my eyes and exhaled slowly, trying to remain calm even though I didn't know what was happening.

Get it together. You've always had control.

I first met Travis at a hospital in the city, a year after the fire. I had moved back home, away from North Valley, after my abbreviated freshman year and started working, first as a cashier at a grocery store, and then at the information desk at Northwestern Memorial Hospital in downtown Chicago. He was in med school, doing clinicals on the pediatric floor. He passed my desk every morning on his way to the elevator bank, evolving from slight head-nod acknowledgments to friendly waves, to saying hello.

One day, before he reached the elevators, he paused and walked over to my desk.

It took me three conversations before I realized that I knew his sister. He was delighted that I had known Nancy and seemed to bond with me over the fact that I had been in Hawthorne Hall for the fire.

It terrified me at first. And also made me wonder why he had stopped to talk to me that first morning.

Was it me, or was it the magic, a love spell, finally working?

I suspected the answer, but I told myself that even if the magic had first made him stop, I had made him stay. My future's being bound to Nancy's also seemed poetically karmic, in a Rule of Three way.

Harper sauntered into the kitchen, her hair pulled back in a ponytail. She grabbed a bottle of water from the fridge.

"Mom, again, when can we go shopping for a dress for the gala?" she said as she sipped the water.

Oh right. The gala. With everything that had happened that afternoon, the event had slipped my mind, the least of my worries. It had not slipped Harper's.

"When is it again?" I said as I brushed a hand along the sparkling white marble countertop. When we'd arrived home after the ceremony, the house was spotless and smelled of lemons. I hadn't done a spell to tidy up while we were out, so I was just as surprised as my family when we walked in and the kitchen dish towels were folded into tiny swans.

I had to pretend I'd forgotten the cleaning service was scheduled, complete with an overexaggerated forehead slap.

"November fifteenth. I'm thinking white or gold for my dress," she said.

"You've already thought about color scheme?" Travis said without looking up from the laptop. "We just found out about it two hours ago."

"Of course," she said as she rolled her eyes. She looked at me. "Mom?"

"Soon," I said.

That seemed to satisfy her, and she turned and walked out of the kitchen. I would have to find a dress, too, and appear next to my family for countless photographs, a perfect smiling composite of rebuilding after disaster. Pictures with Nancy posed in the middle, the rest of us scaffolding her like emotional pillars, the family that couldn't be deterred from their generosity and unconditional love, whether she liked it or not.

But that was what I had cast a spell to receive twenty years before. Unconditional love, a family. A husband. Children. People who wouldn't leave or abandon me. A father for my own children who wouldn't walk out one morning and never return.

When I was fourteen, I flipped through the pages of a *Cosmopolitan* magazine that I had grabbed off the rack when I was sent to the store for 1 percent milk and Wonder Bread. Most girls my age would have read the articles on how to dust highlighter on their cleavage or achieve the perfect cat eye with liquid eyeliner. Instead, being the strange teenager that I was, I stopped on the article about an up-and-coming fashion designer.

The spread began with a photo of the designer's family: her, her attractive husband, and a toddler perched on her lap. They were laughing, surrounded by a beautiful homescape of white couches and brightly colored spines on the bookshelves behind them. A foreign warmth exuded from the pictures—that of a happy, perfect family.

That was what I wanted, what I wished for the night we cast the spell.

Of course, now I understand that no one is ever that happy, that Instagram filters warp reality, and that pictures and social media only show the exterior of someone's life. And that toddlers and white couches are never a good idea, even with the help of my secret personal assistant.

I leaned forward and clasped my hands together on the magazine-worthy kitchen island, careful to keep one chair in between Travis and me.

"What a weird afternoon," I said.

He looked up, a mixture of distraction and concern on his face. "I can imagine. It was strange for all of us, especially Nancy." He folded his arms over his chest. "But I hope the gala will give everyone something to look forward to. And for a great cause. Plus, it gives my mother another project to work on."

I knew that was true. Marcy always needed something to keep her focus on, although it was usually something a little further flung, like rescuing lemurs from an endangered rain forest. Never anything that endangered my secrets.

I loved that Travis had grown up with a mom like Marcy. He was sometimes less than nostalgic about his wonder years, still scarred from when Marcy dressed him in a sequined blazer for school pictures in second grade. But under all of the sequins and sparkles, she had passed down to him her best quality: her heart. She was a weirdo, but no one cared. Plus, she had enough money that she was described as eccentric instead of tacky.

I murmured in agreement and walked out of the kitchen and upstairs, my head slightly pulsing with the leftover magical boost. I pushed open my bedroom door and saw Katy Purry lying on my bed, one eye open.

I walked over to give her a scratch on the head but froze, hand in the air. Because she talked.

Not just telepathically communicated with me, but talked. Out loud.

"How was the ceremony?" Her speaking voice was deep and

gravelly, like she had chain-smoked Misty menthols for twenty years. She sat up quickly, a look of surprise on her face. She lifted a paw to her mouth.

"Did I just . . . talk?" she said. She looked around the room, whiskers twitching, and then back to me.

Struck silent, I slowly nodded. My heart began to thud as I crouched down next to the bed so we were eye level.

"Say something again," I whispered to her as I placed a shaking hand on the bed.

"Something again," she growled out.

Oh shit. Shit. Shit. Shit.

Shit.

"How can I talk now?" she said, raising her voice.

"Shhhhh!" I frantically waved my arms around and began to pace back and forth in front of the bed.

Seeing Alicia and Katrina must have turbocharged all of the magic, to the point where my familiar could now hold a conversation. That anyone could hear.

"Okay, we can fix this," I said, mostly to myself, as I paced back and forth. My knee caught the edge of my nightstand, and the lamp on top of it tipped over, landing on the wood floor with a crash.

"Sarah? What was that? You okay up there?" Travis called from downstairs.

I shot Katy Purry a warning look as I picked up the lamp and called out, "Yes, all good. Just knocked something over. Clumsy me. Oops."

"Very convincing," Katy Purry said with a yawn. Talking seemed to exhaust her.

I steadied myself on the wall, breathing quickly. "Quiet. We are going to figure this out. I don't know what's happening, but you have to keep your literal mouth shut until I do. Got it?"

Katy Purry narrowed her eyes at me and meowed before lying back down on my side of the bed and closing her eyes.

Shit. Shit. Shit.

"Scoot over. I need to lie down and think," I said to her. "We can't just have you talking now."

She opened one eye and hissed at me before rolling her large body over a couple of inches.

"Maybe I like talking," she whispered before she fell asleep. I put my head down and pressed the heels of my hands into my eyes.

This cannot be happening. After how careful I've been—meticulous, even—about keeping the magic private and secret, my cat just can't start talking.

How am I going to hide this?

Then I had a terrible thought. I lifted my head, my chest rising and falling with panicked breaths.

What if this is just the beginning?

Chapter 7

*F*our *seven five six. Key sign.*

The lockbox keypad flashed red at me. I typed in the numbers again, muttering to myself, certain I'd pressed them incorrectly. The red light nearly rolled its eyes as it refused to give up the house key to 325 Muirfield Circle.

Nothing.

"Is something wrong?" said a voice behind me.

I turned and gave my best Realtor Sarah smile to Mr. and Mrs. Johnston. They stood on the expansive front porch, hovering under the wooden awning, out of the range of the spitting rain that fell from the gray sky.

"This little keypad is being temperamental. Just another minute, and we should be right as rain." I internally cringed at my corny turn of phrase.

Mr. Joshua Johnston frowned at me and looked down at his phone in his hand before taking the gesture one step further and exaggeratedly checking the ornate gold watch on his wrist. Mrs. Johnston nervously shifted in her tan strappy sandals, adjusting the hemline of her blue and white medallion-print shift dress.

The couple, in their midfifties, had come to me through a referral from Hunter, of all people. Mr. Johnston was the father of one of Hunter's lacrosse teammates, and I would have thought that might buy me some goodwill—or at least a few extra minutes to figure out why the damn keypad didn't work—but that was incorrect. Mrs. Johnston had called me the day before and told me their family was looking to upgrade their house—"more square footage," even though I knew they already had six thousand square feet of high-end property in a nearby suburb. They also only had one kid.

I'd met them at a listing in Northfield, at a large Georgian with landscaped gardens and a basketball court in the basement, just off the wine cellar and tasting room. A bold choice considering how easy it would be for their son and his friends to move from playing a game of pickup in the basement to raiding the liquor stash. I made a mental note to keep close tabs on Hunter if they bought the place.

Now all I needed was the keypad to accept the code.

I tried again, and the keypad beeped loudly and displayed *Too many attempts. Lockout.* Complete with a circle and a slash through it.

I stood up and gave the Johnstons my best placating smile before pecking at my phone. "The listing agent must have recently changed the code and didn't update the records. Let me call their office."

Mr. Johnston shook his head and took a step toward the edge of the porch. "You were late. And now I have a meeting."

Mrs. Johnston's hands fluttered around as she began to rip into two, torn between waiting to see the house and her husband's apparently very busy, very unyielding schedule. She put a hand out to stop him and quickly retracted it when a large rain-drop fell on it.

Katy Purry had kept up a constant stream of chatter that morning as I got ready to leave for the listing meeting. I had overslept, and the house was empty, so as I rushed around trying to get ready, she took the opportunity to talk to me about everything on her mind, from the raccoon that she'd seen the day before to how much she disliked the navy pantsuit I had picked out. She stopped only to cough up a hairball onto my white bedspread, my hopes that the talking-cat thing had been a one-night occurrence dashed.

I turned back to the keypad as I heard Mr. Johnston creak down the porch steps and Mrs. Johnston's murmurs as she followed her husband.

Panic began to bubble up in my chest, and I felt the magic rise within me. Usually, when this happened, I could tamp it down quickly, a small spark of fire easily contained by a drop of water. But not this time.

The keypad glimmered once and then beeped loudly. The bottom slid open to reveal a burnished gold key to the front door as the keypad read, *Congratulations*. I snatched it out of the plastic prison and held it up as I spun around, ignoring the fact that I'd had no control over the spell my body had just cast without my consent.

"Success. Ready to go inside?"

Forty minutes later, I watched from my car as the Johnstons pulled down the long pavered driveway, the wheels of their Mercedes kicking up puddles of rain. After their car had safely disappeared behind the boxwood hedges that lined the street, I finally exhaled. Sweat poured down my back, and I shrugged out of my suit jacket, head resting against the steering wheel.

They had loved the house. Once we were able to get inside, they'd marveled at the leathered marble kitchen countertops and the first-floor office modeled after the Oval Office. I could practically see Mr. Johnston's chest puff up with pride as he pictured his desk in an office fit for the commander in chief, himself at the helm of the country.

Mrs. Johnston's squeals of delight had reached an eardrum-shattering crescendo when we walked through the master bathroom, with a rain shower big enough to host a football team, not that she looked the type to do anything of the sort. An inappropriate comment about the detachable showerhead nearly came rushing out before I was able to reel it back. At least I was still in control of my own mouth.

Because I certainly wasn't in control of anything else that happened in that house.

In the fake Oval Office, sounds of the presidential march, "Hail to the Chief," began to play softly through the speakers as I opened the door.

"Isn't it a neat feature?" I sputtered out with a smile.

The rain shower turned on by itself, soft steam rising from the marble tile.

"Motion sensors. What a rare upgrade," I said.

Lights turned on automatically as we entered rooms, dimming based on the sun's position. And fireplaces ignited with soft flames as we walked past, turning off when we exited the room.

The oven timer dinged, and when I went to turn it off, I found a batch of freshly made macadamia nut and white chocolate chip cookies ready for guests.

"Newest model. Not even on the market yet," I said.

I shouldn't have been surprised. I had felt the magic coursing through the house as we walked from room to room, like a snake that arrived moments before we did, illuminating everything, spraying its intoxicating scent, luring them into its presence.

Sure, I had used the magic to brighten up a house before a showing before, but nothing like this. Opening roman shades I couldn't reach, or removing fallen leaves from the patio after I couldn't find a leaf blower. Not self-aware steam showers and Martha Stewart recipes.

I lifted my head from the steering wheel and looked at my hand carefully. It looked the same, yet inside, the neurons were firing with small electrical sparks.

I flexed my fingers a few times, trying to shake off the pins-and-needles feeling. I had forgotten about that. When our coven would conclude our rituals, my skin would ache with a peculiar feeling, like I had been too close to a fire and pulled my hand back at the last second.

I'm back, baby, the magic seemed to be saying. Showing off, now that Alicia, Katrina, and I had had our brief reunion.

I had spent the last twenty years being so careful, so meticulous in hiding the magic. Making sure no one was around when I did a spell, always having a cover story for when things would appear, locking the door if I knew someone was home.

Maybe I was deluded in thinking it would always be the case

that I would never be in danger of being discovered. But it had worked for two decades, and I had never seen any warning signs.

Until now.

Until the coven had been reunited.

And now, I feared, the magic was finally exhaling a long, belated breath, ready to show the world what it could do.

It felt like a delayed game of show-and-tell, and I didn't know how to end it.

Chapter 8

The dark blue waves of Lake Michigan crashed angrily against Lighthouse Beach, filling my ears. The coarse tan beach was nearly empty, save for a few joggers down in the distance. I lightly tossed my black kitten-heel slingbacks on top of an old sandcastle, flattening it in the middle. The architect had long ago allowed it to fall into disrepair.

I carefully sat down in the sand next to my shoes, the moisture from the damp ground running up through my navy pantsuit. My dry cleaners would not be thrilled when I brought them our pieces next week. I leaned forward and folded my arms across my knees, looking out at the water.

After I left the listing appointment with the Johnstons, I knew I needed a moment to reset myself, to calm down, and water always did that for me. Harper and Hunter were home from school, and I needed a moment alone to think.

I wondered if Alicia and Katrina were having similarly unsettling moments, if the magic was shouting to them, too. From the safety of the sand, I let my thoughts drift back to college, when we first became friends.

At first, it was being on the outskirts that bonded us, seemingly being the only ones not grabbing cheap beer out of trash cans filled with ice and kissing boys from our English survey course. We were the misfits who had found each other, the square pegs with no desire to fit into the round holes. We were each some iteration of different, and for the first time, I felt seen. Accepted. Not judged or ignored. For the first time, I belonged, not despite who I was or where I had come from, but because of it.

And that was before we discovered the magic.

After we started casting, without much of a guide other than what we found on the Ask Jeeves site and in a few books we checked out of the university library, we were further bonded by keeping the secret, in knowing we had a hidden power, a cheat code to life.

While other students in our dorm worried about whether their boyfriends or girlfriends were cheating on them, or whether their professor would let them turn in their paper late, we were pondering how many candles we should use and collecting cayenne pepper, ground black pepper, and saltshakers from the dining hall to use in our spells.

Jeff Bezos hadn't taken over the world, so the few things we ordered online took over a week to arrive at our dorm. And even then, we had to stand guard by the mailboxes since the men's corridor on the first floor was notorious for package thefts. So, in the beginning, we had to make do with what we could access. Tree branches were collected on the lawn of the quad. The candles were from Walmart runs in the next town over. Herbs were swiped from the cafeteria, and our offering plate was a plastic food tray.

Our spell books from the university library had names like *A*

History of Cunning Women: Witchcraft in New England, but we were able to glean enough—literally reading between the lines—to cobble some spells together. We thought we were just having fun and didn't really expect much to happen.

But it did.

Back then, I could feel the magic moving inside of me, especially after sunset, when the moon rose high above the tall oak trees around Hawthorne Hall. It whispered throughout the day, following me as I took notes or collaborated on a group project, a slight twinge in my shoulders and neck, sometimes in my back. I could ignore it while it was light out. But at night, I would close my eyes, breathe in deeply, and mentally open the gates to the possibilities.

We could feel that the urban legend about the dorm's being built on a magical source was real. The magic exploded forward like water being released from a dam.

Then there was no ignoring it. Once we unleashed it, the sensation rushed through me like I was on fire, every nerve alight, a molten river of magic flowing through my body. I had no idea how apt the metaphor would become.

I thought I had control over it—that we all did. Instead, the magic was playing nice, drawing us in. Grooming us for more powerful spells, bigger wishes. The magic always wanted more.

The night of the fire, we each cast a spell for what we truly desired in our future, wish fulfillment for our adulthood.

Katrina desired fortune.

Alicia wanted fame.

I asked for love.

"Love? Really? This isn't a movie. You can have anything in

the world and you ask for love?" Katrina had deadpanned as she stared at me from underneath the black veil she had draped around her hair. (It was a black cloth napkin we had stolen from Boca.)

"It's so romantic. Simple. Perfectly Sarah," Alicia whispered to me with a smile. A large gold necklace that she'd found at Goodwill hung from her neck. It was more 1970s disco jewelry than anything mystical, but as I said, we were magical beggars, not choosers.

> *For on this night we shall see*
> *The power between us three*
> *As it burns*
> *So shall it be*
> *As it burns*
> *So shall it be*
> *Bring it to me.*
> *Give me the life I've always dreamed.*

☽

We had seemingly received what we asked for, but now my damn cat was talking. I needed to speak to them and find out if they were experiencing their version of talking pets. I pulled my phone out of my pocket and typed out a quick email to both, asking for their phone numbers. They weren't hard to find—they both had professional-looking websites.

Before I could put my phone back in my pocket, it trilled with an incoming FaceTime.

Alicia's face filled the screen with the familiar whooshing

sound. She was holding her phone in an extreme close-up, her heavily made-up features extending to the edges.

"Sarah!" She smiled, and her hot-pink lips stretched to the corners of my screen.

"Well, hello there," said a voice from the box in the lower right-hand corner. Katrina. Unlike Alicia, her camera was set far back, so I could see her upper half. She was reclined in a black chair, in what looked like an office. Her curly black hair was swept back into a knot at the nape of her neck and she wore brick-red lipstick.

My body tightened, anticipating the magic would come rushing forward as it had at the ceremony, but I didn't feel anything other than the chill of the lake air. The magic must have only activated when we were physically in each other's presence. Safety via technology—something I'd never thought I'd experience.

"Both of you?" A particularly strong gust of wind moved across the water toward the beach, the cold air making my eyes water. I swiped a finger under them and looked at the screen to see them both nodding.

"My inbox went crazy last night. I usually use a bit of magic to help organize it." Katrina paused and looked at us, our unsurprised faces confirming that we, too, had used our magic in secret. "But this morning I found it had created seventy-six new folders and sorted through everything on its own." Her gaze was offscreen, and the blue light from her computer flickered against her high cheekbones. "I can't even figure out where to begin. It's moving things around before I can even read them."

"Check this out," Alicia said, followed by quick flashes of the floor, ceiling, and wall, before the camera rested on five striped felines behind her. The animals were tan and had black spots like leopards but looked smaller, closer to the size of a dog. They each wore a pink collar and looked very cute and cuddly, but very much the sort of animal that might rip off someone's face while they slept.

"Are you at the zoo?" Katrina said in a perfunctory tone.

Alicia's phone steadied back on her, once again too close. "No. Those are our African serval cats. They're part of our animal menagerie for my show. We've been training them to perform tricks onstage. They haven't been the most compliant bunch, peeing everywhere and ripping things apart, but after our reunion, they changed. They follow me everywhere. It's thrilling." She adjusted her body, and five heads moved in unison, staring at her. Thrilling, indeed. I didn't want to remind her of what happened to Siegfried and Roy.

"Well, at least they aren't talking to you," I said as I rubbed my forehead. "My cat won't shut up now. She always communicated with me before, but now she has an actual speaking voice. And it's not a nice one."

Alicia nodded, her dangerous animal army bobbing behind her in unison.

"Look, with the attention Obsidian is getting right now in the media, the last thing I need is any extra scrutiny, or anything going awry," Katrina said as she lightly tapped at her keyboard. "Have you heard from that podcast woman, Madisyn? She seemed quite interested in investigating the fire."

"Thankfully, no."

Alicia hummed for a moment before she said, "She sent me an email asking for an interview, but I had to take the cats on a walk."

Katrina slowly locked her gaze on Alicia's image. "You say no. Do not speak to her."

Alicia looked confused. "She seemed nice, though. She said she bought tickets to my new show."

I shook my head, closing my eyes, as Katrina let out a slow exhale.

"Alicia, listen to me very carefully," she said, her voice a low rumble of thunder. "If she finds out that we were responsible for the fire, we could get in serious trouble. Jail-time sort of trouble."

I swallowed hard as I gripped my phone in front of my face. I knew what we had done was terrible, but I hadn't ever imagined a consequence that severe after all this time.

"Really?" I asked in a whisper.

"Really," Katrina confirmed. "I asked my lawyers in a hypothetical, roundabout way—a 'friend of a friend's son' kind of thing—and yes, legally, we could still be held responsible."

Alicia let out a small squeak. "But it was a total accident."

Katrina looked away, back at her computer screen. "Doesn't matter. Accidentally set fires are still a crime. As are reckless endangerment and property destruction." She leaned forward and shook her head. "Shit. Seven more folders just appeared."

Shapes began to form behind Alicia, the herd of savanna cats crowding around the screen, trying to peer at us. She turned and waved her hand, and they backed off. Slightly.

"How could this have happened?" I said.

The same question we'd asked each other as we'd watched our dorm burn to the ground.

There was a long pause, and I saw Alicia cast her eyes down, her eyelids decorated in purple glitter.

"We need to be careful. Maybe it's just some residual effect, and everything will calm down soon," Katrina said. "That podcaster will find some other topic. There have to be a million other crimes she can investigate. If none of us talk to her, there isn't a story."

While I agreed with her, I wasn't willing to have my open houses devolve into some kind of magical carnival while we waited. I couldn't risk anyone's finding out, not just about the fire, but about any of it. The magic inside of me.

"Should we try to get together and . . ." I waved my fingers but didn't finish the sentence. They knew what I meant: *Use magic to try to stop all of this.*

"Sounds fun. What about lunch here? I could make a fun butter board or charcuterie tray at my place," Alicia said with a smile.

Katrina shook her head quickly. "No. It's not safe," she said. "Look what happened the last time we gathered. I say we stay in contact and figure out next steps based on what happens." She cocked her head to the side, considering. "Unless . . ." She smiled. "We want to stop Madisyn preemptively." Her grin widened. "That could be fun. We never got to try it back in college."

I knew exactly what "it" she was thinking of.

A hex.

It was her unattained goal back in college. She had suggested hexing more than a couple of people back then, which Alicia and

I had always refused. The Rule of Three meant that the hex could come back to us, threefold, and it was a price we weren't willing to pay.

And I still wasn't.

But before Alicia or I could respond, I saw a woman in a pink tracksuit jogging down by the waterline. Her arms punched the air as she moved, like a female Rocky training for a fight.

"Oh no. I have to go. Staying in contact sounds good," I said quickly as I reached for the End Call button. Katrina frowned, and Alicia waved an enthusiastic goodbye.

I shoved my phone into my pocket as I stood up, my heels dangling from my fingertips. The woman in pink slowed when she saw me, as I knew she would, and then her face brightened and she jogged over, uppercuts swinging.

"I thought that was you," she said. "What are you doing out here? Not going for a run, I assume." My neighbor Taffy Redfield put her hands on her hips, surveying my wrinkled, sand-dusted body. Taffy was in her fifties, although she looked a bit older. She and her husband had a second home in Scottsdale, and it was clear that she didn't believe in sunscreen. She probably thought it was a government conspiracy, planned right after they hid JFK Jr.

"Just enjoying the scenery," I said. "A moment of quiet." I took a step toward the parking lot, hoping Taffy would take the hint.

Unfortunately for me, she was not one for picking up on social cues.

"What are you and Travis doing next weekend? Tucker and I still want to have you both over to see the Shelter," she said. She glanced down at her Apple Watch and swiped a few times. "Six p.m. Saturday?"

I chewed on my lip and pulled out my phone, pretending to look at my calendar as I tried to think of an excuse. Taffy and Tucker lived three doors down from us, in a sleek modern house they'd built two years ago. I had represented them in their purchase of the lot, a referral from another client. They'd built a monstrosity, a narrow, tall rectangular house that looked like a shoebox standing on one end.

The pièce de résistance was what was belowground. Taffy and Tucker were doomsday preppers, certain there would be an outbreak of domestic terrorism or a civil war coming soon. So they'd outfitted their basement with the Shelter, a cross between a high-end survival bunker and a panic room, where they claimed they could live up to three years when the time arose.

Never mind that, according to social media posts, the deadline for this apocalypse kept getting pushed back. That didn't stop them from trying to convince Travis and me to build our own shelter.

"Oh, shoot. Cheer competition this weekend." I wasn't lying—Harper had an all-day competition at a suburb an hour away, on the edges of cornfield territory. I smiled at her as I put my phone back in my pocket. "Sorry, but thanks for the invite."

Taffy shook her head sadly. "I understand, but we're worried about your family. You don't have much time to get your affairs in order before the main event. You did start collecting canned goods like I said, right?"

I made a murmuring sound, and she took a step forward. "We

want you on our side." She lifted a hand and placed it on my forearm before I could move away. "Please."

Annoyance flashed through my body as I wondered why she and Tucker had chosen to focus on us. We were just nonconfrontational enough that she and her other equally deluded friends wanted to include us in their LARP fantasies of being the true heroes.

I felt the magic start to tingle, ready to unleash on Taffy. After the chaotic house showing, I knew I didn't have much time before it got rid of her, one way or another.

"Look, I really should get going. This isn't a good time," I said quickly.

"Never" is a good time, I silently added before I turned and jogged toward my car, leaving her standing on the sand.

After I reached my car, I realized I hadn't put my shoes back on, and the bottoms of my feet were bleeding. The debris and rocks in the parking lot had cut into my bare feet as I booked it across the parking lot. I dabbed at the blood with a napkin from my console, wincing as the cuts stung.

My eyes lingered on the scar on my arm.

Chapter 9

SEVEN THOUSAND THREE HUNDRED AND FIVE MOONS AGO

Let's go. What's taking so long? You two are always late." Katrina stood outside my dorm room, a hand on the doorway as she leaned in. She smacked the door frame three times for emphasis.

I leapt up from the bottom bunk. The fact that I had scored the bottom bunk was nothing short of a miracle. My randomly assigned roommate, Clementine Corliss, was a Southern transplant who had left me a message before school began, trying to coordinate matching toile comforters and Lilly Pulitzer throw pillows. I never called her back. When she walked into the room on move-in day, she frowned when she saw my things already on the bottom bunk, including a plain navy comforter with exactly zero throw pillows. I'd claimed the bottom bunk because while I wanted to get along, I wasn't that nice.

Clementine was at a Pi Beta Phi sorority mixer. Rush week had just finished, and the sororities would be handing out their bids soon. I only knew about it because it was all she could talk about, spending long hours on the phone with her mom back home in Charleston. Apparently, Clementine was a legacy; her entire extended family had been Pi Phis and there would be hell to pay if she didn't get accepted.

I wore headphones a lot and still knew all of this.

"Finally," I said. As night fell, I had been waiting for Clementine to finish getting ready and leave for what felt like years. I wasn't sure how long it was supposed to take to apply MAC Lipglass, but she somehow managed to stretch it to twenty minutes.

"Where's Alicia?" I asked Katrina as I opened my particleboard closet door and bent down to retrieve our supplies. I pulled out the black vinyl duffel bag that I kept hidden behind my collapsible laundry basket.

"She snuck into the community garden to steal some basil leaves. Make sure everything's there," she added impatiently, drumming her fingertips against the door frame. She wore black yoga pants and a black zip-up hoodie, Adidas shower sandals on her feet.

That night, I wore a black tank dress that had been washed so many times, it had faded to a dark gray. It was the best I had to work with. I slid my feet into fluffy slippers.

I looked inside our bag of goodies from the curiosities shop: tarot cards, candles engraved with sigils, a crystal pendulum, obsidian stones. Shit was getting real. No more cafeteria trays and Walmart candles.

The first time we'd played around with the magic, it had been like a slumber party. We brought our comforters down into the rec room and, laughing the entire time, used whatever we could find near us.

We had decided to cast a spell for something innocuous, silly. Ridiculous, even. We asked that the dining hall serve chicken fingers every day, not just on Chicken Finger Fridays (which resulted in very inappropriate jokes and wordplay).

The moment we lit the candles in our circle, closed our eyes, and called forth the magic, we stopped laughing. It felt like an invisible wind had swept through Hawthorne Hall, encircling us, illuminating our circle.

"It's the underground magic, like the urban legends say. It's all real," I whispered as I watched the lights.

We felt like we were in an episode of *Charmed*.

And the next day, we saw a note taped up on the door of the dining hall announcing chicken fingers were permanently on the daily menu.

"You're welcome," I whispered when I saw the other students read it with glee.

And so it all started with chicken fingers.

But that night, we were ready to try something far more ambitious—it was the night we would try to shape our futures.

"Well? Is it all there?" Katrina said. She didn't wait for me to answer and impatiently stepped into my room, nudging my body aside with her leg as she grabbed for the bag, checking the contents. "Good. Just as I asked."

Typical. Even though we had all agreed on the ritual, created it together, listed out what we needed as a group, she still acted like the one in charge.

"Let's go find Alicia," she said, and didn't wait for me to answer before she walked out of the room, slinging the bag across her shoulder as I followed.

"Sarah, hi. I thought I heard your door close. Staying in tonight? Another juggling club meeting?" Our RA Nancy's head popped out of her door, and I jumped, crashing into the wall next to me. I had been silently repeating my part of the ritual, making sure I had the words memorized for when it was time.

Then I realized we actually at some point would have to learn to juggle if we wanted to keep up appearances. But not tonight.

Nancy had taken her contacts out and wore her glasses, thick black frames, and a matching pink velour Juicy Couture sweatsuit, the silver J hanging from the zipper. I suspected that her parents were wealthy because she had four Juicy Couture tracksuits and a new MacBook, but she was so normal that I never would have thought otherwise.

I nodded, my eyes shifting toward where Katrina had already rounded the corner down the hallway. "I think we're going to practice a little and then maybe watch a movie in the rec room."

"What movie?" she asked brightly.

"Um, *Blue Crush*," I said.

"Fun. I love that movie." She paused, an awkward moment passing between us without an invitation for her to join. "Well, have a good time. Do you guys want any popcorn?"

Before I answered, she turned and retrieved a bag of unpopped microwave popcorn and held it out, looking at me expectantly, still hoping for an invite. A wave of guilt ran through me. Any other time—when we weren't doing magic—I would have invited her. She was only a year older than us, but taking on the RA role had kept her on the outskirts of the North Valley social scene, too.

I took the flat bag from her. "Thanks," I said, averting my gaze as I turned and walked down the hallway, feeling terrible. Nancy was so nice and seemed as though she really wanted some companionship, but this wasn't the night to cultivate new friendships.

I found Katrina and Alicia on the floor in the rec room, seated on the navy blue fleece blanket Alicia kept on her bed. It had glittery spots on it from when she fell asleep at night before she washed off her body powder. Around Alicia's neck was a plastic circle, filled with a few of the sea monkeys that she kept in her room. Technically, we weren't allowed pets in the dorm room, but brine shrimp and her betta fish, Franco, were somewhat outside of that policy. She often put a few of the shrimp in a necklace or a bracelet and wore them to class, as though people needed another reason to find her strange.

Alicia was busy laying out the basil leaves she'd collected in the garden, placing them on the perimeter of the blanket in a circle. The leaves were used to call forth the power of nature to amplify our intentions. She placed dried hydrangea blooms on top of the leaves for extra protection.

Katrina began to drip oil on the candles we had charged with energy by placing them on our windowsills during the full moon. She then placed the tarot cards in the center of the circle, put the obsidian stones on top of them, and held the crystal pendulum in her hand.

I took my seat in between them, forming a triangle with Katrina facing north, and Alicia and I facing east and west. With the candles set up in the center, we began the ritual as we always did: by taking three deep breaths and then calling out to the elements.

> *We call to the elements: water, fire, earth, and air*
> *We ask you to help us with utmost care*
> *We each have a wish or a dream*
> *From now on we ask it is granted it would seem*

I opened one eye and glanced at Katrina, reacting to the clunky incantation she had written, and then quickly closed it to lock in on the spell.

> *For on this night we shall see*
> *The power between us three*
> *As it burns*
> *So shall it be*

Time to get specific.

Alicia slowly opened her eyes, which were rimmed with black liquid eyeliner and purple glitter.

"I ask the magic to grant me my most desired wish: fame." She smiled broadly as she spoke the words, unable to maintain a neutral, calm demeanor. I imagined she pictured finally being noticed by the world. She'd grown up in the shadows of her two older, beautiful, successful sisters, and she was the unplanned, much younger addition. She had tried to differentiate herself, but all it had done was make her the freak of the family.

Socially, people noticed her, but not in a good way. They stepped out of her path on the sidewalks that crisscrossed the quad.

Weirdo.

Loser.

She looked at Katrina, who nodded.

"I ask the magic to grant me what I know is my life's purpose: Victory. Success," Katrina said, her voice booming.

"Shhhhh," I hissed, glancing over my shoulder. Although the

dorm was fairly empty, the last thing we needed was another student stumbling into our ritual.

Katrina shot me an angry look and then relaxed her face.

"Victory and success," she repeated confidently.

We knew why Katrina coveted such things. Her parents had money, but her mother was like her father's servant. He was the businessman, the one with the power at home, and his word was law. Her mother only existed to make sure his demands were met. A voiceless fixture, like the custom-made furniture or the designer wallpaper.

Useless.

Powerless.

Then it was my turn.

I closed my eyes and took a deep breath, afraid my dream would sound stupid. But I was able to whisper my truest wish: to find love. My mother watched romantic movies the way someone might watch a sci-fi film set on a distant planet.

Unloved.

Lonely.

I wanted whatever was the opposite of what my mother had. I wanted someone who loved me, who would support me, who would have children with me, who would make sure I didn't spend nights crying over the electric bill that I couldn't find a way to pay. Someone to make me laugh. Someone who thought I was the whole world.

I wanted the blue-box mac and cheese, not the generic store brand.

I wasn't even sure that kind of love existed; I had only seen it in movies and TV shows. But I still wanted it.

After I whispered my incantation, I slowly opened my eyes. Alicia passed each of us a short match to light the candles in front of us. We struck our matches at the same time, moving our hands together so the candles would be lit simultaneously.

The times we had done it before, the candles would be lit, and then the flames would reach higher than they could naturally, the fire extending just above the circle, offering up our intentions.

Yet this was different.

We lit the candles, and at first, the flames did nothing.

"Huh." I cocked my head in confusion. Maybe we had forgotten a step or missed something.

Maybe what we had asked for was too big.

A hollow thought rattled through me as I wondered if what we had asked for was unattainable. I wasn't meant for the kind of love I so wanted. An impossible ask, even for the magic.

"What the hell?" Katrina said as we continued to stare at the flames, which danced as innocently as the L'Occitane candles a girl down the hall had in her room, artificial lilac stinking up the corridor every Sunday night.

"Maybe we . . ." Alicia trailed off as she felt around behind her for the brown notebook we kept to record all of our rituals. "Forgot . . ."

"Why isn't it working?" Katrina's voice amplified. "Are they dud candles?"

"I don't know! Please give me a moment," Alicia said, her voice cracking as she flipped open the notebook.

I didn't say anything as I stared as the flame in front of me. It looked different. Darker.

"You guys," I said. *I think something is wrong*, I wanted to say.

Before I could, one of the candles began to spark. Small embers flew off my candle, bouncing off the tray and onto the fleece blanket underneath.

Small burn holes surrounded the candles as sparks flew off the flames and landed in front of us. I crab-scrambled backward to get away from the fire. Katrina turned and flung her body across the yellow linoleum floor like an army commander, while Alicia's eyes were open wide, frozen, as she stared at the candles.

The sparks didn't fizzle out, and flames began to eat the blanket, the red and yellow fingers of the fire quickly reaching across the worn material.

"Alicia!" I shouted, and wrenched her arm.

She snapped out of her trance and rolled off the blanket just as the fire began to consume where she'd sat.

I stood. "Water! We need water." I ran into the small kitchen off the rec room as Katrina and Alicia tried to pick up the edges of the blanket to smother the fire.

Katrina stopped and I heard her saying the words for an incantation, asking for the power of water, to calm the flames.

"Are you crazy?" I screamed. This wasn't a time to use more magic; this was a time to involve emergency services and a fire hose. To stop, drop, and roll.

I flung open the maple cabinets, searching for a fire extinguisher or a container to stick under the faucet. They were empty. Out of the corner of my eye, I could see that my friends weren't having any luck with putting out the fire. It ignited the edges of the blanket as they folded it over, rather than suffocating it.

Desperate, I cupped my hands under the faucet and filled them with cold water. It dripped through my fingers as I ran toward the blanket, and I flung it down. Only a few drops of water pathetically landed on the blanket, evaporating immediately.

Sweat poured down my back, from both panic and the rising heat in the room. The thick smell of burnt plastic filled my nose as the flames consumed our ceremonial pieces. The dried hydrangea blooms only served as an accelerant.

"What should we do?" Alicia said. Her face was streaked with tears and sweat, glittery makeup falling down her cheeks like track marks, giving her the look of a horror movie clown.

"Run," Katrina said. She grabbed Alicia's upper arm and began to drag her toward the exit. "Sarah, c'mon!" she shouted.

I hesitated, not wanting to leave what we had created, to allow it to grow into something worse.

Why aren't the smoke detectors going off? They must be ready to blare. The sprinkler system has to activate soon.

We stumbled up the gray carpeted stairs to the first floor of our dorm building, shouting that there was a fire downstairs. But no one came; everyone was at the Saturday night parties.

"Help!" I shouted in the foyer as smoke began to waft up from the basement stairs. Then I remembered someone. "Nancy—she's upstairs."

I took a step toward the stairway, but Katrina pulled me back. "You won't get there in time."

"She's right. Look," Alicia whined. Her gaze was fixed on the stairs to the rec room, now thick with smoke and alight with dancing red and yellow flames. We were several feet from it, but the intensity of the heat was already beginning to redden my skin.

"We have to try," I said as I moved toward the stairway to alert Nancy. Just then, a burst of fire swept up the stairway to my right, burning my arm. I didn't feel any pain, just stared at it in wonder as my skin turned red and I smelled the burned hair and skin.

I allowed Katrina and Alicia to pull me outside as we shouted into the building for anyone who could hear that there was a fire, to call 911, get help.

Over the next two hours, we watched as the flames climbed up the building, scorching the ivy that grew on the side of the red brick building. We smelled the smoke as it poured out of the windows and saw as the heat exploded glass onto the pavement below. More and more fire trucks lit up the dark night, the firefighters shouting instructions to each other, and the water hoses sprayed, seemingly in vain.

"No one is going to believe we're a juggling club," Alicia said.

Stretchers were brought out of the building, ladders erected to rescue our fellow students after ambulances arrived. Katrina and Alicia were in separate ambulances, oxygen masks strapped on as they were treated for smoke inhalation.

An EMT wrapped my arm in a thick, white bandage where I was burned. One of them told me I needed to go to the hospital to have it checked out, but it was like listening from underwater.

The last thing I saw before they closed the ambulance's door was a stretcher carrying a woman with blond hair, her face streaked with black and her skin reddened. They hurried her to a waiting ambulance, shouting instructions. Her eyes were closed. She looked dead.

Her arm dropped off the stretcher as they loaded her in, the remnants of a tattered pink Juicy Couture sweatshirt floating off her body.

Chapter 10

A yellow dotted bathing suit flashed around the side of my house as I pulled into the driveway after leaving Lighthouse Beach. I could hear the sounds of teenagers having probably a bit too much fun as I got out of my car and walked to the backyard.

The music increased in intensity as I unlocked the gate and heard someone yell, "Cannonball!" before it died down when the group saw an adult had arrived.

Harper and her cheer squad friends were spread out on the loungers around the pool, surrounded by towels and beach bags, sunscreen spilling out onto the pool deck. She was on her stomach, lying on an aqua and white striped Turkish towel spread next to the edge of the pool, her knees bent, heels toward her head, aimlessly fluttering her feet with a magazine open in front of her.

Hunter's crew had commandeered the hot tub, half of them submerged in the water, the other half sitting on the edge, their hands trailing in the bubbling water. There was foam at the top of the water, giving the hot tub the appearance of a pot about to boil over on the stove.

I closed the pool gate loudly, and their heads jerked up in unison. Someone turned down the music, and Harper gave me a cautious wave. I couldn't see her eyes behind her aviator sunglasses, but her body language was tense; she was waiting to see if it was okay that they'd had a party without asking first.

Normally, I might have questioned why they didn't seek permission, but the day had been too long to fixate on small grievances.

"Hey, guys," I said with a casual wave. I walked over to the edge of the pool, slipped off my shoes, and sat down, sticking my scraped feet in the water. There was a palpable sense of relief as the teens' shoulders collectively relaxed.

"Mom, you should come swimming," Harper said as she flipped a magazine page.

I smiled and shook my head. "No, thanks." I trailed my feet in the pool. "How was practice, girls?" The water was a translucent gray from the cloudy day. My shoulders hunched forward as I kept my feet submerged under the surface.

Georgia, a flyer on the squad who could seemingly bend herself in half when hoisted up, sighed. "We still can't get the heel stretch right. It keeps wobbling." She cocked her head ever so slightly toward the two girls who based her stunt, allowing the blame to carry through the wind over to them. They pretended not to notice.

"You guys will get it, I'm sure," I said. Harper twisted her mouth in disagreement but didn't say anything.

Her squad had been working on that particular stunt all summer, at sleepover camps and long practices after which she came home limping and sweaty. They still hadn't perfected it.

"Hunter. Hello. Nice to see you," I said with a laugh as I waved over to the hot tub.

He stopped the story he was relaying to his lacrosse team-mates, hands poised in the air. "Hey, Mom. Thanks for setting out all those snacks for when we got home from school," he said.

I frowned, trying to understand what he was talking about. I didn't remember setting anything out before I left for the listing meeting.

Unless . . .

I swallowed hard and nodded. "Sure thing." I tried to keep my face neutral as I craned my neck toward the house, attempting to peer into the kitchen and see if the magic had laid out an after-school snack spread for my kids. I couldn't see into the house, but I spotted Katy Purry lounging under the hydrangeas that lined the pool deck. Her eyes darted around as she looked for a small creature to torture. She made eye contact, and I gave her a warning look that said, *Remember, everyone can hear you.*

"Hey hey," said a voice from behind the gate.

I turned and saw Travis dressed in scrubs, walking across the pool deck, home early from the hospital. He laughed as he surveyed the scene around the pool.

"Taking advantage of the time between the rain, huh?" he said.

I saw Harper's friends straighten up, a titter going between them. I knew, because I had overheard, that they thought Travis was cute, "for an old person, obviously." He wasn't like their fathers, who were relegated to thinning hairlines and increasing waists.

Hunter's friends brightened at the sight of their favorite dad, who always got them tickets to Bears and Bulls games—courtesy of the hospital—and let them order as much food as they wanted in the corporate suite.

"What's up, Dr. Nelson?" Luke Tobin, the goalie on the lacrosse team, called out, lifting a hand.

"Not much. Tell your dad I said hey," Travis said with a wave. Luke's dad was an in-demand plastic surgeon—one who did good work, properly placed belly buttons and all.

Travis walked over to me and smiled. "How was your day?"

I nodded, pushing down the memories of the magic. "Good. I think the Johnstons are going to move on the Northfield house."

"Well, that's great." He looked around the pool deck, squinting. "We should celebrate, then."

He held out a hand and I allowed him to pull me close. "Twist my arm," I said with a laugh. "I'm not really in the mood to cook dinner tonight." I looked over at the kids. "Looks like you're ordering Domino's."

Travis slung an arm around my shoulder. With the weight of his body next to mine, I felt safe again. Protected from my past, protected from what might have been happening again.

"They're so cute," I heard one of Harper's friends say.

"Mom, can you get us some more snacks? Like a bunch of sandwiches?" Hunter called out, clasping his hands in prayer.

"Sure." Only sixteen-year-old boys would consider a bunch of sandwiches a "snack."

Travis kept an arm around me as we walked inside.

"Just let me change," he said before he turned to walk up the stairs.

"Sounds good. I'll get on those 'light snacks' for the boys." I turned and headed to the basement to grab the food.

I opened the basement fridge, ready to pull out the Boar's Head turkey and sliced cheese, but stumbled back when I peered inside, tripping over an errant Nike one of the kids had left in the basement. I fell down hard, and pain jolted up my arms as they tried to brace my fall. I stared at the inside of the fridge.

Inside were stacks upon stacks of plastic bags filled with deli meat.

I leaned forward and crawled slowly, my eyes widening as I looked at the tower of lunch meat. The bags filled an entire shelf of the fridge, pushing upward into the grate above it. There must have been forty pounds of it in there.

"No. No. No. No. No. No," I sputtered as I slid one of the bags out and looked at the label.

Salsalito turkey, very thinly sliced. The same kind I always stocked. Somehow the magic had gone into overdrive with that, too, and just rotely stocked the turkey until it ran out of room, the Energizer Bunny finally running into a wall. I tried to slip the one I'd extracted back into the fridge, but it seemed the hole had been instantly filled.

Thank God Travis or the kids hadn't spotted it first.

But I didn't have long to reflect on what I would have said if they had, because I heard shrieks and screams coming from the pool deck, the sounds of teenagers all being spooked at once.

What now?

I scrambled up, slamming the fridge door closed to hide the flock of turkeys who had died in vain, and ran up the basement stairs.

"What's wrong?" I called out as I yanked open the sliding glass door.

I saw Hunter and his friends jogging away from the hot tub to the grass nearby.

"What is that thing?" Hunter said as he ran toward his twin. Despite sibling bickering, they always found each other in honest moments of emotion—fear, love, laughter.

A small brown animal was army-crawling across the pool deck, sniffing around and scampering underneath the pool loungers, Katy Purry following in close pursuit, tail twitching.

Harper and her friends screamed and stood up, flapping their arms like stereotypes of teenage girls.

"I think it's a rat," Georgia screamed as she ran toward the gate, still in her bathing suit.

The boys laughed while stepping away from where the small animal hid. It was brown with white spots and peered out from under the lounger, shaking.

Katy Purry smiled at it, ready to claim her next victim. The year before, we'd counted at least twenty lawn creatures that she had maimed, bringing each inside as a gift, an offering, to us, a look of pride on her orange face.

"What's wrong? I heard shouting." Travis appeared, half dressed in a white T-shirt and scrub pants.

"Katy Purry found another one." I nudged Travis with my elbow. "Go see what it is."

Travis crept toward it, slowly bent down, and peered at the animal, then stopped and laughed. He turned back to me, his shoulders shaking. "It's a squirrel. A baby squirrel. It must have fallen out of the nest."

At the mention of squirrel rather than rat or possum, Harper and her friends smiled and began to cautiously walk over from where they had congregated near the pool gate.

"I want to see," Hunter said, and padded over to where Travis leaned down. Harper lined up behind her father, peering around his shoulder.

"It's so cute!" she squealed when she saw it. "He's so scared." She held out a hand for it to approach, despite my protests. I saw Katy Purry's eyes flash in annoyance and jogged over to her, scooping her up before she could pounce again.

"Bullshit," she whispered to me. "That thing is mine." I clutched her to my chest, hoping no one heard.

Hunter turned around, eyes wide. "Mom, what did you say?"

"Nothing. I didn't hear anything," I said quickly as I speed-walked toward the sliding glass door and dumped Katy Purry inside.

"No Temptations for you tonight," I hissed at her as I closed the door. She began furiously pawing at the glass, meowing in protest.

"What are we supposed to do with it?" I called out from the door. "Find the nest and put it back?"

Travis shrugged and pulled out his phone, typing away at the screen. "It says here we should call a wildlife center."

"Aunt Nancy!" Harper said. She swept her blond hair over her shoulders and turned back to smile at her friends. "My aunt runs a wildlife center, so we can give it to her." She raised her eyebrows at Hunter. "Go get a box or something."

He turned and jogged inside without question, past the cat. Harper had always been the leader in their relationship, and he was the one who kept her humble with pranks and teasing, the yang to her yin.

Travis turned to me and said, "I'll text my sister," as Hunter reappeared with a Nike box. Katy Purry stared at me from inside, a look on her face that said she was definitely going to pee in my closet later.

I watched as Travis held the Nike box and crept toward the squirrel, and it inched away from him, a silent dance.

"Hang on," he said. He paused, and the squirrel cocked its head to one side before Travis lunged for him, thrusting the box forward.

But the squirrel was too fast and narrowly escaped, running around the side of the pool deck, past Hunter's friends, who yelled in protest; past the hot tub; straight toward me. I froze. Two small back eyes fixed on me, a small, pathetic tail trailing behind.

A screech caught in my throat as it ran full throttle to me. I lifted my arm across my chest for protection, leaning away from the animal. I closed my eyes as I waited to be attacked. But, instead of an attack, I felt it curl up in my arms.

"Mom!" I heard Harper call, and I slowly opened my eyes.

The squirrel's sharp claws tickled me as it climbed up my chest, before resting on my shoulder. It chirped a few times, and everyone tittered.

"It . . . likes you," Harper said, her voice low.

"Um, what now?" I said in a hissed whisper. "Help!"

Katy Purry went into a tizzy inside, and I could hear her alternate between meows and *Oh hell no.*

Travis slowly walked over, hiding a smile behind his hand. "Snow White and the woodland creatures."

I pointed a finger at my shoulder. "Help," I whispered again.

Travis held the Nike box against my shoulder as he slowly slid the squirrel off me and inside, closing the box.

"Are you the squirrel whisperer now?" Hunter said.

I hoped to the high heavens that wasn't my fate. Alicia would have her herd of African serval cats, and I would be left with rodents and felines.

"I hope not." I looked at Travis. "Let's get it to your sister."

Chapter 11

"D on't forget to breathe through your mouth," Travis reminded me as we walked up to the doors of Nancy's workplace, the Woodbluff Wildlife Center.

"Already on it," I said. I had only visited Nancy's work a few times, yet the memory of the smell had never left me. It was a combination of ammonia, coyote urine, and cedar chips.

I held the box with the squirrel inside. A few times on the car ride over, it had scratched on the side of the box, and I'd peered through the holes in the side. I could have sworn the damn thing smiled at me. At one point, it raised a clawed paw and waved at me.

At least it did not talk. Although Katy Purry had certainly had a lot to say before we left, when Travis was upstairs finishing changing.

"How would you like it if I stole *your* dinner? Keep pissing me off, and I'm going to tell the kids about your hidden boxes of mac and cheese."

I placated her by opening one of the million bags of sliced turkey from the basement fridge and placing it on the ground. She grumbled but thankfully shut up.

Travis opened the glass door with *Woodbluff Wildlife Center* stenciled on the front in white lettering. I stepped through, into the foyer filled with glass cases of animal skulls and a large plastic tree with a cut in the center for kids to burrow into like the center's residents. I looked to my right and nearly dropped the box with the squirrel inside as I came inches from the taxidermied, outstretched mouth of a bobcat, its fangs pointed and ready to sink into my skin.

I also forgot to breathe through my mouth and inhaled sharply, the pungent smell of animal urine burning my throat.

I started sputtering just as Nancy appeared. She wore a long-sleeved tan polo with the center's name embroidered across the chest, tan cargo pants caked with dirt, and black work boots.

"There you are," she said. She eyed my black dress and Travis's tan pants and blue and white checkered button-down. "You guys are a little overdressed." We were dressed for our celebration dinner, ready to head to the restaurant after we made a quick stop to drop off the squirrel.

Nancy fixed her gaze on the Nike box in my hands, held out like an offering plate, the burn scars on her neck peeking ever so slightly out of the collar of her shirt.

"Let's see what we have here."

I gingerly moved it toward her, and she took it from me, her reddened hands strong and confident as she brought the box to her midsection.

"How's work today?" Travis said as we shuffled toward the glass case filled with bird skulls.

She laughed. "It's been quite a day. The wolf pack got into a fight and we had to separate them—bad blood from when we didn't put enough frozen mice in there and Chester hoarded them all. Then Misty, the raccoon who was hit by a car last year, escaped her enclosure and tried to open up the dumpster out back." She shook her head. "And it's not even closing time yet."

The creepy blue jays screeched from their six-foot enclosure just inside the animal-viewing area.

"Quiet." She rolled her eyes. "Tom and Jerry have been in quite the mood today."

I looked over at the two birds, which were perched on the side of the cage, cocking their heads back and forth like a pair of metronomes, their small black eyes staring at me. I had brought Hunter and Harper to the center more than a few times when they were little, as it was a good place to walk with them in the double stroller, traversing the dirt trails past the animal cages, pointing out the story behind each one.

All of the animals at the center had come there for rehabilitation, due to either abandonment or injury, from being hit by a car or some other human interference. Most of them had been deemed unfit for the wild and unable to be released, so the center was their forever home.

"Is Lawrence still here?" Travis asked as he leaned against the glass counter.

Nancy pointedly looked at him, and he quickly removed his elbow, brushing off the thick layer of dust now on his shirt.

"Sorry," he said, and lifted his palms in the air. "Don't want to disturb the skeletons."

She put a hand over the Nike box and frowned at him. "They might come back to haunt you. They all met terrible ends from humans. I'm sure they haven't forgotten."

Her eyes slowly slid to me for the briefest of moments, so quick that I was sure Travis didn't notice, but I did.

"Yes, Lawrence the turtle is still here. Prosthetic shell still working." She peered into the box. "Hello there. Just a little guy, aren't you?" Nancy cooed into the box. She extended a finger inside.

"So you can take it, then?" Travis said as he checked the time on his black Apple Watch. He nodded and looked at me, without waiting for her to answer. "We figured you would know what to do with it."

"Her. Know what to do with her. She's female," Nancy said, almost to herself. She looked up, her clear blue eyes glinting in the waning sunlight of the foyer. "Of course I know what to do with her."

She carefully picked up the box and jerked her head toward the back. "Follow me. I have just the habitat for her." She turned and walked through the doorway to the animal-viewing area.

Travis poked my arm behind her back. "We are going to be late. You know how she gets. We could be here for hours."

I shot him a warning look. "Stop. It's just dinner. We can eat at the bar if we miss our reservation."

We followed Nancy through the doorway beneath a dusty sign proudly welcoming us to the center, which looked like it had been painted circa 1975, in orange and red with stenciled green ivy encircling the letters.

The emotionally unstable blue jays squawked as we approached their cage, which was just a tall, thin wire enclosure. They screeched as they flitted from wall to wall, their heads jerking even more rapidly.

"Quiet," Nancy commanded as she pushed ahead toward the back of the building. As I walked past Tom and Jerry, one flew over to the cage's side and stuck his pointy beak through the wire opening, squawking loudly as he tried to peck at my coat.

Travis whispered behind me, "Think Hitchcock visited here?"

I smiled but didn't respond as I kept walking along the tan linoleum, my gaze trained on Nancy's back. Her hair was in a messy ponytail at the nape of her neck, secured by a black elastic that looked like it had seen better days.

To my left was a bank of aquariums filled with frogs and turtles. I stopped and peered into one of the tanks. Lawrence, the painted turtle who had come in with a cracked shell and received a new prosthetic one, floated lazily to the surface of the water.

I smiled and tapped at the glass. I'd always wanted a turtle. When I was growing up, there was a pond in the forest preserve just past our apartment building, and sometimes turtles would float up to the surface as I peered into the water. They always seemed so friendly, so harmless. My mom had nixed my requests for any kind of furry pet, so I fixated on getting a turtle. I even picked a name: Tully. Tully the turtle. I never got my pet turtle, my mom instead compromising on a goldfish that I named Cracker (after the Pepperidge Farm snack). I was overjoyed at first, watching Cracker swim back and forth in his plastic fishbowl. But I quickly lost interest in him after cleaning the bowl a couple of times. He died after a month, and neither my mom nor I shed a tear when we flushed him down the toilet, the pet experiment over.

Lawrence's name was displayed on the placard to the right of the tank. *Sponsored by the Breen family* was displayed in small letters under his name. Travis and I had donated money for the library a few years back, but I started to wonder if we should sponsor an animal next time. One that didn't have to live with us . . . or talk.

I leaned in closer to Lawrence, and he slowly turned his head to look at me.

"Hey there, buddy," I said.

Lawrence's eyes bulged—something that I didn't know was possible—and he ducked his head into his plastic shell with a flourish, sinking to the bottom of the tank.

"Guess he's a little shy," Travis said with a laugh.

"Oh." I stood up, frowning, a whisper inside my core telling me that it wasn't nerves from a turtle that had been terrorized in the wild. It was me. He knew.

I kept walking, keeping my gaze trained forward. As I walked through the building, out of the corner of my eye I could see the animals in their tanks scurry away from the glass, desperate for a safe place to hide . . . from me. It seemed as though while some creatures embraced me, like the wayward baby squirrel, others were afraid.

The animal kingdom is more in tune with magic than we are.

Alicia's words popped into my brain. She had said this decades ago, when we first started experimenting with the magic. We were outside in the quad, gathering fallen sticks and spent buckeyes to use as decorations for our altar, when we heard an owl call out in the night air. We never saw it, but it continued to hoot as we collected our things, like it was trying to tell us something.

Alicia took it as a good sign. Katrina ignored it. I wasn't sure.

In the back room of the center, Nancy placed the Nike box with the baby squirrel in it on a white linoleum counter. She pulled a white box out from a cabinet under the counter, opened the shoebox, and gently transferred our woodland visitor.

"There you go. You'll be much more comfortable here." Her voice was full of warmth and compassion, neither of which she ever displayed when she talked to humans. Not that I could blame her after everything she had been through.

She brushed the top of the squirrel's head with a slightly gnarled finger and then looked at us. "I'll make sure she's safe."

"Thanks a lot," Travis said as he took a slight step toward the door, more than ready to leave.

I thought of the placard by Lawrence. "We'd love to sponsor her, if that's okay," I said quickly.

Nancy's lined face brightened and she smiled, and for a moment, I remembered the girl from freshman year. It hadn't escaped me that my in-laws had chosen to raise money for a scholarship fund rather than for the wildlife center. A scholarship fund was splashy, bigger, more worthy of the society pages than a linoleum-tiled center where raccoons came to die. Despite my love for Marcy and Thomas, I wasn't blind to the fact that they could be achingly shortsighted when it came to their daughter.

"Wonderful. Why don't you come outside and I can show you what we're building for the coyotes? We would love some help with that, too."

Travis made a sound, no doubt ready to just write a check rather than stomping through the mud to see the coyote enclosure.

"We'd love to," I said.

. . .

I shifted my heels as they sank in the dirt and wet leaves outside the half-constructed coyote pen. "It's great, Nancy. I'm sure they will love it."

She nodded, and I saw Travis take a quick step toward the parking lot again, ready to go.

"Thanks for showing us around, Nance, and for taking the squirrel. But we really should get going. Dinner reservations," Travis said, hooking a thumb over his shoulder and giving her an apologetic look.

She frowned and shook her head slightly, in a gesture that said she couldn't fathom why we wouldn't want to spend any extra minutes at the center. She took one last glance at the coyote enclosure before she nodded and turned, gesturing for us to follow her back down the dirt path to the parking lot.

A breeze blew through the woods as we followed, carrying my hair off my neck and cooling the sweat that had started to pool under my arms. The tree canopy above us rustled, leaves gently floating down to the path.

"Sarah, look at this," Travis said from behind me.

I turned and saw him standing in front of a chicken-wire-encased enclosure, about twelve feet high. I tiptoed around forest debris on the path as I approached. Inside the cage were a few hollowed-out logs, some old car tires, and shiny-looking dog toys. Wooden steps led to a second level, with soft bedding and bowls of water.

A sign next to the cage read: *Raccoon Habitat.*

No name after them—I guess no one wanted to sponsor the trash pickers.

"Their house looks nicer than ours," Travis said with a laugh.

"Figures," I said.

Nancy walked back and came up to my left side. "Isabelle and Hannah. They were brought here after their mother abandoned them." She took a step forward and made a clicking sound, and two gray heads popped up out of the cozy bed.

"Aren't they sweet?" she said as their beady eyes fixed on us.

I thought of our trash cans, of picking up rotten food off the driveway and holding my nose as I corralled week-old yogurt containers. Thankfully, the spell I had done on the morning I received the reunion invitation had held, and they had stayed away. But I was sure they would find a way to come back—they always did. "They're certainly crafty animals," I said.

I slid my eyes to Travis, who stifled a smile. We both knew better than to say anything negative about wildlife in front of Nancy.

"Come on, Isabelle. Come here," Nancy cooed to one of the raccoons.

I smiled at her tone, full of warmth and love. A glimpse into the softer side of her personality, one that she kept hidden under lock and key, away from everyone. A secret, carefully buried.

We had more in common than she knew.

The raccoon slowly stood up from its warm bed, glancing at its friend, Hannah, before stepping over to the stairs and beginning to descend.

"That's it," Nancy whispered. "Come say hi." She made a motion with her hand for Isabelle to continue.

I frowned as I noticed her claws, much longer up close than I had anticipated. They looked sharp, ready to scratch and attack. I shivered as I thought of her teeth. And rabies.

"She's really cute, Nance," Travis said quickly. He caught my eye and jerked his head toward the car.

Let's go, he mouthed.

Nancy didn't—or pretended not to—hear her brother, her gaze still fixed on the raccoon. With her urging, Isabelle continued down the stairs at a leisurely pace, with all the time in the world. She apparently didn't have dinner reservations starting in fifteen minutes.

I gave Travis a look that said, *Just a few more minutes*.

Isabelle stepped over the old car tire in her pen, making her way toward Nancy.

"You should have garbage cans in here for them to play with," Travis said with a chuckle, putting his hands in his coat pockets.

I made a harrumph sound. "Our trash is not a toy. They need to stay away."

I gave Isabelle a withering look. Her head snapped to me and she froze, her eyes wide.

"C'mon, girl. What's wrong?" Nancy said. When the raccoon didn't move, Nancy looked from her to me. "What did you say?"

"N-nothing," I stammered, warning bells beginning to go off in my head. "Just that they like to get into our trash."

Or *used* to. Before I did the spell.

At the sound of my voice, Isabelle turned and ran back up the stairs, leaping into her cozy bed and hiding. I swear, I saw a look of shame on her face before it disappeared into the fleece material.

I don't know how, but she knew. She knew I had done a spell to banish the raccoons from our house and was afraid to get near me.

Travis laughed. "Well, let's hope the ones in our neighborhood feel the same way about us."

Nancy glared at him and shook her head. She gave me a critical, appraising look before she whispered a few soothing words to Isabelle and Hannah.

As we followed Nancy back down the dirt path to our car, Travis leaned over and whispered, "Well, that didn't go how I thought it would."

"No kidding," I said. I glanced back over my shoulder at the raccoon enclosure. Isabelle's black eyes found mine, and she ducked back down into her bed.

I had done small spells to keep pests away from our house before—before the reunion, before the magic amplified—and they had always worked, without any truly lasting effects.

But this? This was new. It seemed I had alienated an entire species of wildlife by asking them not to knock over our trash cans.

Not entirely the worst possible consequence, but it felt like a warning. One that said the worst was yet to come.

Chapter 12

Several hundred dollars lighter, after a check written to the center to sponsor the baby squirrel, Travis and I drove home. My dress was streaked with dirt and the backs of my legs had clumps of drying mud stuck to them. Not exactly prime attire for La Marche.

He put the car in Park when we reached the top of our circular driveway.

"Well, that was an interesting night out," he said. He put a hand on my knee, and the warmth melted my tension ever so slightly. "I'm sorry. That wasn't the way I wanted our date night to go, obviously."

"Not your fault," I said. "Hopefully our donation will help the squirrel live a long, happy life."

I started to reach for the car door to go inside, but Travis didn't remove his hand from my knee. I turned toward him, and he put a hand on my cheek, bringing his face to mine and kissing me.

Despite my shoddy appearance and possibly traumatizing animal encounter, my body began to tingle. He slowly moved a hand down to my rumpled dress and started to unzip it.

I leaned back and shook my head. "Not here. Inside." I nervously glanced around and sure enough, Lois Greenglass's watchful face was peering out of her window, mentally recording any neighborhood disturbances. We were a few moments away from being the subject of a neighborhood telegram.

Inappropriate activity at the Nelson house. Stop.
Called the police to report indecent exposure. Stop.

We walked inside, holding hands and laughing, falling against the door as we closed it. We ran upstairs, and I heard Harper whisper to Hunter from the television room.

"Ew. What's wrong with them?"

"That was incredible," Travis whispered in my ear as we lay in bed, sweaty and exhausted.

He was right—it was the kind of sex that we hadn't had in years, since back after we had first met. When it felt like my body would die if he wasn't close to me. When we couldn't wait to get inside somewhere private, we found the most discreet place nearby to fool around.

I didn't want to give the turbocharged magic any credit, but that was one side effect that I certainly didn't mind.

After I put my muddy dress in the dry-cleaning pile, I lay in bed next to Travis, unable to sleep as he lightly snored.

I stared at the text message Nancy had sent us after we got home.

Isabelle and Hannah are still skittish. Not sure what spooked them so much. I will make sure to add your names to the sponsor placard next to our newest resident squirrel.

I didn't want our names on anything. It seemed like the least we could do. Too bad I couldn't pay for therapy for Isabelle and Hannah. I'd had no idea the raccoon-deterring spell would have such lasting, traumatic consequences for an entire population.

Travis rolled over, the white noise of his snoring never changing in volume, and I caught a glimpse of his neatly folded scrubs on the tan leather chair in the corner of our room. The moonlight shone through the French doors to our private balcony, almost like a spotlight on the work clothes.

It was a photograph, a mental snapshot, a symbol illuminating that he always thought of everything. I had friends who complained that their husbands never picked up their clothes, never thought to empty the dishwasher, barely knew where their kids went to school. He always picked up his things, put the glasses in the cabinet according to size, and was on the Boosters Board at school. He secured the hospital's sports tickets for the silent auction at the school fundraiser each year and always volunteered to drive our kids' friends home after a practice.

A sinking feeling washed over me like a waterfall as I thought back to Nancy's confusion at the center. I felt exposed, as if the world were ready to reveal my secret not just in front of him, but in front of Nancy. The amplified magic was so close to exploding everything I had. Travis wouldn't want to be married to a witch.

And Nancy would surely make the connection between my power and what had happened twenty years ago.

My throat began to close up as my panic rose, and I walked into the bathroom for a drink of water. I flipped on the light and tripped over Katy Purry, where she sat on the bath mat in front of the shower.

"I was trapped in here," she said in her raspy voice.

"Shhhh! And I had no idea. I'm sorry—I must have accidentally closed the door before we left," I said.

She flattened her ears against her head, and her whiskers twitched down. "I was forced to listen to you, and those . . . noises."

I laughed and covered my mouth, cheeks flushing. "Sorry about that. I was only worried about Hunter and Harper hearing, not . . ." I gestured toward her on the floor. She continued to glare at me, so I sighed. "Um, I saw some salmon filets on sale at Whole Foods the other day. Would that make it up to you?"

She closed her mouth and cocked her head to the side in agreement. A truce. Then she sauntered out of the bathroom and army-crawled under our bed, her claws straining to pull her body along the carpet.

I slid back into bed and picked up my phone, loading my work email. Twenty-two messages popped up, mostly inquiries from other real estate agents about listings or feedback from my clients after showings. But in the middle was a different message, sent at 10:31 p.m.

From: Madisyn.Parks@gmail.com

Subject: Following Up

My heart started racing before my brain registered her name. The famously tenacious podcaster.

I tapped it and scanned the body of the email.

> Hi there,
> I hope this email finds you well. I wanted to connect with you, and apologies for not contacting you sooner.

Apologies? When did I say I wanted to talk?

> Anyway, I would still love to talk to you about your experiences at Hawthorne Hall during the time of the tragedy. I am hoping to set up times to talk to several other residents of the dorm but would love your input. Please email me back, or call my cell at the bottom of the email at your earliest convenience.
>
> Best,
> Madisyn Parks

I pictured Madisyn sitting at a desk, probably her first big splurge after the success of the *Morgantown Murders*, in her apartment, writing and rewriting the email to hit the right professional yet casual and chatty tone. Her glasses were slipping down the bridge of her nose, and the glow from her computer was giving her a headache. Her heart beating a little too fast, she hit Send and stared at her inbox, as though waiting for an immediate response.

I clicked away from the email, intending to delete it, then saw two other unread emails. One was from my in-laws, who had sent a formal invitation for the scholarship fundraiser. I clicked it open.

> We are pleased to announce the 1st annual winter gala celebration benefiting the Thomas and Marcy Nelson Scholarship Fund at North Valley University.
>
> We invite you to join us on November 15th at 7 p.m. at the Chicago Botanic Gardens.

With all that was currently happening, I would be lucky if the centerpieces didn't come alive or the silverware start to dance on its own.

Then I noticed the email wasn't just an invitation but a forward. At the top of the screen was a note from Marcy.

> Sarah, my love!
> Let's put our heads together next week to start the planning. It's going to be such a fun party!
> —Marcy

I noticed I was the only one she'd sent it to. Not Travis, or Nancy, or anyone else. Her surrogate daughter, the one who indulged her, found her quirks charming. Mostly. After all, she was the only mother I had anymore.

The other unread email below it was from Obsidian Corporation. It was a forward, sent to Alicia and me from Katrina. **See below,** she had typed. **Thoughts?**

I scrolled down and saw that Madisyn had emailed her, as

well. It was generally the same as the one she sent to me, but with one additional line: I've uncovered some new information that I would love to discuss and get your take on.

"New information?" I whispered as I reread the email. My breathing quickened as I remembered what Katrina had said about being held legally responsible for the fire. If Madisyn started to raise suspicions about our involvement, things could get really bad, really fast. Everything we had, everything we wanted, everything we loved, was at risk.

The kids, Travis, my career, my in-laws, not to mention my love of not being incarcerated.

My fingers flexed and then froze, and my phone tumbled forward, smacking me in the nose.

Travis rolled over again in his sleep, sighing deeply. I rubbed my face and looked over as the snoring stopped and he lifted his head.

His eyes still closed, he mumbled, "Gas bill." Then he lay back down and started snoring again.

I guess he got to dream about paying the gas bill, while I would certainly have nightmares about my life quickly crumbling into rubble.

I tapped Reply All.

> I think we need to meet and discuss how to handle
> Madisyn. After what happened last time, we need to meet
> somewhere safe, where we aren't exposed. Weekdays
> are easiest, but my house is out, as, I'm assuming, is
> Katrina's work. Alicia, why don't we come to you?
> —Sarah

I knew they would look at the phrasing—*how to handle Madisyn*—and think of the options, as the dark corners of my brain were already doing. We would have to think of all possibilities, even the ones I was afraid to use again.

We had to meet somewhere quiet, somewhere private. Alicia's house felt like the safest to have a magical discussion, far from my unsuspecting family.

Besides, I didn't want Katy Purry to inadvertently gain any more people skills.

Chapter 13

If a sore thumb is something that sticks out, Alicia's office building, which was also her home, was more like a severed appendage. I parallel parked my car into a tiny spot in front of 3482 Walnut Street, nearly blinded by the hot-pink brick exterior with lime-green trim. Bright white lettering was stenciled on the windows out front—Eudora Enterprises—with a design of stars and the moon around the words. It was a sort of Palm Beach-after-huffing-glue vibe. Lilly Pulitzer would have been horrified.

Yet blending in had never been something Abracadabra Alicia was very good at.

I pushed open the glass doors and stepped into a chaotic space. The carpet was bright pink, and the walls were painted in deep purple with robin's-egg-blue trim, like the designer just couldn't decide if the entire color wheel should be used or only 90 percent of it. Soft sitar music wafted through the empty room and the smell of incense assaulted my face. I sneezed four times, and as I was wiping my nose, Alicia's head popped through a white velvet curtain strung with glittery beads.

"Sarah!" she said as she stepped through the material, her

gold-coin headband catching sightly on the beads. She adjusted it with one hand. "You're early."

I sniffed, willing my body not to give out another cartoonlike sneeze. I placed my hands against my midsection and waited, listening to see if the magic would spark. Nothing. Everything was still.

I shook my head. "We said noon."

She frowned and then looked at her watch. "Oh, who can keep track of time? Not me."

I smiled, remembering how in college she treated movie times like a suggestion, leading to her, Katrina, and I being late to see Lindsay Lohan in her heyday star in *Freaky Friday* at North Valley's only theater, missing the beginning. Alicia had never seen the movie, or apparently heard of the concept, so she spent most of the night whisper-asking why the mom and daughter were acting so weird.

"Apologies for being late," Katrina said from behind us as she pushed open the door. She confidently strode into the room, her eyes flicking back and forth among all of the metaphysical paraphernalia. "I had an interview with *Chicago Magazine*. They're doing a profile on me, possibly for the cover." She smiled, her face softening, true joy radiating across the room.

Alicia clasped her hands together. "Oh, that's just simply wonderful." She looked over at me and smiled. "I have good news, too. We're in talks to do a residency for my show in Las Vegas." She spread her arms wide, an invitation to each of us.

I took a step forward to hug her, just for a moment, before I stopped, nervously glancing out of the large window. We were visible to any passerby. We needed to be careful.

Katrina's face looked the same as mine, and it took Alicia a moment before she understood.

She nodded and crooked a finger at us, beckoning us to follow. "Come."

We filed behind her through the waterfall of beads. One of the strands smacked Katrina in the face as it rebounded off my head, and she muttered a few choice words. I stopped quickly as I walked into the room, Katrina running into me, cursing more.

"Holy shit," I whispered as I looked around.

Alicia stood in the center of the room, nearly glowing with pride. The walls were painted black, and shelves lined the walls, holding candles and crystals bundled together. At the front of the room was a makeshift stone altar covered in a purple cloth adorned with sigils. Gold offering plates had been placed on it, along with a sage stick and dried herbs.

She had her own magic room. No doing spells in private, behind a bathroom door or from the safety of her car, like I did. She had her own dedicated space to cast spells.

"Welcome," Alicia said. "Oh, hey!" She waved to someone behind us.

Cressida stuck her head in the door and smiled at Katrina and me. "Hello, ladies. Glad you could make it. I just wanted to say hi before I go feed the cats. I'll leave you to your reunion and rituals," she said before she disappeared again.

I guess that answered one of the burning questions I had for each of them: does anyone know about your magic?

A guttural animal sound came from somewhere deep in the building, and I shivered.

"Still no talking?" I said, and Alicia shook her head.

Katrina folded her arms over her chest and slowly walked the perimeter of the room, taking in the scene. "Alicia, this is remarkable."

She beamed. "Thank you. I've been a busy bee."

My gaze fell to a framed picture on one of the shelves. I walked over and ran a finger along the edges. It was a picture of the three of us, taken a couple of days before the fire. Before we scattered.

We were in the quad, seated on a blanket laid out in the grass. I remembered it was an unusually warm, sunny day, so we had on shorts and tank tops, trying desperately to get any semblance of a tan. Alicia had brought a disposable camera, the kind where you had to hold down a button to charge the flash. We had asked someone walking by to take our picture—selfies weren't really a thing yet—and she had promised to get doubles of the photo to give us as we dropped it off at a Walgreens after.

But then the fire happened and I never saw the photo. She must have picked up the pictures sometime after.

I studied the girls in the picture. Our smiles were wide, our eyes bright. We looked like ordinary college girls, full of youthful excitement and maybe a little naïveté. Yet you could see a little twinkle behind our expressions, the knowledge that we had a secret no one could guess.

A wave of emotion ran through me. We'd lost all of that—the feeling of being safe, the pride in what we could do, the confidence in our abilities, the trust that the magic could never turn dark, the belief in ourselves that we would never harm anyone else. We had lost one another, too.

I turned to them, feeling the pressure in my chest build. Katrina's eyes remained on the photo as she studied it, and Alicia nodded to me, understanding.

"Once again," she said.

Katrina broke away from the photo, misty moment of reflection over. "Have either of you figured out how to control it, calm it down, yet?"

I shook my head. "Not really. It's like a wild horse that I'm slowly learning how to tame. Before, it was easy, small. Now it's like a tsunami, and I'm trying to steer a rowboat."

Alicia cocked her head to the side, and we heard another growl from her serval cats. "Somewhat. But I've been practicing more than you both have, I think?"

I nodded and looked at Katrina, who did the same.

"I've always done it in secret," I said. "But now it's like I can't stop it at all. I've always done small spells here and there, but this? This is all new," I said.

Katrina cleared her throat. "Same with me. Nothing formal, just a few incantations throughout the day, but nothing proper or official."

"Well, no time like the present," Alicia said. She gestured toward the rug on the ground. "Come. Let's commune."

We took a seat in a triangle, as we always had, naturally moving to our respective corners. It felt like putting on a comfortable sweatshirt I had forgotten in the back of my closet, muscle memory working more than conscious choices.

Alicia reached behind her and opened a drawer in the apothecary cabinet against the wall. She carefully picked up a worn brown leather book and placed it in the center of our triangle.

"Is that a grimoire?" Katrina said as she leaned in closer, one manicured finger outstretched.

Alicia laughed. "You could call it that. But it's more like a magic diary, where I've written down what's worked and what hasn't over the years." She smiled, crystals sparkling. "It's how I've been able to perfect my shows."

I had no doubt Alicia would be offered that residency in Vegas, and who knew what else. After all, she had the actual magic.

Katrina's eyes widened and she moved closer, looking almost as if she wanted to grab the book and pull it into her lap. I recognized that look. She was a thirsty traveler stranded in the desert who had just spotted a waterfall.

I knew we needed to remain focused on the reason we were here, before Katrina went off the rails and began paging through the book to absorb all of Alicia's work.

I cleared my throat. "Madisyn. What are we going to do about her?" I turned to Katrina. "What did she tell you?"

Katrina moved back, although her gaze lingered on the book. "It's not good news," she said carefully, looking at each of us. "She said she was particularly interested in the 'occult' items found in the fire and thinks they might be a clue to solving what happened. She suspects that someone was messing around with the magical items because they heard the urban legends about the dorm. She said she found an occult store in—get this—Millville, and is going to visit it to see what she can find out."

My blood froze and my stomach clenched. "No one will remember us, right? It was twenty years ago," I said, my voice a whisper. We had only visited that store once and couldn't have been inside for more than fifteen minutes.

Alicia placed her hands over her mouth, speechless.

Katrina frowned. "Apparently, the owner, Madame Serena, is alive and well. Must have found an antiaging spell."

Alicia shook her head. "That's not even—"

"I was kidding," Katrina said quickly with an eye roll. "Anyway, I'd bet Obsidian that someone remembers us. I'm sure college girls don't go wandering in there very often. It won't take long before Madisyn is knocking at our doors again, this time armed with accurate information."

I had a flash of Madisyn's voice on her podcast: *Culpability, reckless actions, sister-in-law of one of the victims. Arrest. Incarceration.*

The air between us seemed to crackle. The familiar guilt swelled in my stomach, acid burning up my esophagus. Even though we had never meant for anyone to get hurt, they had. We all knew that.

"We have to find a way to stop her," Katrina said, the pitch of her voice rising an octave. She looked at the grimoire and raised her eyebrows.

I could practically see the word *hex* scroll across her forehead, projecting her thoughts.

"Are you sure there's not another way?" I said quickly. "Throw her off the scent somehow?" My anxiety spiked as I thought of Alicia's office and house going up in flames, windows bursting, ambulances wailing. More burn scars.

"What do you have in mind?" Katrina said.

After a moment, Alicia closed her eyes, lips pressed together. Then she slowly placed both hands on the book for a moment before opening her eyes and placing them palms-up on her knees.

An invitation.

Almost as if my hands belonged to someone else, I outstretched my fingers and slowly grasped her hand first, and then Katrina's. The circle was complete.

White-hot magic shot through the circle, moving like a snake through each of us, spinning, gaining power. An electrical charge, like the one we had felt a few days ago.

But instead of pulling away, Alicia said, "Just breathe through it, and it will calm down."

I was nearly hyperventilating, and my chest felt like it was going to burst, but I took a few deep breaths, and she was right. The volume turned down, and then the magic crackled like the white noise of static on a radio station.

"Binding spell?" Katrina said, one eye open.

Alicia shook her head. "Those go wrong too often. I recommend a freezer spell. It will stop her from finding out anything else, like water turning to ice cubes."

Water.

I nodded. "Let's do it."

Alicia broke from our hands, reached into her grimoire, and pulled out a stack of yellow legal paper and a ballpoint pen. She wrote *Madisyn Parks* on the paper, folded it, and then put it in the circle.

"Legal paper?" I said.

She shrugged and smiled, reaching for our hands again. "Still works. Now, repeat these words: We hereby freeze Madisyn Parks and her actions against us three. With the power of us three, so shall it be."

We repeated the words, and I felt the magic wake up again, pushing through us, illuminating the paper.

"Now for the freezing," Alicia said. She stood and brought a gold pitcher of water over from the altar, and a plastic sandwich bag. She poured the water into the bag and then stuck the paper in it before closing the seal.

"Oh, you were being literal. That really works?" I said, brows knitted together, as Katrina and I followed Alicia to the kitchen. Alicia placed the sandwich bag in the freezer after carefully moving aside a few boxes of Lean Cuisine meals, waiting for the water to freeze around Madisyn's name.

"Yup," she said as she stood and faced us. She laughed when she saw our expressions. "Magic doesn't always have to be smoke and crystals."

"Well, now we wait," Katrina said. Her expression very much told me she didn't think it would work. But it was all we could do, for now. She looked down at her watch, pausing for a moment to stare at her fingertips. I knew they must have been tingling, like mine were, the boosted magic still pulsing in her veins.

"I should go. I have a meeting this afternoon," she said.

"Me too—well, sort of," I said. Hunter had a lacrosse game after school, and magic or not, I still had to be a mom.

Alicia nodded, glancing at the fridge one last time before she gestured for us to follow her to the front. She went behind the reception desk and pecked at her phone.

"Before you go, to close out our circle, listen. Remember this?" She looked up, and Christina Aguilera's voice replaced the sitar music. Before my brain registered what it was, I started whispering the lyrics to "Fighter," our favorite song from twenty years ago. Sung many times in our dorm rooms, complete with overexaggerated dance moves that we thought at the time would be backup-dancer worthy. (They were not.)

A warmth moved through my chest, and I allowed myself to remember the good times with my friends, not when we were casting spells, using each other for what we could gain together, but when we laughed, danced, sang, complained about professors and boys. Just scared college students, finding safety together.

Katrina broke first and began to move, to dance to the song.

"Yes!" Alicia said, and held her arms out, hands moving in a dance that resembled more a woman on LSD than one of Christina's backup dancers.

I joined in, ridiculously swaying my hips and overemoting every lip-synched word. For those four minutes and six seconds, "Sarah Nelson: wife, Realtor, mom" ceased to exist. I was back at NVU, dancing with my new friends.

I had forgotten how much I needed that.

☾

After saying goodbye and leaving Alicia's, I sat in bumper-to-bumper traffic on the Edens Expressway, heading back to my suburban bubble. On the drive, I realized how much I had missed them. Missed being with people who knew my deepest secrets. A part of me that I hadn't known existed had exhaled at the opportunity to show all of my scars without fear.

My right hand resting on the steering wheel, I slowly pushed up the sleeve of my shirt with my left hand, staring at the pink and red burn mark on my arm. I could barely remember what the skin looked like without it. It was ugly and rough, but I could cover it with expensive shirts and blazers. With airbrush makeup and waterproof powder.

But it was always there, waiting.

Chapter 14

The sun rose high over the lacrosse fields at Forest Hills High School, illuminating every Botox-needle prick and rogue gray hair of the high school moms in the stands. I had brought a wide-brimmed straw hat to hide my own. I was nearly blinded by the flash of a thousand carats on the hands of the women who waved as I sat down on the metal bench.

I spotted David and Stephanie Tobin, Luke's parents. Even though David was one of the most well-respected and liked plastic surgeons in the Chicago area, Stephanie hadn't succumbed to the knife. She had lines on her forehead and a soft jawline; she was aging naturally and gracefully. She warmly waved to me as I sat down.

"You look amazing," she called out across the stands. "Like, nearly glowing."

My smile and wave faltered for a moment. I hadn't used a spell to improve my appearance.

Was the magic obvious? Did it look like I had dipped myself in body glitter?

I mouthed a thanks and then shrugged, trying not to notice as other moms nudged each other and whispered about my appearance. I pulled a pair of sunglasses out of my bag and leaned forward, resting my elbows on my knees, as the game began.

Hunter's school, the Forest Hills Hornets, were about to face their biggest rival, the New Trier Trevians. The schools were only two miles apart, and since the families and students of each were intertwined by blood, geography, and business, they were each other's biggest threat. Only one school could be top dog on the North Shore, and every year New Trier came out the alpha.

Winning this game was all that Hunter had talked about when the season first began. "Mom, even if we lose every other game, if we beat New Trier, it will be a great season," he had said, in all seriousness, before the first practice of the school year.

And now it was time to see which dog would eat first.

Unfortunately, Stevie Honeycomb, president of the Forest Hills Neighborhood Beautification Committee, sat down right next to me. She was an interior designer best known for her traditionally Southern style. Not the beachy blues and whites with natural rattan chairs, but more the wallpaper heavy enough to strangle someone if the correct glue wasn't used, and the terrifying portraits of long-dead dogs wearing tartan bow ties. It was the rich person's version of haunted house décor.

I smiled hello, which she took as an invitation to air her neighborhood grievances.

"Sarah, so good to see you. I must say, I've had quite the struggle lately with enforcing the bylaws on exterior illumination." She rubbed her forehead in despair.

I tuned her out, briefly nodding and murmuring to pretend I was listening. Pissing off Stevie wasn't a good idea. As tenacious and opinionated—and bored—as she was, she could destroy lives and careers with a few phone calls. A couple of years ago she had run an incense shop out of town after some perceived slight when she shopped there, waging a campaign against the store, claiming it brought the "wrong kind of people" to Forest Hills.

It went out of business two months later.

"So then I asked Ransom, why on earth would anyone use oak for a closet? They're supposed to be cedar. Everyone knows that." Stevie shook her head, her black hair wafting around her shoulders like a cloud. I watched, mystified, as it moved as one organism, all the strands held together by hairspray.

I murmured and trained my eyes back on the lacrosse game, and she took that as a request to continue.

"How do we expect our community's home values to keep rising if people won't properly tend to their gardens? Just yesterday I saw the Dickemanns' weigela hedge hadn't even been deadheaded yet. It must frustrate you as well, doesn't it? Since you're the one selling the neighborhood to your clients?"

I was about to murmur again when a small voice inside my head reminded me that while Stevie may have been irritating, she knew everyone in town. Although I was dealing with my own issues, I still needed to keep my career intact, magic or not.

I turned toward her and smiled. "Yes. Of course. You're so right."

I didn't have to say any more, because Hunter's team scored a goal and the bleachers erupted with parents standing up to cheer, purses and bags falling from laps and overturning into the grass below.

A gaggle of girls ran up from behind the stands, waving their arms and cheering. It was Harper's cheer squad, finished with practice in the field house. They were dressed in their sleeveless white practice shirts and black spandex shorts. White cheer bows perched on their heads, hair spilling down around their faces.

"Let's go, Hornets!" Harper's voice wafted up from the chain-link fence where she and her teammates stood. She turned and shielded her forehead with her palm and spotted me, waving enthusiastically before trotting over.

"Mom! Guess what? We finally landed that heel-stretch stunt," she said, her face wide with glee. "Not just that but the twisting basket toss, too! It was like a miracle practice."

I clasped my hands together. "That's so amazing! You guys have been working on that for months." I had only stayed for one practice, two months ago, and watched them try again and again to land the skill, holding my breath each time the girls launched Georgia into the air to turn twice, do a center split, and then spiral down to be caught.

"I know, right? Just in time for the first competition." She shook her head proudly, still basking in the glow of their cheer victory, before she turned and jogged back to her friends.

My heart stopped as I watched Hunter break away from the group on the field, the ball twirling in his lacrosse stick as he gunned toward the goal. New Trier's goalie crouched and braced, ready to block the shot.

Hunter launched the ball, and it sailed through the air as the goalie leapt to block it. It looked like it was directly in the goalie's path.

"No!" I shouted from the stands, clenching my fists. "Get in the goal!"

Time seemed to stop, a collective breath held. The noises on the field melted together into white noise. And I felt the magic rip through me, breaking away from my body and bolting across the field.

Just as the goalie reached for the ball, it changed direction at a right angle in the air, before sailing into the opposite, unoccupied corner of the goal.

Silence enveloped the crowd as everyone tried to process what they had just seen, while the players on the field scratched their heads. The New Trier goalie looked back from the ball to the field, trying to understand.

Oh shit.

In an effort to distract everyone, I jumped up in the stands and began cheering. "Goal!" I shouted.

After a moment, the rest of the crowd followed my lead. The stands rose, the parents high-fiving and hugging each other, shouting toward our kids on the field. Hunter turned and found me in the stands. He shrugged and then gave me a thumbs-up.

I waved and returned the gesture, clapping a bit too much and cheering a bit too loud, trying to will everyone to forget the strange trajectory of the ball.

Chapter 15

No one saw me.

How could they?

If they did, it wouldn't be blamed on me.

My secret is still safe.

Soothing mantras ran through my head as I turned down my street after Hunter's game. New Trier hadn't scored at all, and the Hornets had won 3–0. Finally, North Shore bragging rights were ours for the year.

I just hoped that would be all anyone would remember.

My stomach clenched as I approached my house and saw a red BMW SUV parked out front. In the driver's seat was Madisyn Parks. Her head was bent down toward her phone, light brown waves framing her face. When she saw my car approach, she lifted her head and waved. She opened her car door before I had parked mine.

My breath quickened, and I was very thankful that Harper and Hunter had decided to go out for Andy's Frozen Custard with their friends after the game to celebrate.

She strode across my cobblestone driveway, forging ahead despite her heels' catching in the stone seams.

I guess the freezing spell didn't work.

"My apologies for surprising you like this!" She stopped in front of me and brushed her hair back from her shoulders. She wore a tan belted trench coat and far too many gold bracelets.

"I'm sure. What can I do for you? I'm still not interested in being interviewed. My answer is still no." I remained against my car, without fidgeting, hoping she understood that "No" was a complete sentence.

She shoved her hands into the pockets of her coat and lowered her chin. "Of course. I understand. But I was hoping that you'd reconsider. More than your friends"—she lifted a toe of her shoe, digging the heel into the stone—"I think you're relatable."

I sputtered a loud laugh. That was a new one. I shook my head and smiled. "Not really sure what gave you that impression, but I'm really not." I gestured toward the house. "All an illusion, I promise."

"If I could just have one—" Madisyn started to say when she was cut off by a voice on the sidewalk.

"Sarah! Sarah! I'm so glad I caught you." Taffy, the doomsday prepper, came jogging up my front lawn, dressed in black capri leggings and a matching tank top. Her surgically enhanced chest bounced in the right places. "Our new vertical garden with simulated light for the Shelter was just installed. Would you like to come see it?"

She then seemed to notice Madisyn's presence. "Oh. I didn't know you had company." She looked at me and then back to Madisyn again, no doubt debating whether or not to launch into a spiel about the necessity of having one's own bunker. She must have decided Madisyn wasn't worthy of the postapocalyptic world, because she looked at me and gave a slight head shake.

Don't tell her. When the apocalypse comes, she's expendable.

"I don't have company. I have . . ." I trailed off as I tried to explain Madisyn's presence. *A problem*, was what I wanted to say.

"Hello, I'm Madisyn Parks. You might recognize me. I was the host of the pod—" she started to say, hand outstretched.

I stuck an arm in between them and looped it around Madisyn's shoulder, turning her to face the front door. "Let's go inside."

Brushing off Madisyn was one thing. Brushing them both off was another. And it wasn't like I was confident enough to use the magic to get rid of both of them. Too many witnesses and no room for error.

"Next week, then!" Taffy called as I hurried Madisyn up the front steps.

"You have a lovely home," Madisyn said as she craned her head around, stopping temporarily to peer up at the floating staircase for a long beat.

"Here." I pointed toward the living room just off the foyer. It had a large white stone fireplace that stretched up to the vaulted ceiling, two pale blue couches facing one another, and a blue and white area rug underneath. No one ever really went in there. When the twins were little, we gated it off to keep their hands away from the expensive fabrics. The living room was a relic left over from the days when people entertained in their parlors, yet every buyer I had still wanted a formal living room, if only as a place to keep their nicest furniture. I thought the room was mostly useless, but I was grateful to have it at that moment. That morning, the kitchen had looked like it had exploded before I left to go see Alicia and Katrina, and I'd figured I would clean it up when I got home.

"Listen—" I'd started to say when I heard sounds from the family room. It sounded like the television was on, which wasn't how I had left it that morning.

The damn cat.

I lifted a finger. "Hang on."

I speed-walked past Madisyn, through the foyer, and into the family room. I inhaled sharply as I saw Katy Purry on the couch, lounging on her side, belly spilling over the remote control next to her. Her eyes were fixed on the screen, watching *Ratatouille*.

I grunted at her and narrowed my eyes before I snatched the remote from under her.

"Hey!" she said.

I shook my head furiously as I turned off the television, making a hissing sound.

"Did you say something?" Madisyn called from the other room.

"Nope," I called back. I gave Katy Purry one more glare as I put the remote in a drawer. She harrumphed and scampered out of the room.

I steadied my shoulders as I walked back into the formal living room and sat down on one of the couches. Madisyn did the same opposite me, her gaze moving around the room as she unbelted her trench coat. I didn't offer to take it from her; I hoped this sit-down wouldn't take that long.

I clasped my hands together and leaned forward. "I appreciate what you're trying to do—really. I know you think there's probably a lot of interesting material to explore about the fire. But I don't think you're grasping just how difficult and traumatic it was for those of us who lived it." I raised my voice to keep her attention.

Her eyes were wide as she nodded, her face serious. "Yes. Yes, of course. I hope you don't think I'm trying to be disrespectful in asking for these stories."

I raised my eyebrows. "Showing up at my house isn't disrespectful of my privacy?" I leaned and put an arm on the back of the couch.

"Well, I do apologize about that. But I uncovered some new information and wanted to ask you about it." She continued. "If I could start by sharing some of what I've learned with you, then you could decide how much you want to talk. It's up to you."

New information. *She couldn't possibly have already visited the occult shop in Millville, right?*

And why the hell *didn't the freezer spell work?*

"Again, there really isn't anything to say. It was an awful night, but there really isn't much to investigate. I—" I stopped when I heard a scratching noise coming from the kitchen. I cocked my head to the side, listening. The sound continued, a rhythmic shushing.

"What is that?" Madisyn said as she turned her head toward the sound.

I held up a finger. Again. "I'm not sure. Stay here. Let me check." Madisyn, surprisingly, did as she was told and remained seated while I hurried out of the room again and down the hallway toward the kitchen.

I stopped quickly when I walked into the kitchen, frozen. The broom had broken free of the cleaning closet and was slowly moving back and forth, sweeping up the crumbs from breakfast on the white oak floor.

It was like something out of Cinderella's deranged life.

Stop, I thought. *Stop right now.*

But it ignored me and kept going.

I jogged over and grabbed it, but it twisted out of my grasp, moving toward a pile of dust behind the kitchen island.

I hurried around the island, grabbing for it over the marble countertop, throwing my body forward. My arm wasn't long enough, so I pushed away from the island and skidded around the counter corner.

"Everything okay?" Madisyn called. She sounded like she was where I had left her, thankfully.

"Yes! One second," I called, my voice high and squeaky.

I lunged for the broom and hooked a finger around it before it slipped out of my grasp, moving toward the hallway.

"No. No. No. No. No," I muttered as I stumbled toward it, tripping over the piles of dirt it had gathered.

I had just about reached it when it stopped and fell to the floor with a snap, clattering back down onto the wood with a loud bang.

Just as Madisyn appeared in the hallway.

She looked down from the broom and back to me again, her mouth parted in a little O. "Are you sure everything is all right in here?" She frowned.

I was still in a half lunge, arm stretched toward the wayward broom. "Yes." I stood up, pulling my shirt down over the waistband of my pants and smoothing my hair behind my ears. "Yes. I just tripped over the broom."

Not even a believable lie.

"Listen, this really isn't a good time, and like I said, I don't want to talk. I'm sorry." I took a few steps toward her, gesturing to the door.

She didn't move for a moment, remaining as motionless as the fucking iceberg that hit the *Titanic*, if it had been self-aware and just purposely did not want to scoot out of the way. When she glanced once more at the broom, I kicked it, sending it sliding back toward the kitchen. My foot tingled where it made contact.

She finally nodded and walked toward the front door. As she reached for the knob, she stopped and turned. "I can be available anytime and meet you wherever is best."

"I'll think about it," I said out of desperation. Anything to get her out of the house for now. I was reaching for the door to open it wider so I could hurry her outside, when my foot brushed against hers.

A residual spark of magic traveled from me to her, like an electric shock after walking across shag carpeting.

She jumped and looked down at her leg.

"Sorry. Lots of static in the house. You know how dry it is right now," I said quickly.

It had started to rain outside.

"Bye." I threw open the door and stepped forward, a physical block between her and my home.

She gave me a strange look but turned and walked toward the porch stairs. I watched as her brown waves bounced around her shoulders while she made her way toward her car. I was so busy making sure she left that I didn't notice Katy Purry had crept up behind me.

She made a hacking sound, like she was going to cough up a furball, and I jumped, accidentally slamming the door shut loud enough for the neighbors to think Stevie Honeycomb herself had delivered a violation notice.

She threw up on the floor and then licked her lips. "That's for making me miss the good part of the movie."

Chapter 16

The North Lake Country Club jutted out of a steep hill overlooking Lake Michigan like a fortress or prison. I wasn't sure if it was to keep the rich in or the lowly poor out. Probably both. It was designed as a stone Gothic castle, with turrets pointing out of the roofline and an arched entrance at the end of a gated driveway. The club was the most exclusive in the area, with waiting lists generations long, and any slight social infraction was grounds for removal from the list. Thomas Nelson's family had been founding members.

The Nelson family was old money, North Shore elite. They had gained wealth from investing in railroads, and it had led to summer estates in Lake Geneva; boarding schools with the reputation that if you had to ask the tuition amount, you couldn't afford it; and multiple country club memberships.

Well, Thomas was old money, and then he married Marcy, who had been a bartender at a college sports bar. Their marriage was "wealthy trust fund kid gets hitched to Jennifer Coolidge in *Legally Blonde.*"

"Club sandwich with extra bacon. I need bread." Marcy nodded to the waiter dressed in a black suit with a bow tie. "Thank you, Albie." She wore a pale pink pantsuit with a white blouse underneath, a black Birkin bag on the chair next to her. Her blond hair was blown out around her shoulders, brushed back to show off her diamond earrings.

Albie nodded and turned to me.

"Sounds good. Same," I said. I internally chuckled as I realized we were likely the only women ordering carbs—not to mention handheld ones.

We were two oddballs in a room full of St. John and Chanel knit suits, our pasts paved with struggle and difficult choices. As I had many times before, I said a silent thank-you that I had been granted Marcy Nelson as a mother-in-law. Because I really liked carbs.

Twenty minutes later, our sandwiches were half-eaten, and I had a stack of files at my elbow, tasks and people for me to contact regarding sponsorships for the gala.

"Do you think your juggling club will come to the event?" Marcy asked. "It was so nice that you were able to reunite at the ceremony."

If only she knew.

I wasn't sure if Nancy had seen us together, and if she had, if she'd paused for a moment, remembering when she'd last seen the three of us together.

"I'm not sure if they'll come," I said casually, although inside I was thinking that was very much not a good idea, considering it was a public place, with way too much room for error if something magically went awry.

"Oh, bummer. So, I had a little thought," Marcy said as she twisted her enormous engagement ring around her left ring finger. "We should have Madisyn Parks host a table. She's just so wonderful, isn't she?"

Anxiety rippled through me. "I think she's been a little pushy."

Marcy's eyes went wide, and she reached across the table and put a hand on mine. "Oh no. How did you get that impression? She's so talented." She sat back and took a long sip of her chardonnay.

"Well, she showed up to my house, for one," I said. "After I asked her not to."

Careful, Sarah.

Marcy smiled, exhaling in relief. "She's just excited, is all. Remember how much she pursued the last story? She's . . ." She stopped and tapped a finger against her cheek, brightening. "Tenacious."

You have no idea.

"Anyhoo, I'm talking to her next week and I can't wait to hear what she has to say," she said.

"I didn't realize you had been in contact with her," I said, my voice low. I glanced outside at the gray sky over the water. Dark waves moved toward the shoreline with white peaks like fingers reaching for the building.

"Oh yes." She waved over to Albie, signaling for another glass of wine. She leaned forward and put her hands on the table. "I want Nancy to speak to her, too." She leaned back and sighed. "I think it will be good for her. She should talk about it more. I think it would help." Her eyes looked faraway.

I nodded and swallowed my response. I couldn't imagine

Nancy's speaking to Madisyn. She so rarely engaged in any look-back conversation about what had happened. It was as though her scars were enough to remind people. She didn't need to show her emotional wounds to the world as well. Those were for her. Private. The months spent in the hospital. The years of therapy.

She had never talked to me about her dark memories of that night, and part of me hoped she had blocked it out. That she didn't remember the flames licking her door and the smoke filling her lungs. The terror as she realized there wouldn't be a quick rescue. That she didn't remember what her body had looked like before we caused the fire, or what she used to be like.

Nancy had her own story to tell from that night, and she had every right to share it how she chose. I wanted her to gain healing in any way she needed, but I prayed it was with someone other than Madisyn.

"Maybe not for a podcast, though," I finally said.

Marcy looked confused for a moment before she nodded in agreement. "Sure. But maybe she'll change her mind," she said, brightening.

Not a chance.

After lunch, we walked outside, Marcy holding my hand. Her white Jaguar was already waiting out front, Albie having signaled to the valet when we paid the bill.

"My chariot awaits!" she said before she leaned over and kissed both of my cheeks in a cloud of flowery perfume.

"Let's do pedis soon!" she called out before she drove away. "Maybe we can invite Madisyn."

I waited for my car to be brought up, shifting from side to side in my heels. I checked my phone and saw I had missed texts from

Alicia and Katrina. Alicia had changed the text group name to B.A.W.—Bad Ass Witches. Katrina remarked that it should be B.W. since "badass" was one word yet abandoned that fight for more pressing matters. She wanted to meet that afternoon to discuss the failed freezer spell (and, I suspected, lay out her case for hexing Madisyn again), but Alicia's daughter, Joelle, was home sick. I looked at my watch and saw I had some time to spare. I had planned on heading to my office to finish up work, but this seemed more pressing.

So when my car finally arrived, I set my navigation for the Obsidian office instead of my own.

Chapter 17

"Welcome to the battlefield." Katrina stood in front of her silver and black desk, leaning back with her hands on either side of her body. She wore a black skinny three-piece suit with tuxedo cuffs and collar. She crossed her ankles in front of her, showing the red bottoms of her black stilettos. Her dark hair was pulled up into a tight topknot, giving her the look of a ballet dancer ready to kick some serious ass.

"Your office is gorgeous." I craned my neck around from my vantage point of one of the dark blue velvet chairs in front of her desk. Steel, black, and glass dominated every surface in the warehouse-style office, giving it an almost unfinished look, like construction had stopped midway to allow for the employees to rush in and conduct serious business.

She held her palms in the air and smiled wide. "Thank you. Things are really happening over here." She crossed her arms in front of her chest and cocked her head to the side. "The past few weeks have certainly been prosperous. Obsidian has raised all of the capital we need. Soon our surgical knives will be in every hospital in the world. We were already doing well, but recently it's like a switch has flipped."

The statement lingered in the air. I pushed myself up and walked over to the enormous glass wall overlooking Chicago. I studied the people down below, small black flecks scurrying to and fro.

"Like ants in an anthill, going back and forth automatically. Building something, but not sure what exactly," Katrina said as she stood next to me. She straightened her back and gazed out at the horizon before she exhaled and looked at me, smiling. "But we know the truth."

"How come you don't seem as rattled by the magic taking control?" I said.

She regarded me and lifted her eyebrows. "Of course I am. But you can't tell me that it's not exciting to think of the possibilities. Of what we could do if we really committed to practicing."

I turned away from the window, looking at the Obsidian employees bustling around outside Katrina's office. "And what about what happened before? Our power came at a price. A big one."

"We were young, immature," she said.

"So was Nancy." I said it more to myself than to her. I didn't need her permission to feel the way I felt about the magic's returning. I needed to remember it. Because the pit of anxiety was growing in my stomach as I realized how badly I wanted to be like her and Alicia and truly lean into what was possible.

But I lived with the daily reminder of how badly things could go wrong, how easily magic could be used to hurt, even accidentally, every time I saw my sister-in-law.

"It was twenty years ago. I'd like to think that we are all different people." She took a step back and held her arms out. "Do you feel anything now? Are the outlets sparking or the glass cracking?" She smiled, dropping her arms. "No. We're older. We can control it, shape it."

I thought of the broom activating when Madisyn was at my house. "Not always. It still seems to do what it wants at times."

"We'll learn," she said confidently.

"And what about Madisyn? Why didn't the freezer spell work with her? I can't figure out what we did wrong."

"Well, we've had some wobbles before. Remember the Frankenstein incident?"

I smiled. The Frankenstein incident was our first spell gone wrong. Alicia had said she wanted a few pink streaks in her hair. Of course, we couldn't do the normal thing of going out and buying hair dye.

It was a Thursday night—Fraternity Fight Night, a big boxing match between the fraternities that was supposed to be for charity but was really about slugging back bathtubs full of liquor concoctions, or so I had heard. It wasn't an invitation-only event, so we could have gone, but the thought of squeezing myself into low-rise jeans to watch a bunch of drunk guys punch each other sounded like my worst nightmare.

We flipped through the witchcraft books we had from the library, and a few we had ordered online, and decided to modify a spell for hair growth that included cutting an onion in half and mixing it with a shot of vodka and a tablespoon of honey. The onion and honey we bought at Walmart, and the vodka we co-opted from the meathead guys who lived downstairs by pretending we wanted to pregame.

Alicia had been nearly squealing with glee as we used a paint-brush to paint it on, trying not to gag at the smell while whispering the words to the spell.

> As we paint this hair
> With perfect care
> Turning what was dark into fair
> Pink is what we will see
> By the power of us three
> Hear our words
> And so shall it be

It should have worked. Instead, as we said *pink*, Alicia misspoke and said *zinc*.

That, by our best guestimate, was where things went wrong.

Instead of bright pink streaks, Alicia's hair turned green. All of it. Frankenstein style. Like when someone wears a cheap ring and it turns their skin green.

"Is it amazing?" Alicia said as she clasped her hands in front of her. Katrina and I were behind her and mouthed *Oh my God* to each other.

"How does it look?" Alicia said impatiently. She whirled around and caught a glimpse of her hair as she turned her head. "What the hell?" she whispered as she picked up a strand and held it out.

She started to screech. "Fix it!"

Katrina and I looked at each other and stumbled over our words, apologizing and explaining that we didn't know how to do it.

"Maybe we can try another spell? Come up with something else?" I said as I grabbed for the books scattered around us.

"What if her hair falls out if we mess with it again?" Katrina said, and Alicia moaned.

We finally calmed Alicia down and she put her hair in a baseball cap that I dug out of my tiny dorm room closet, and we went back to Walmart. Instead of supplies for another spell, we bought Clairol hair dye, like we should have done in the first place, and two hours later, Alicia's hair was back to normal. Well, mostly. It did have a green cast to it for a few weeks before it washed out.

Thankfully, we were all able to laugh about it later.

And we learned the importance of precision during our rituals.

In her office, Katrina leveled her gaze at me, and memory gave way to the present. For a moment, she looked exactly as she had back in Hawthorne Hall, silently advising me not to tell Alicia her hair was the color of vomit. "I've been thinking. I think we should do a bigger spell to get Madisyn out of our way."

"Such as?" I asked, even though part of me really, really didn't want to know the answer.

She leaned forward and whispered, "A hex, of course."

I took a deep breath, shaking my head. "Rule of Three. No way."

A hex could quite possibly ruin someone's life. It could cause injury, illness, maybe even death. It was too extreme, especially considering the Rule of Three. If we tried to hex Madisyn, we could end up hexing ourselves into something far worse.

Katrina frowned and exhaled. "Think it over. If she succeeds, we lose everything. It's a risk I'm willing to take if it comes down to it. It's good to have a plan."

I hadn't just driven to Katrina's office on a whim—that much I knew. She always had an answer for everything, a plan in place that was so thought out, it made me wonder if she had an infinite number of scenarios mapped out in her head for every twist in life's path, and her job was simply to select the appropriate contingency plan for the moment.

"Don't you ever wonder why us? Plenty of people experiment with magic, and they don't burn buildings down," I said.

Katrina nodded. "Of course. That's why I choose to look at it as a gift. We awakened something natural, something buried deep in the universe, and it can't be put back to sleep again. It will always just be. It's like a wild horse. You don't want to break its spirit, but you have to harness it. So we all need to grab a bridle and saddle."

"Yes, but it was actually in my control before. Now?" I lifted my eyebrows.

Katrina nodded. "I know. I, too, used it in small ways before our reunion. To get investor meetings or compose tricky emails. But now? It's showing us what we can do. It's time to see what we're really capable of."

She slowly moved her gaze down to my arm, lingering on my pink burn scar, before she looked up at me again.

"And take down whoever stands in our way," she said.

Chapter 18

My conversation with Katrina was still on my mind as I drove home, heading on autopilot to Whole Foods to pick up dinner for that night. I wasn't sure if the magic had planned anything—I'd forgotten to check the fridge before I met up with Marcy. I thought of Katrina's gleaming, bustling office as I grabbed stuffed shells and a large Caesar salad. Throwing a bottle of wine into the cart, I could almost hear the magic judging me for making a frozen dinner when I could have magicked up something from scratch.

As I walked through the store, I waved hello back to a few clients and parents from the twins' school. I then stopped at the fish counter for the promised salmon for Katy Purry.

Back in my car, I glanced at the brown paper bags in the backseat and reached for the button to turn on the engine. I caught sight of the scar peeking out from the hem of my sleeve and paused. I slowly lowered my hand and rested it on the gearshift. With my other hand, I slid up my sleeve and ran a finger along the ragged edges of the scar, feeling the bumps and puckering in the skin.

I looked up and saw that in the same strip mall, in a space

that had once been an overpriced art supply store, there was an orange banner with black lettering.

COMING SOON: SPIRIT HALLOWEEN STORE

From my car, I could see workers inside the empty space, carrying around ladders and setting up shelves. Soon they would be filled with costumes and decorations, animatronics waiting patiently to greet visitors at the door with a variety of macabre sayings. Just to the right of the door, a large sign hung: *Toil and Trouble*. Two black witch figures with pointy hats and brooms were on either side of the lettering.

Bullshit. We never had hats.

They would have made our statements to the fire department and police on the night of the fire much more interesting, that's for sure.

On Halloween night, there would be little girls dressed up in long black cloaks, with sparkly pointed hats and matching brooms. Black lipstick and dangly star earrings. Maybe a black plastic cauldron used as a prop for their parents to take a picture before uploading it to social media. And none of them would know it was real.

That the magic existed.

Instead, they would treat it as a fun exercise for one night and then go back to laughing at the women who believed in astrology and the power of the moon cycles.

Most people don't want to know. It's safer that way. Like clicking on a terrible news story about a war somewhere far away, before switching to the Starbucks app to order a latte.

But I knew. It was my secret. My power.

I looked down at my scar again and felt a tightness in my chest, just as a text from Harper dinged on my phone.

> Mom! We added another basket toss to the routine, just in time for the comp next weekend. Such good energy around all of us. I don't know what's going on, but we're all loving it. It's finally happening!

I knew what had given them the extra push.

See? It can do good things. Bigger things than stocking the fridge or sweeping the floors.

I closed my eyes, allowing the thought to settle over me. What if I really could make things right? What if there wasn't any harm in stealing a glance at the eclipse?

Even though the freezer spell against Madisyn hadn't worked, maybe we were just out of practice. I opened my eyes and looked again at my scar, the physical reminder of what we had gotten wrong.

I felt magic push against my chest and took a deep breath. I lifted my left hand and whispered: *"Away, this burn."*

I felt the tip of my pointer finger grow hot, pressed it to the hardened skin of my scar, and focused my intention on healing.

Without overthinking it, I continued:

Away, this burn
For the lessons I have learned
Magic come forth and make me heal
With these words as the seal

For all to see
By the power inside of me
So shall it be

A warmth spread through my body, radiating from my chest down to my toes and pulsing toward my index finger like blood pumping from the heart. A faint glow appeared around the scar, with a jagged line encircling the damaged skin. It flooded the area until the entire patch was glowing.

The light moved inward, folding in on itself. As the glow contracted, it left behind perfectly healed skin.

When the light disappeared after contracting to a tiny dot, I lifted my arm and held my breath.

Where once had been gnarled, tightened skin was now a perfectly smooth surface. Tiny hairs flecked the skin, and the two moles that I had forgotten once existed were back.

"Holy shit," I whispered as I touched the new skin. I felt the nerve endings activate, like flipping a light switch, bringing feeling back to what'd been numb for twenty years. I flexed my fingers a few times, seeing the bones and veins move beneath the surface.

I laughed and held my arm up in a waving motion. A man in a tracksuit carrying two Whole Foods bags stared at me from his car, parked facing mine. He placed one of the bags next to his car and slowly waved back, looking bewildered.

I laughed again and shook my head, realizing how ridiculous I probably looked. His expression said, *Lady, you're scaring me*, before he hurried into his car, throwing his bags onto the passenger seat. I needed to get out of there before I terrified anyone else who hadn't been sufficiently traumatized after buying ground beef at fifteen dollars a pound.

I drove home, staring at my arm and sneaking glances at the road, wondering how I was going to explain it.

Chapter 19

So you shot lasers at your arm?" Hunter's face scrunched in wonder as he looked from my arm to my face as he sat on his bed.

"Something like that. Not a space laser or anything," I said lightly.

"Wow. Cool," Hunter said. He leaned back against his headboard and put a hand behind his head, his other hand holding his phone.

That was likely to be the extent of his reaction. "Thanks." I closed the door behind me as I left his room. I figured it was best to just rip the figurative Band-Aid off and proudly display my arm in a dramatic fashion to my family rather than try to hide it.

It was easier than I'd thought.

Travis had simply said, **Looks great! Impressive! I didn't know you had an appointment for that**, via text between surgeries.

I was in the clear.

As I put away the rest of the groceries, I kept holding my arm up, turning it toward the light, admiring the skin. I still couldn't believe the magic even knew about freckles I'd forgotten.

It knows more than you do.

The thought was both comforting and deeply unsettling. A force that I had somehow managed to harness was smarter than I'd thought yet seemed to be on my team. If only I could get it to refrain from activating when people like Madisyn were around.

I heard a frantic padding coming down the stairs and turned to see Katy Purry standing in the doorway. I held up my forearm to show her.

"Look," I said, showing off my arm.

Her mouth dropped open and her tail twitched. "Incredible."

I smiled and walked over to give her a scratch behind her ears. She purred loudly and fell on her side in blissful submission. I crouched down and absentmindedly petted her.

"Please stop ordering movies," I whispered. "I had to claim I ordered that movie—five times—because I love it so much. I can't keep covering for you."

"Can we order *Cats and Dogs* tonight?" she said.

"Not tonight. We have plans," I said with a sigh.

We were due to attend a dinner party next door, at the Redfields' house. Travis was picking up a bottle of wine on his way home from work.

Too bad we hadn't done a freezer spell on Taffy.

For a moment, I was tempted to use magic to wiggle free from the invitation, but I stopped before I thought too deeply on it. It wasn't right to use it in a way that didn't benefit people, and I knew Taffy had likely been looking forward to that night for a long time. Showing off her canned goods and intricate generator would bring more fulfillment to her than the relief I would feel in the inverse. Not to mention the Rule of Three.

So Doomsday Dinner it was.

. . .

"This is where we keep the gas masks," Taffy said proudly as she waved a coral fingertip toward a row of black shelving, army gas masks proudly on display. She wore a blood-red wrap dress and matching red heels, contrasting with the gray interior of the Shelter.

"Very nice," Travis said as his eyes slowly slid to me for a moment before they went back to Taffy and her husband, Tucker.

When we'd arrived, we'd seen the front of their house was already decorated for Halloween, with two large skeletons standing guard on either side of the door. In the upstairs windows, holograms of ghosts and witches moved past the glass. Small black animatronic bats hung from the trees lining the walkway, screeching as someone walked past, unnerving visitors all the way to the front door. And that was all less spooky than what was in the basement.

We turned as we heard a slap from across the room. Tucker had a hand on one of the bunker's walls, smiling broadly.

"Hear that?" He slapped the wall again. "Nine-foot epoxy-hardened concrete walls. Can withstand the blast from a nuclear fallout." He gazed up at the wall with admiration. He wore a navy blue blazer and khaki pants, looking better equipped to sip a gin and tonic at the country club than survive a nuclear winter.

Travis caught my eye, a smile playing on his lips, and I pressed my mouth tight to keep a laugh from escaping.

It was surreal to be in the Redfields' house for many reasons, more than just being in the presence of people who'd deemed it necessary to duplicate their entire wardrobe to fill the closets in the Shelter, as though the apocalypse would require custom-made suits and designer bags. It was being around people who were convinced the world was out to get them. People who were expecting to isolate out of fear that they called preparedness.

Tucker turned to me and narrowed his eyes. "Do you have twenty/twenty vision?"

I furrowed my brow. "No, I wear contacts," I said, and glanced at Travis, who discreetly shrugged.

Tucker folded his arms over his chest and nodded. "I would consider getting LASIK. When the end comes, we might not have access to contacts or glasses for a while. Best practices, and all that."

His face told me he was serious. I murmured as Travis hid a smile. We'd been brought down to the Shelter as soon as we had arrived, barely crossing the threshold of their house before Taffy, face flushed with excitement, gestured for us to follow her downstairs, glass of chardonnay in her hand. I still had my coat on.

The first stop had been the decontamination room, followed by their three-year supply of canned goods and prepared food, then the generator room, and the bedroom with a blast-resistant dead bolt locking the door. In their shelter bedroom was a metal sign that read *TNT*.

When Tucker saw me looking at the sign, he laughed. "That's what everyone calls us: TNT. Tucker and Taffy, because we are firepower together. Feel free to use it."

I declined.

Taffy gulped more of her wine with each room that we walked through, the pitch of her voice rising octaves in excitement. This was her moment to show us what we had been missing, how short-sighted we had been by not constructing a shelter of our own. Instead of enticing me, it just made me sad and uncomfortable.

As we walked out of the gas mask room, Taffy whirled around, her glass of wine now empty. She leaned forward and put a hand on my forearm. "The most important thing to remember is that you need to protect yourselves. Only you can save yourself. Using personal power."

If only she knew.

I nodded politely as Tucker clapped. "Well said. Now, who's hungry?"

"Food sounds great," Travis said quickly, clearly ready to move this evening along.

We followed Taffy and Tucker back upstairs into their kitchen, where the catering staff was buzzing around a charcuterie table like honeybees in the springtime. We were the only guests that night, but the Redfields could have fed an army with the food—or survived in the Shelter for a month. An embarrassing amount of imported cheeses, meats, olives, and fig jam was artfully arranged on a long wooden board, the center spelling out *Prepare* in garlic and rosemary crispy bread sticks. I briefly wondered if I could rearrange the letters into something offensive.

"Travis, come with me. I want to show you the new crossbow I picked up the other day," Tucker said. He stood up, bourbon in hand, and gestured toward the den before turning and walking away.

Travis shot me a helpless glance before he followed him out of the room.

I filled a plate with some accoutrement from the charcuterie board and had just popped a piece of blue cheese in my mouth when Taffy leaned forward conspiratorially.

"I've heard something," she whispered, voice full of glee she couldn't conceal. "A secret." She put a hand on my shoulder. "Don't worry. I'm keeping my mouth shut."

I raised my eyebrows and didn't say anything, waiting for her to very much not keep her mouth shut.

"Someone's been leading a double life. Someone who lives very, very close to here." She took a long sip of her wine, eyelashes fluttering.

I swallowed the blue cheese whole, feeling it stick in my throat. "Who's that?" My voice came out hoarse.

She made a pip sound and then slowly put her wineglass down on the island before she looked up. "Well, it concerns the family of a very well-respected physician who lives in this neighborhood."

I felt my stomach clench, and the blue cheese wanted desperately to come right back up, all over Taffy and her expression of glee.

After a beat, she decided she had kept up the charade of suspense long enough. "The Tobins," she said, waiting for my reaction.

Relief whooshed through me for a moment before I reset. "David? What do you mean?" I couldn't imagine anything scandalous with him. His plastic surgery practice seemed to be thriving; his son, Luke, nearly lived at our house; and his wife was one of the few normal women in Forest Hills.

She tapped a finger against her wineglass. "Well, seems that David was partaking in some extracurricular activities a few years ago." She leaned forward. "With a patient of his."

I stepped back and folded my arms over my chest. "Wow. I never would have guessed. They seemed so happy. That's terrible."

She waited for me to ask more questions, but I didn't give her the satisfaction. It wasn't any of my business. And Lord knew I certainly wouldn't have wanted people asking too many questions about my own past.

Taffy frowned. "Just so sad. Stephanie found out, and I heard they're staying together, but no way will his practice survive now that it's public knowledge. Who would trust a doctor who sleeps with their patients?"

She had a point, but I was about to argue that it might not be that catastrophic until I reconsidered where we lived. If an incense shop was run out of town for being too out-there, a public scandal involving a married doctor would easily fall into career-ruining territory.

"Just awful. So terrible," she said in a tone that implied she could not have been more pleased to come across this information. "I'm just glad we didn't invite them to join our group." She smiled at me. "You and Travis are much more our kind of people."

Again, if only she knew.

If Madisyn was able to figure out information about the fire, and if our culpability came out, Taffy wouldn't have to lead the charge in an actual witch hunt. The entire community would join her. Travis would be ruined by association, not to mention what would happen to me.

Tucker and Travis reappeared in the kitchen, my husband looking like he had just survived waterboarding.

"Shall we sit in the living room and enjoy a drink together?" Tucker said.

Travis's eyes slid to me, pleading for an early release. *Play along.* He pulled his phone out of his pocket.

Got it.

Travis furrowed his brow. "I would love it, but you know what, we really need to get going. I just got a text that I have an early morning surgery now on the schedule, so I should get some sleep," he said. He gave Tucker his megawatt smile.

Out on parole from the Redfields', I whispered to Travis as we walked to our car.

"You don't have to work tomorrow," I said, and he tapped my arm with a finger as an answer.

We quickly stopped and turned, almost military style, to smile and wave goodbye to the Redfields, who were watching from the windows in their foyer like rich Peeping Toms. They waved back and continued to stare at us.

"I'm not tired. Are you?" Travis said as he closed his car door.

"Tired of talking about filtering our own water, yes. But otherwise, no," I said. I looked back at the house. "Oh no, they're still staring. Drive before they show us another weapon."

He hurriedly pushed the Start button and pulled to the end of the driveway, waiting for the security gate to open. Then he turned left instead of right. When I began to question this, he put his hand over mine on my knee.

"A surprise," he said.

☾

"Another round?" A waitress in cut-off jean shorts and a crop top gestured toward our empty beers. She didn't wait for us to respond before she nodded and lifted a finger to the bartender, who began pouring two more pints.

"We're going to have to Uber home," I said with a laugh as I trailed a finger along my empty beer glass.

"We can share an Uber with that guy," Travis said as he pointed a finger toward a guy in jeans and a flannel shirt warbling out "Livin' on a Prayer" in the center of the dance floor, eyes closed.

I laughed. "I'll pass. Although nothing could be as bad as that dinner party. You're my hero for getting us out of it."

He nodded. "It was too weird. They were looking at us like they wanted to eat us instead of that charcuterie board."

"The Donner dinner party?" I said with a smile.

"Exactly."

I settled back into my bar stool, body turned toward Travis as I hooked a foot on his stool. I had chuckled as he pulled into Woodpecker's, a karaoke bar three towns over that sported buzzing neon beer signs, an overflowing ashtray of cigarette butts outside, and a sticky wooden entryway.

One of our first dates was at a karaoke bar called the Hitching Post. Travis had never been there before, and his mouth dropped open as we pulled into the parking lot, glancing down at the directions printed out from MapQuest.

"One of the residents said this was a good date place," he said quietly, mostly to himself.

"He or she sounds fun," I laughed as I popped open the car door. "Let's check it out."

It became a joke between us. He had pictured a cozy cocktail lounge, an out-of-the-way secret place that would impress me. To be honest, nothing impressed me more than sharing a pitcher of beer with him in a place with peanut shells on the ground. The admiration continued when I met his parents and fully understood where he came from. He came from privilege, albeit with a few extra quirks and rhinestones than most.

Two decades and two kids later, we were back at a karaoke bar.

After the waitress brought over our fresh drinks, he took a sip and turned to me. "Things have been really good lately, don't you think?"

I quickly looked at my drink and fixed my gaze on the foam floating above my beer. "They have."

I felt his hand on my knee and looked up at him. "They have," I said again.

He leaned forward and kissed me, and then hugged me tight.

I wished more than anything in that moment that I could tell him everything, show him the ugly parts of me, of what I had done. What I was afraid might happen. But I knew I couldn't. It would destroy everything.

I made a vow, again, to do whatever I needed to keep my past where it belonged: behind me.

Chapter 20

I will have to remove both kidneys to fit into this," I muttered as I struggled to pull the red bodycon dress over my head. My shoulder nearly dislocated as I tried to shimmy it down my waist. Sweating, I looked into the dressing room mirror and frowned. I looked like an overfilled pastry bag. If the pastry bag cost $800.

"No," I called over the dressing room curtain. I pulled on my black jeans and white long-sleeved T-shirt before I left the torture dress in the dressing room.

Marcy tapped a finger against her cheek as I walked out and then shifted her gaze to the dressing room next to mine, where Nancy was trying on a purple monstrosity that her mother had insisted she model.

A saleswoman with a silver tray of champagne glasses hurried over, and Marcy eagerly grabbed two. I thought she was going to hand one to me, but she quickly downed one and held the other.

I retracted my outstretched hand, desperately wanting an escape.

We were at Eduardo's Boutique, a small designer dress shop on Michigan Avenue in the Gold Coast of downtown Chicago. Marcy had insisted on a "girls' day" for us to go shopping for our dresses. She'd wanted Harper to join us, but my daughter was mortified at the idea of going to an "old lady dress shop," so I had to lie and say she had cheer practice.

I took a seat in a blue velvet armchair next to my mother-in-law.

"Yoo-hoo, Nancy! Let's see it, honey," she called. Marcy had already picked out her own dress—a bright green sequined, strapless mermaid gown that she thought would look perfect in the botanic gardens. She said she wanted to look like a living plant, albeit one that was fond of fake eyelashes and pink lipstick.

The heavy white dressing room curtain quivered before it slowly parted and Nancy walked out, frowning.

The dress was a deep violet ball gown with a satin bodice encrusted with black sequins. It looked like a 1980s prom dress, and not in a cool, nostalgic way. In a Glamour Shots-at-the-mall way.

Marcy cooed and clapped her hand against the champagne glass, while I tried to hide my look of horror.

"Absolutely not," Nancy said as she slouched forward, letting the puffy sleeves frame either side of her lined face.

I gave her a sympathetic look and then slightly rolled my eyes, but she didn't react. She turned to look at herself in the large mirror behind a small white pedestal, and I caught a glimpse of her back. I swallowed hard as my gaze trailed along the angry red skin.

I saw Marcy's gaze stop on Nancy's back, her eyes lingering.

"I think you look beautiful," Marcy said, too quickly.

A high-pitched whine moved across the room. "What's wrong with her?" a child's voice wailed.

A young girl modeling a flower girl dress huddled in the corner with a group of bridesmaids and pointed at Nancy. The women moved around her, trying to block the little girl's view, keep her out of sight. I heard hushes and low tones and saw reddened faces flashing apologetic looks to our group.

Nancy's face remained stony and she swept back through the dressing room curtain. Then, rustling noises as she shed the eighties prom dress.

I looked at Marcy, who shook her head and then took another sip of her champagne, trying to pretend that nothing was happening. While she loved drama, she hated conflict.

Sweat pricked the back of my neck and anger burned in my midsection as I saw the women comforting the little girl as though she had been through something traumatic by seeing burn scars.

Before I could stop myself, I walked over to the group. The girl whined again as she saw me, the little stinker.

"That was really rude," I said to a bridesmaid wearing an awful ruffled hot-pink gown. "You need to keep her quiet or leave."

The bridesmaid pressed her lips into a thin line and slowly nodded. I turned and walked back to Marcy, who was still pretending that nothing was wrong.

"I pulled a few more dresses," the saleswoman said as she walked in with a rack of silk, taffeta, and sequins next to her, oblivious to everything that had just happened.

"I'm done," Nancy said as she reappeared in jeans and a wild-life center T-shirt. When she saw her mother's mouth open in protest, she held up a hand. "I'm done," she repeated. Her gaze flicked to me and I nodded in solidarity.

As we gathered our things and turned to leave the boutique,

I saw Nancy's eyes land on a beautiful blue silky dress on the rack. It was backless, cut low in the front.

"Did you want to try that—" I started to say, but Nancy pretended she hadn't heard me and kept walking.

I hesitated before following her, an ache forming in my chest. We all knew why she wouldn't wear it. I reached out and ran a finger down the soft material, my healed forearm sticking out from my jacket sleeve.

After lunch, I drove Nancy back to her house, mostly in silence. My futile attempts at conversation had fallen quickly to the floor of my car. She barely looked at me as she got out, mumbling a thank-you before she walked inside.

Tears formed as I watched her walk up the path to her building and disappear inside. I wished that there was something to do for her.

The magic nudged me, reminding me that there was, in fact, a way to help her. But it wasn't as though I could heal her scars overnight—it would be too inexplicable. And even if I wanted to tell her what I might be able to do, there was no way she would believe me. The magic had to stay a secret.

After it had first happened, I had sleepless nights of wondering the same thing—if I could use the magic to heal her. Or even just to take her pain away. But I was terrified of using it again after the fire, terrified I would make it worse for her. Katrina and Alicia had long left North Valley and gone back home to their families, and I didn't think I could do anything by myself even if I tried.

But now we were together again, and the magic seemed to be within our abilities to harness, if only we could get it right. Maybe we had enough magical juice to do something remarkable.

I drove home through the twisting hills of the North Shore, glimpses of Lake Michigan reflecting off my windshield, my mind lost in the past and the future.

By the time I arrived back home, I had a plan.

A big one.

I picked up my phone and texted my coven.

☾

The night after the afternoon in the dress shop, I had a nightmare. I was back in the fire at Hawthorne Hall, flames licking the walls of my dorm room. The fire climbed up the walls, turning my posters and pictures taped to the walls to ash, curling the papers upward until they fell to the carpet, gone forever.

I was rooted to my bed as I watched it all, unable to move. The fire melted my desktop computer like candle wax, a mixture of gray and black rivers running down my scarred wooden desk. It made dust of the clothes hanging in the closet, split my shoes in half, and broke the mirror.

I couldn't move to run out of the room, that much I knew. But I didn't try. I just remained there, waiting for the heat of the fire to reach my bed. I closed my eyes and allowed it to consume me, surrendering to its power.

Allowing the fire to flood through me, ready to harness it.

Chapter 21

The harvest moon was a bright orange as it cast a glow over the empty playground in Kelly Park. Moonlight shone over the quiet plastic slide. The swings swayed gently in the evening breeze as though phantom children were lazily twisting in the darkness. The rubber tire material flexed and bounced as I walked across it to the old oak tree where Katrina, Alicia, and I had decided to meet at midnight. Well, I had picked midnight, but Katrina had asked for it to be closer to twelve forty-five because she'd be coming from a charity fundraiser.

I'd snuck out of my house after the kids were in their rooms and Travis was lightly snoring in bed, shooting a murderous, threatening look at Katy Purry to keep her quiet.

"Where—" she started to whisper before I shushed her and kept descending, stepping over her on the stairs.

Twelve forty-two a.m. displayed on my Apple Watch. I dropped a black backpack at my feet, wrapped my arms around my waist, and waited for them, hoping they'd arrive before I lost my nerve.

Katrina arrived exactly three minutes later, pulling her black SUV onto Elm Street and parking in the cover of the tree line. I suspected she had been idling around the corner to arrive exactly on time. She got out of the car, striding toward me in heels and a black shift dress, with a red blazer set atop her shoulders.

"How was the fundraiser?" I asked as she slowed her approach to me.

She smiled, the corners of her red lips moving upward. "Very successful." She took the blazer off her shoulders, arm muscles rippling in the moonlight. She looked down at the black back-pack at my feet. "Is that everything?"

I nodded and swallowed quickly. "Everything but Abraca-dabra Alicia."

She rolled her eyes. "Of course she's late. We should have told her eleven forty-five."

Twenty minutes later, after five unanswered texts and two phone calls, Abracadabra Alicia arrived. On an electric scooter. She stopped it when she saw us and climbed off, setting the scooter down in the grass near Katrina's car.

"Did you ride that the whole way here? That's like twenty miles," I said as I watched her strut toward us in full cow-boy regalia—boots, jeans with a wide leather belt, long-sleeved flannel.

She shook her head, and I saw that in addition to her country-western attire, she had affixed crystals to her cheeks, which caught the moonlight like tiny facial sequins. Vegas makeup.

"Cressida and I were at a country-western bar not too far from here. She's still there, learning a new line dance, so I just decided to scoot here. We always keep our electric scooter in the back of our car," she said with a giggle. She leaned forward and gave us each a quick hug, smelling like combustible dive-bar fumes.

She rubbed her palms together. "This is so exciting!"

A strong night breeze blew through the playground, slowly turning the spinner. The swings jostled lazily, kissing one another, and a handful of leaves blew across our feet.

I took that as a good sign.

Alicia lifted her arms to the sky in the wind, rejoicing. "Yes! Nature agrees with our intentions."

The wind picked up again, and I laughed. "Or it's just autumn in Chicago."

Katrina looked at the ground and shifted on her feet, thrusting the heel of her stiletto into the dirt. I saw that she looked nervous, wondering what we might affect by casting this spell. It was so much bigger than anything we had tried, which was exactly why I wanted to do it.

We were going to do a spell to undo the past. To reverse the damage that had been caused by the fire. To prevent Nancy from being hurt and leave the dorm standing. And then Madisyn would have no reason to investigate us.

Before, we had cast spells for the future. Now we would attempt to change what had already happened, to make things right.

"We could do something even bigger," Katrina said, eyes gleaming. "Like—"

"No. Just this," I said quickly, willing her to channel her power into good.

I had always done that. Back in school, she wanted to use magic to kill off the wasps that kept finding their way into our dorm rooms. We would find them flitting around after class, banging futilely against the screens. We never had any bug spray, so we first started by spraying them with hairspray until they were immobilized, then killing them. But she suggested we try a spell to kill all the wasps on campus in one instant. I told her I didn't think we had that kind of power, but I was afraid we did. And certainly afraid of the consequences for the ecosystem if it succeeded. So I walked to the hardware store in town and bought wasp traps to hang outside our windows. A nonmagical solution that actually worked.

Tonight the solution would have to be magical. I looked around at my friends. "We can make things right. No burn marks, no hospitalization. Make it so that everyone who had injuries recovered just fine. No lasting effects. No scars. The spell will take effect overnight, and by the time the sun rises, everything will have been made right."

"And that bitch will be off our backs," Katrina added. I knew she was still wishing we would agree to hex Madisyn, but I had found a magical workaround that benefited all. I was sure Madisyn could find some other mysterious tragedy to investigate. The world was full of them.

Alicia's eyebrows knitted together. "Katrina, be careful. Rule of Three. We need to have only the best intentions." She looked trepidatious, like she thought this wasn't a good idea.

"Hey." I tapped Katrina on the elbow. "Are you with us? Only white light?"

Katrina's face relaxed and she nodded. "Of course."

"Then it's time to get started," I said.

I knelt down and opened the black bag at my feet, and my hands began to tremble. I had been full of confidence and determination when I was the one pitching the idea, throwing myself behind convincing them. Now that it was done, the worry that something would go wrong began to creep back in.

I took a deep breath as I reached for the white candles in the bottom of the bag, pushing aside the moon crystals and the herbs that would go in the center, remembering Nancy's face as she tried on the cocktail dress and that horrible little girl in the shop.

We caused that.

We can undo it.

We have to at least try.

Slowly, I began to pull out the supplies I had gathered, mostly from memory and some from intuition. I was setting the candles down on the ground when I was startled, nearly falling backward as Katrina's phone trilled.

Her screen lit up and she held up a finger. "Sorry. I have to take this."

She answered the call, hissing into the phone that the unfortunate employee would have the spreadsheet on her desk first thing in the morning if they knew what was good for them, then she slid it back into her pocket.

She put her hands on her hips and watched as I unloaded the materials. Alicia bent down to help me, carefully turning over the offering plate in her hands, her cheeks slack with anxiety.

"Are you having second thoughts?" I whispered to her.

She closed her eyes and exhaled for a long moment before shaking her head. "No, my body is ready."

I swallowed and nodded, continuing to unpack the bag until everything was in front of us, splayed out like a magical autopsy. We considered it for a moment before Alicia bent down and began arranging the stones in a triangle, with a crystal at each peak, pointing to where we should stand.

I leaned over and lined the inner portion of the triangle with the candles. Wordlessly, Katrina picked up the rose hip oil and began anointing each one. Then she struck a match and lit them carefully as my chest tightened at the sight of the flames. I glanced around again, making sure we were far enough away from any trees or bushes that might catch fire. We were. If one of the candles toppled over, we would be able to stamp out the fire before it left the circle.

No blankets in sight.

When it was done, we stood. I took a deep breath and held out my hands. I felt theirs slip into mine, Katrina's smooth and polished, and Alicia's rough with jeweled rings scratching at my hand.

And I felt the flutter already begin.

We closed our eyes, and I began the incantation that I had written.

> *Return our spell*
> *To where it came*
> *To return life to the same*
> *Reverse the hurt and the pain*
> *Let only the light still remain*
> *Protect the good that we have now*
> *And everything else we disavow*
> *By the power of us three . . .*

My skin began to prickle, and I squinted open my eyes and saw small dots of light fluttering around us like supernatural fireflies, stopping to consider each of us before continuing to swirl.

I paused, and Alicia and Katrina joined in, a muscle memory of doing spells together decades ago.

Hear our words
From the power of us three
As it burns . . .

The pinpricks grew more intense, and I opened my eyes wide. In the center of the circle, the glowing dots began to gather, slowly turning from white to lavender to purple.

"Beautiful," Alicia breathed next to me.

Katrina's face was like a mannequin's as she stared at the lights, and a wave of fear ran through me. I wanted to stop. Stop before something terrible happened again. The sparks began to clump together, like mercury from a broken thermometer, until they were one big ball of rotating light, with us on the outskirts, barricading it in.

"Do it," Katrina said, nearly shouting.

I closed my eyes, ready to complete the spell.

But before I could speak, a gale-force wind whipped through the park.

We heard a creak and a ripping sound, and our circle broke apart.

Chapter 22

Everything went black as I flew backward and landed on the ground with a thud, my head hitting the hard dirt. A small tree branch came down next to me, and I lifted my forearm to my face in protection. The wind still whipped around us, pushing leaves and dirt over my body as I squinted, my vision blurry.

My head turned to the side, I saw shapes starting to form in the tree line in the distance. First, it was shadow people, their images floating above the grass. Travis, Hunter, Taffy Redfield, Harper. They blinked in and out, coming into focus before turning blurry again. Then, finally, a woman with wavy brown hair whose face I couldn't make out. My head began to pound.

As my eyesight started to come back, I saw the tree line was just that—trees—without people. I heard a yell.

"Alicia!" I heard Katrina say from somewhere to my left.

I slowly sat up, every muscle straining and bones aching, and blinked a few times. Pain coursed through my back and legs, radiating outward.

Alicia was on the ground to my right, a large tree branch covering her face. Katrina crawled toward her, calling her name.

"Oh my God," I said as I scrambled over to her. Smaller twig offshoots were covering her face, but the thick branch was luckily just above her head. Blood trickled from a deep cut on her forehead.

"Alicia! Alicia, wake up!" I said as I touched her shoulder.

She moaned but didn't open her eyes.

"That branch must have knocked her out," Katrina said as she reached for it. She pointed to it. "Help me get it off her."

As my body still screamed in pain, panting, we rolled the heavy branch away from her, careful not to scratch her face.

She moaned again, her face streaked with dirt and tiny cuts.

"Alicia, can you hear us?" I said as I knelt next to her. "It's Sarah and Katrina."

Her eyes slowly fluttered open, and her pupils dilated as she looked up at us.

"What happened?" she croaked out.

"The wind. You were hit with a branch," I said. I hovered my hand over her forehead. "You have a cut on your head."

She lifted her palm to her forehead and touched it, wincing. When she pulled away her fingers, she looked at the blood.

"Is it bad?" she asked.

Katrina and I exchanged a quick glance. "No," we said in unison.

She smiled, her lips trembling. "Liars." She put her hands on the ground and slowly sat up, despite our protests. She shook her head.

"What was that?" she said.

I glanced around, seeing our magical items scattered throughout the park, candles extinguished and crystals buried in the grass. I again looked to the tree line, where I had seen the shapes.

"I'm not sure. Wind, I guess."

Katrina and Alicia looked at me silently. A moment passed where we all acknowledged that it had very much felt like something other than wind.

"We should take you to the hospital," Katrina said, putting an arm around Alicia.

My stomach clenched at the memory of the last time we were all at a hospital together: After the fire. After another spell gone awry.

She shook her head. "No. I'm fine. Really." She pulled her hand away from her head and looked at her palm, streaked with less blood than before. "See? It's already stopping," she said, holding it up.

"We could maybe heal . . . ," Katrina said, trailing off.

Alicia quickly said, "No. No more magic tonight."

I took a deep breath and whispered, "We didn't finish the ritual. What do you think that means?"

Alicia winced as she stood up, swaying slightly. "Nothing. It wasn't completed, so nothing happens."

More than anything, I wanted to believe her.

"C'mon, let's get you home. I can drive you and put the scooter in the back," Katrina said. She looked at our items scattered around the park.

"I got those, don't worry. Just take care of her," I said.

They left, with Alicia reclining in the passenger seat of Katrina's car, leaving me to hurry around the park and search for everything. As I packed candles and crystals back into my black bag, a warning feeling moved through my body.

At home, I snuck back into bed next to a sleeping Travis, hoping that when I woke the next morning, nothing would be different.

At least not anything we didn't ask for.

Chapter 23

"Are you guys going to the homecoming float-building party tonight?" Pamela Jacobs asked, her eyes wide. In her hands she held a clipboard, pen poised above it. "We still have room for a few more volunteers, especially with making the paper rosettes." She shifted her weight from side to side, wearing low-rise 7 for All Mankind jeans and a studded belt, a swath of stomach exposed below her tight baby T-shirt.

Katrina, Alicia, and I stood in the crowded cafeteria, plastic trays in our hands. It was lunchtime, and the summer heat of the early September afternoon, coupled with the number of bodies in the room, made the space feel particularly stifling, despite the air-conditioning cranking.

Katrina's eyes widened in horror, and I stifled a laugh as I pictured her wrestling with tissue paper and a hot glue gun.

"Well, maybe," Alicia said, chewing on her lip, and our heads snapped to her.

"No, sorry," I said quickly. "We're busy tonight." I smiled, waiting for Pamela to walk away.

But Pamela did not get to be head of the float planning committee by accident. She wouldn't be deterred that easily. "Really, what are you three up to?"

"Club meeting," Katrina said as she folded her arms over her chest.

Pamela cocked her head to the side. "What kind of club? I'm not aware of any club that holds meetings on Saturday night."

"We just started it," Alicia said. "It's really a new thing."

"What's the activity?" Pamela said.

Katrina and Alicia looked to me.

"Um . . ." As I stalled, a tall, lanky figure in a trucker hat walking across the cafeteria caught my attention. His name was Scott Harrington, and he was in my freshman English class. He had never so much as looked in my direction, but I had certainly noticed him, tall and tanned and corn-fed. He'd borrowed a pencil from me once, and that was all it took for my eighteen-year-old self to crush, hard.

"What?" Pamela said as she leaned in closer. Katrina and Alicia shifted, their panic rising, still looking at me.

But I stared at Scott and watched as he plucked an orange from the basket of fruit. As he walked to the register to pay for it, he tossed it back and forth between his hands in a light juggle, his hands expertly flexing with each toss. I nearly collapsed as a swoon washed over me.

Katrina elbowed me in the ribs, and I jolted. I shot her a look and turned back to Pamela.

"Juggling," I said finally. "We're forming a juggling club."

It was the best I had.

((

"We should actually learn how to juggle in case anyone asks us to," Alicia said as we walked off the bus later that afternoon. Her skin sparkled gold in the sunlight, thanks to her Urban Decay Honey scented body powder. We'd left a half hour late because she'd meticulously applied it to every exposed part of her skin. It was supposed to be lickable, yet I doubted she would want anyone on the city bus to lick her.

"I still can't believe that was the best you could think of," Katrina said as she bent down to brush dirt off her UGGs.

"Sorry, guys. Don't put me on the spot next time then," I said as I hitched a black messenger bag over my shoulder.

The bus pulled away, and we looked around the town of Millville. It was twenty minutes by bus from North Valley, a sleepy small town with one gas station, a neon-lit tavern that had apartments above it for rent, and a laundromat. Not the usual destination for a group of college girls.

Yet there was something here for us.

We walked across the street and around the laundromat to a small purple door marked *Madame Serena's Curiosities Shop.* White stars and a crystal ball were stenciled in white below the name.

I hesitated for a moment before pushing open the door, and Katrina grumbled and put her hand over mine, shoving it forward. We stepped inside Madame Serena's lair, and our eyes adjusted to the darkness. Crystal beads hung on the walls, and incense smoke made our eyes burn. I coughed and looked at my friends. Alicia's eyes looked like a kid at Disney World's, and Katrina's face held a small smile. Lining the walls were glass cases filled with crystals and gemstones, candles and jewelry, tarot cards, and divining rods.

We had found the store on the internet. Katrina's desktop computer had an Ethernet port, which was worlds faster than dial-up. We started by searching for candle stores nearby, then crystal shops, and finally found a listing on a message board for Madame Serena's store. After studying the bus routes on a map I had shoved into my backpack on orientation day, we figured out how to get there, since none of us had a car.

"Greetings, ladies," said a voice from the corner.

We jumped, and a very short woman stood from a black velvet chair, a purple headscarf clasped with a crystal brooch wrapped around her hair. She wore a black robe with silver moons on it.

"What brings you girls here?" she said. Her fingers were decorated with gemstone rings, and her wrists clanked with layers of bracelets, like wind chimes tinkling in the breeze.

I shifted my black messenger bag to the side and nervously tucked my hair behind my ears. "We're looking for some items for a few . . ." I glanced at my friends, unsure of the proper word choice.

"Spells," Katrina said confidently.

"We're witches," Alicia said, her voice light.

And there it was.

Madame Serena folded her arms over her ample chest, appraising us. We certainly didn't look like witches, in our velour sweatpants and T-shirts. And we hadn't yet called ourselves that, at least not out loud. We had only done spells twice, small ones, for things like passing a test or pushing back the due date for a paper. Even though both of those spells had worked, we couldn't tell if it was the magic or luck. So we had decided we needed to level up and acquire actual magical items to assist us, and a witch field trip it was.

"I see," Madame Serena finally said, and uncrossed her arms. She walked behind one of the glass counters and tapped a finger. "Here are some things that you might be interested in."

Ten minutes later, we'd bought tarot cards, candles engraved with sigils, a crystal pendulum, and some pieces of obsidian. Katrina had spotted the black volcanic glass objects and crouched down.

"What are those?" she said.

"Obsidian," Madame Serena said with a smile. "One of the most magically powerful substances on earth."

Unblinking, Katrina said, "We'll take those, too."

As we pushed open the door to leave, ready to catch the bus back to North Valley, Madame Serena called out, "Girls, a word of warning: Be careful who you tell what you're doing. They still burn witches, you know."

We froze, and then she tilted her head back and laughed, revealing missing molars.

"Um, okay. Thanks," I said quickly, and pushed open the door, flooding the room with sunlight.

In the gravel parking lot in front of the laundromat, Katrina stopped, face serious. "She's right. We can't tell anyone. It has to be our secret."

"But—" Alicia started to protest, looking conflicted.

Katrina shook her head. "No one can know. We have to promise not to tell."

I nodded, and Alicia finally did, too. Of course, we didn't know just how many secrets we would have to keep.

Or for how long.

Chapter 24

A thunderstorm rumbled in the distance over Lake Michigan, nudging me awake. Before I could open my eyes, I felt Travis roll over in bed next to me and put a hand around my waist. He scooted his body closer to mine, fitting us together like two spoons. He began kissing my neck, making it clear that it wasn't a simple good-morning wake-up kiss.

With the storm cocooning us inside, I turned over toward my husband, forgetting all about the night before.

He grabbed me with the intensity of a castaway spotting a rescue plane, like I was the last drink of water in the desert.

"Whoa," I said with a laugh. "What's gotten into you?"

I closed my eyes as he kissed my neck but snapped them back open as I answered my own question.

Last night.

I tightly shut my eyes and tried to block out any warning bells going off in my head that said something was different with my husband as I put my arms around him and mentally returned to the moment.

Twenty minutes later, slick with sweat, my head felt like I had just gotten off a roller coaster, unsteady and buzzing with adrenaline.

The sex was good. Almost too good.

"That was fantastic. I'll go make some coffee," Travis said as he bent down and kissed me on the top of my sweaty head. "Just stay in bed and relax."

Before he left, he turned and looked at me. "You're so perfect," he said.

"Um, thanks." I shifted uncomfortably under his expression. It was as though he had cartoon-heart eyes.

As though he was under a spell.

Bewitched.

After he left the bedroom, I closed my eyes again. I just needed a few moments to think, to process what might have been happening. After a few seconds, I heard a loud crack of thunder outside. My heart racing, I shot up, threw off the cover, and peeked out of the bedroom window. Another sonic boom rattled the windows in the house.

As I stepped away from the window, the events of the night before flooded my memory.

Alicia had said that nothing would happen since the spell had been interrupted, but I wasn't entirely convinced. The magic had felt so powerful, so aware, before we were stopped, I had to wonder—where did all that energy go?

Nancy.

I ran over to my phone and swiped at it but then paused. It wasn't like I could call her up and ask her what happened the night of the fire. I realized I could Google it and see if any news articles came up, and find out what exactly had transpired, but I couldn't bring myself to do it. Not yet.

I looked at my phone in my hand and saw that there was so much dirt underneath my nails that it looked like I had gone feral. Maybe a shower would help me decide what to do next.

In the bathroom, Katy Purry was curled up on the bath mat. She opened one eye and then stood at attention, her tail twitching back and forth like a cat clock's.

"What in the world is going on?" she said, her voice a low rumble.

I stepped over her to reach into the shower and turn on the water. "Thunderstorm. I'm shocked you aren't hiding under my bed. Do you mind?" I said as I nudged her away from the shower with my foot. "It's weird to be naked around you now that you can talk."

She didn't move, a wall of orange fur. "Not that. Something feels different. Off."

My hand paused above the water, half in, half outside the shower. "Oh really?" I hadn't told her of the plan the night before, figuring she would try to talk me out of it.

She made a growling sound, and I looked down. Her ears moved like antennae, trying to pick up the magical signals in the air.

"Did you guys fuck something up?" she said, blinking slowly.

"Um, what do you mean?" I said as I adjusted the shower head and she moved away to avoid the spray.

She didn't answer, just walked out of the room, glancing back once to give me an appraising look.

I was about to step into the shower when my phone began to light up, buzzing with nonstop texts. I picked it up and saw it was downloading texts that had been delayed for some reason, maybe due to the storm.

My stomach clenched. I slowly leaned over to turn off the water and sank down onto the marble bathroom floor, terrified to open them up. Something was going on, and I wasn't sure that I would be pleased to find out what.

As suspected, they were all between Katrina and Alicia. I tapped on the B.A.W. conversation, scrolled up, and began to read.

The first unread message was from Katrina, at 5:03 a.m.

> Is this morning weird for anyone else? I opened my
> inbox to over a hundred new emails from investors
> inquiring about Obsidian. Not that I'm complaining,
> but . . .

Alicia: I might have to call the police. There's a man buzzing my doorbell over and over again, asking for me to come down so I can sign a program from a show I did two years ago. I'm scared.

Katrina's response was: Call the police. Then, Where the hell is Sarah? She can't be sleeping in after last night, can she?

It was seven forty-five a.m., not exactly the definition of sleeping in on a Saturday. But I typed out a response, telling them that things were normal at home for me, as far as I could tell.

Minus the overeager husband.

I started to put my phone down, as it was mostly a back-and-forth between the two of them arguing over what I was doing, when I saw a notification from Instagram. Curious, I clicked on it.

It was a message from a C-list reality star.

Hey there. You have a great profile. How are you doing?

"Gross," I muttered as I clicked Ignore and deleted the message. I told myself that there were plenty of weirdos on social media, yet something inside me said that this was different. New. A warning sign.

I decided to go ahead with the shower to clear my head, and turned the water back on and pulled off my pajama pants. As I did, another loud boom of thunder sounded, and another crack, followed by a fizzling sound, like fireworks on the Fourth of July.

I jumped back and looked out my bathroom window, but I couldn't see anything through the torrential downpour. Running into my bedroom to look out the bay window at the front of the house, I saw the once-beautiful weeping willow tree in the Greenglasses' front yard had been struck by lightning. The long, bow-shaped branches were scattered around their front yard, and the center of the trunk had a jagged black scar down the center. *Well, that's definitely not a good sign.*

Small orange flames shot from the blackened area where the lightning had hit, the little fires that could, despite the rain.

I ran downstairs and flung open the front door, rain hitting me in the face. Travis was already outside, running toward the Greenglasses' house to make sure they were safe.

I saw then what I couldn't have seen from the vantage point of my bedroom window: a tree branch had crashed through a nearby power line, and it snaked on the ground, sparks flying, like it was challenging invisible enemies to a ComEd duel.

"Shit!"

I turned around and realized my house was eerily silent, no refrigerator buzzing or HVAC system blowing. Our power was out.

"Kids?" I shouted up the stairs. "Hunter? Harper?"

Where were they? Had the magic done something to them?

I again called for them, standing in the foyer. I was about to go upstairs when Harper appeared at the top of the staircase, hair tangled around her shoulders, rubbing her eyes.

"What? What's wrong?" She dropped her hands from her face and looked at me, cocking her head back. "Why aren't you wearing any pants?"

Hunter walked up behind her. "Why is everyone shout— Mom!" He covered his eyes with one hand.

I looked down and realized that not only was I wearing just underwear on the bottom, the rain had soaked the front of my white T-shirt, making me look spring break ready.

The front door was still open, and I heard the wail of fire trucks in the distance, heading toward the Greenglass house. I relaxed my shoulders and hung my head.

Thank God. That was fast.

I started to close the door, but not before I saw a neighbor drive by our house, presumably to check out what the lightning had struck, and do a double take as they saw me in the doorway, half naked and in transparent clothing. I quickly slammed the door shut, rattling the wood around it.

I crossed my arms over my chest and faced the twins. "Storm knocked the power out. You guys okay?" But they had already grunted their acknowledgments and turned back to their bed-rooms to return to sleep.

My arms were slick with water, and I started for the kitchen to dry off as Travis walked through the front door, shaking water off his head.

"No pants? Round two?" he said with a smile as he looked me up and down.

"I'm good, but thanks," I said stiffly, but tried to smile back. "Bigger things to think about—no power."

He walked over and hugged me for longer than usual, and I had to peel myself away from him. He wasn't usually this . . . persistent.

What's gotten into him?

"I'm going to change," I said. I slowly turned and walked up-stairs, peeking outside at the flashing fire trucks parked in front of the tree. Thankfully, the fire already seemed to be dissi-pating.

"I'll miss you," he called after me. "Try to hurry back."

I gave him a wavery smile as I climbed the stairs to the bed-room in my silent house, the hair on the back of my neck stand-ing at attention as the strangeness of the morning swirled around me.

Was this our fault?

Chapter 25

My hair dripped around my shoulders onto the T-shirt I'd slipped on after my shower, as I sank down at the end of the bed while holding my phone. Across the lawn, the shrill of the sirens had quieted as the fire had been extinguished. The power was still out, and my bedroom was nearly black from the rain clouds. The twins were still in their bedrooms, and Travis was cooking breakfast in the kitchen, calling upstairs to see if I needed anything—twice.

The text stream between Alicia and Katrina had continued, devolving into all-caps sentences and messages sent one thought at a time. Before I could respond to them, I had to know.

I had to find out if we had affected the severity of the fire. And if Nancy had still been hurt.

I closed my eyes for a moment and took a deep breath before I opened up Google and typed in *North Valley University fire*.

My finger shaking, I clicked on the first link, an article from the *North Valley Chronicle*.

I scrolled down and skimmed the article.

A peaceful autumn night erupted in a blaze around 10:56 p.m. in the basement of Hawthorne Hall at North Valley

University, a freshman coed dormitory. Initial reports were called in to 911 that students were trapped inside the building, although many were out for the night.

Greg O'Callaghan, director of public relations for North Valley University, said the fire was isolated to the basement of the dormitory.

The blaze was successfully extinguished just after midnight, with the North Valley fire department, police department, and emergency medical services all reporting.

Frustrated, I clicked back to the search and scrolled through, looking for more articles on the fire. The only ones I found I had already read, with the same information.

I looked out the window, shoulders rolled forward. I could have called Nancy, but I couldn't figure out a way to ask her what had happened without sounding every alarm bell west of Lake Michigan. I'd be put into memory care faster than I could decline another bunker tour from the Redfields. I knew I would find out the next time I saw her, but I wanted to know right then.

I went back to the text stream with Alicia and Katrina, skimming it for any answers. It was all just texts about how Alicia woke up to being harassed and Katrina's oddly timed Obsidian investors.

And then there was Travis. His lovesick-puppy demeanor was definitely not normal. It was like he had been hit over the head with something.

I heard him downstairs, whistling and banging around pots and pans to make breakfast. It sounded like he was making a seven-course feast.

"You still doing okay up there?" he called from the kitchen.

"Yes. I'm fine," I quickly called back.

I was about to go downstairs when my phone buzzed with an appointment reminder.

Shit. I had to host an open house at 4723 Lawn Avenue. I would have asked a colleague to cover for me, but the sellers—the Baroneviches—were very particular about my being the one present at every meeting, every showing. They were certain someone would come in and root through their belongings when they weren't home, as though people often made visits to houses for sale to go through some stranger's underwear drawer.

Although, I did have that happen once. At an open house, I found a man in the kitchen, pulling snacks out of the pantry. He said he had missed lunch and needed something to eat while he walked around the house. He wasn't happy when I snatched the box of Annie's organic cheese crackers out of his hands.

I walked back into my closet to find something to wear to the open house and saw a pile of dirty laundry in the corner. I paused, wanting to test the magic in a small way, like I used to do before everything exploded after the coven's reunion. Just a minor thing—something to reassure me that the magic was still there. That we hadn't entirely corrupted it during our ritual.

I leaned over to make sure I still heard Travis in the kitchen, and no sounds from the twins, and looked over at the laundry, focusing my intention and whispering a few quick words.

The laundry rose up suddenly, clean, and folded itself before floating over to the dresser and resting inside the drawers.

I nodded, feeling a tiny bit of relief as my shoulders relaxed.

Maybe it's just a weird morning. The storm threw everyone off. Maybe there's no real cause for concern.

I dressed and went downstairs to the kitchen. Travis proudly stood in front of the kitchen island, where a gluttonous display of breakfast food was laid out. Eggs, hash browns, bacon, pancakes.

"Sorry," he said with a frown as I walked in. "Since we don't have power, all I could use was the burners, not the oven."

I didn't know what else he had hoped to make. "Oh, wow. Thank you. Are you expecting company?" I laughed.

He walked around the island and put his hands on his hips. "Just you." He looked down. "Are you going somewhere?"

I took a quick step backward, grabbing a pancake. "Unfortunately yes. I have an open house over on Lawn Avenue." I gave him an apologetic look. "I completely forgot." I gestured to the food. "I'm so sorry. I'm sure the kids will love all this, though. But I have to run."

His shoulders sagged but he nodded. "Of course. Got it." He grabbed a piece of bacon off the island and bent down, placing it in front of Katy Purry, who had been waiting for the spoils. "Guess it's your lucky day."

She closed her eyes and began happily working at the bacon.

The rain slowed to a drizzle as I drove to the Baroneviches' estate across town, taking small bites from the pancake. A ray of sunshine even peeked out as I navigated the stone paver walkway up to the front door. I squared my shoulders before I punched in the key code, ready to have a few normal moments that morning.

Chapter 26

ooking good. Looking *real* good today." The shouts came from
across the street and down two houses from the Baroneviches'
front yard.

I paused, holding the *Open House* placard to attach to the *For
Sale* sign in the front yard, confused.

They weren't talking to me, were they?

I was well past the age where men catcalled regularly.

I shaded my eyes from the sun and looked down the street, to
where a group of men was gathering around a truck from the
electric company, no doubt servicing lines that had been downed
by the storm.

"Good morning!" one of the men called to me with an eager
wave.

Confused, I gave a half wave back before hooking the *Open House*
sign onto the post and then speed-walking back into the house.

"Can I get your number?" was the last thing I heard before I
quickly shut the door.

I wasn't sure what the spell had done—other than not the
things we had asked for—but my original love spell was definitely going haywire.

Leaning with my back against the front door, I took a couple of slow, deep breaths, desperately trying to convince myself it was all a coincidence.

I heard the shuffle of someone walking up the front steps, the first visitor to the open house. I squared my shoulders and then turned around and opened the door, ready to greet the potential buyers. My smile wavered and I nearly fainted as Scott Harrington, my freshman-year North Valley University mega-crush, walked through the Baroneviches' door.

I hadn't seen him since freshman year, in English class.

He was the reason I'd blurted "juggling club" that day back in the dining hall.

We never had a full conversation that first semester, and since I left after the fire, I never saw him again. But man, did I remember him. He was my only college crush. My first glimpse at all the other boys out in the world, instead of the jerks who went to my high school.

His face brightened as he walked in the door, then his eyebrows lowered, and he tilted his head to the side, as though deep in thought, and stopped after he crossed the threshold into the estate. The years had been good to him—very good. He had a head full of blond hair and no sign of any middle-aged paunch around his middle. With the addition of a few lines on his forehead, he looked exactly the same.

He won't remember me. Of course he won't. Why would he?

But I must look familiar.

"Sarah Nelson," I said, straightening up and walking away from him across the marble foyer floor. "I'm the listing agent for this home." I lifted my palms in the air and smiled.

He took a listing sheet off the entryway table (that the Baron-eviches had had custom-made in Spain, per a forty-five-minute conversation that I would classify as a hostage crisis), glanced at it, and then looked up.

"I know. We went to college together," he said with a smile. He walked toward me and held out his hand. "Good to see you again."

He didn't notice me in college but recognizes me now? Again, not normal.

"Good memory. Freshman English, right?" I said casually, as though I were trying to remember. I stuck out my hand to shake his.

He shook mine, holding it for a beat longer than was normal. "Yes, of course. You look exactly the same."

I laughed nervously, taking a step toward the rest of the house. "I doubt that, but thank you."

He put his hands in his pockets and watched me, not in a creepy way, but with friendly interest.

This is definitely not normal. Men from my past don't usually just pop up, unable to look away. Especially ones from my Hot Tools–curling-iron years.

Just keep it together. Be professional.

I lifted a hand, raising my voice in what I hoped was a busi-nesslike, authoritative manner. "It's a wonderful estate, perfect for a large family, or for entertaining. There are lots of open spaces and rooms for guests." He followed me into the foyer, craning his neck up at the oversized glass chandelier that hung in the center. It had been designed by Dale Chihuly, the artist who created the glass sculptures at the Bellagio in Vegas.

"Do you live in the area?" I said lightly as my heels click-clacked on the marble floor leading into the kitchen.

"Right now I'm downtown, in a condo off Oak Street," he said as he followed me.

I stopped in front of the Sub-Zero fridge and clasped my hands behind my back. It was one of the cardinal rules of show-ing a house. Make yourself look bigger in a space that needed a lot of work—like an illusionist. An Alicia. In a space that was large and spoke for itself, blend into the fixtures, guiding the cli-ent to see things for themselves. Manipulation tactics, ones I was sure Katrina employed as she was bullying her colleagues.

"A dream kitchen, great for entertaining and hosting family gatherings," I said, hoping he would say he had a wife and family.

Scott chuckled. "Well, I haven't really been entertaining that often lately." He looked at me, his mouth cocked to the side. "I'm going through a somewhat complicated divorce."

"I'm sorry to hear that," I said. "A fresh start, then."

His nod confirmed it as he ran a hand along the quartz coun-tertops, peering down at the busy pattern. Then he looked up at me, hair falling over his forehead, looking exactly the way he had back in college. Looking at me exactly the way I wished he had twenty years before.

Except this was now, and he was about two decades late. I already had a husband at home, furiously cooking me breakfast in a house without power and waking me up for morning sex.

"Let's keep moving, shall we?" I said. I turned toward a vaulted family room and let him take in the thirty-foot stone fireplace and inlaid flooring.

"As you can see, this is a wonderful family room, with lots of space for custom couches and a large television. And this comes with the house." I swept an arm toward the large, built-in saltwater aquarium in the wall opposite the fireplace. It was 180 gallons and sunk into the wall so that the edges were flush. In the center, four lionfish lazily drifted around, their brown and white striped bodies waving in the water.

"Well, that's pretty cool," Scott said as he walked over and bent down to peer at the fish. "Aren't they venomous?"

I nodded in confirmation. The Baroneviches had told me so at the first listing meeting. Poisonous as a nest of cobras.

I leaned forward to get a closer look at the dangerous fish, and as I did so, they stopped and stared at me. All four fish, nearly in a line, their fins waving gently in the water, eyes alert.

"I think they like you," Scott said with a laugh as the fish stared at me. They waited, like I was about to give them instructions.

Then they puffed up, looking twice as big as before, and began to strike the glass, one at a time, moving down the line, so hard that it looked like they were trying to break it.

Familiars, they were not.

Scott laughed again, and my body went rigid as I watched the lionfish butt against the glass, ready to sink their poison barbs into my skin.

"Weird," I said quickly, and turned away, the tapping on the glass continuing.

I gestured toward the windows that showcased the back of the property. "A wonderful view with mature trees for lots of shade."

He walked over and gazed out at the backyard, at the expansive Rainbow playset, in-ground trampoline, and custom playhouse.

"Those all come with the house," I said.

He chuckled. "No need. I don't have any kids," he said. He looked at me, eyebrows raised. "Do you?"

I felt my face flush. "Yes. Twins. But way too old to use things like that anymore."

His head moved back a little, as though he was recalibrating. "Ah."

Thank goodness.

The fish were still hitting the aquarium glass as Scott followed me upstairs, ready to tour the expansive master bedroom and the two-person shower.

We walked back down the bridal staircase, toward the front door. I was about to show him the lower-level entertaining space when he stopped.

"You know, I don't want to waste any of your time. I really don't think this house is for me," he said. The front door framed his body, like he was a doll in a box, waiting to be opened by some eager woman. He would have been the most popular gift of the season.

"Of course," I said as I clasped my hands in front of my body. "It's important to connect with the right one."

"It is," he said, and his eyes met mine for a bit too long.

"Um, yes, of the utmost importance," I said quickly.

"Of the utmost importance"? Stop talking like you've just arrived on Earth.

"To be honest, I'm not even working with a broker right now, but I should probably have someone. Are you taking on new clients?"

Always. I was always taking new clients.

I hesitated before I nodded. "Of course." Warning bells went off in my head, screaming that I was making a mistake. That everyone was off-kilter in some Mercury-in-retrograde-on-speed way, and no decisions should be made. Yet my pride and denial pushed that voice of reason aside.

Scott smiled. "Great. I'm looking to put down roots in a neighborhood. As I said, I'm living in the city now, but this morning I was looking at real estate listings and saw this house. I can't really explain it. I had to see it." He gave a quick laugh. "And then when I saw your name on the listing, I just had to come. Right away."

While I appreciated the magic's bringing me new clients, this did not seem like the way.

My phone began buzzing in my purse on the entryway table. I ignored it.

Trying to keep my composure, I folded my arms over my chest. "Are you considering other areas, or just the North Shore?" I said, my eyes flicking to my purse, which vibrated again.

"Probably just this area. I'd love something near the lake." He looked up, his gaze moving toward the second floor. "But I think this might be too much house for one person." My purse jumped again, and he pointed to it. "Do you need to get that? Sounds like an emergency."

I waved my hand around as I quickly walked over to the table. "I'm sure it's nothing. Seems like there's always some urgent matter going on with my teenagers. We probably ran out of Zbars or something equally life-ruining."

I pulled out my phone. When I saw the text messages on the screen, I quickly put it facedown on the table.

"Just as I expected: nothing. Well, I'd love to discuss this further with you, to sit down and go over your priority list for a property, and then we can start really digging in."

He looked from my phone to me, clearly not buying my lame attempts at diversion.

"That sounds good. I'll be in touch." He took my business card from my outstretched hand, looked at it and then back up to me with a smile. "It was so good to see you. Again."

I watched him walk down the stone pathway, open his car, stop to wave, and then get inside. It wasn't until he started backing out of the driveway that I turned, my smile gone, the panic building.

I picked up my phone and looked at the messages again. The top one was from Katrina.

It read: **I think we're screwed.**

Chapter 27

I sank down on the floor of the Baroneviches' foyer, my back sliding against the gaudy black and gold wallpaper, as I tried to reach Katrina and Alicia.

Katrina was the first to answer the FaceTime, her office in the background. Before I could ask what was going on, she started shouting.

"Sarah! Where have you been? This morning has been a shit-show," she said. Her gaze flicked to something offscreen, and she whispered a few unintelligible words before her eyes narrowed and she looked back to me. "Sorry. Had to pause my inbox from loading. I'm getting about ten emails every second, more inquiries on Obsidian."

"Isn't that good?" I said, my voice full of false hope. From my vantage point on the floor, I saw Scott's car drive past the Baronevich house again slowly. I wanted to believe he was checking out the house, taking it in one more time. But I feared he was looking for something else. *Someone* else.

She laughed bitterly. "No. Not at all. So many orders are coming in that we won't be able to fill them all. There's no possible way, even if we relocated our factories to China and pumped out product faster than Shein."

Alicia's face popped up on my screen, joining the call. Her cheeks were red, puffy, and streaked with tears.

"Girls, I had to keep Joelle home from school." She sniffled and wiped her nose with a finger. "There's a police cruiser parked outside for protection. It was a really frightening morning. Cressida saw a man lurking around in our lilac bushes. He said he was a fan."

Katrina let out a loud grunt and hung her head before snapping it back up, looking in the direction of her inbox, and whispering another quick spell to calm down her emails.

"Sarah?" she said as she looked back to our call.

I glanced up at the glass chandelier hanging in the foyer and sighed, briefly closing my eyes. "Nothing that extreme, but it's definitely weird. It's like the love spell kicked into overdrive. Remember Scott Harrington from North Valley? Well, he just showed up at one of my listed houses."

Alicia's face brightened. "Oh. He was so handsome. How is he doing?"

I just stared at her, while Katrina shook her head.

"Why would you—" Katrina said.

"Katrina . . . ," I said, warning her.

Alicia looked confused for a moment before she understood. "Oh."

"Alicia, you said nothing would happen with the spell since we didn't complete it," I said, my voice shaking.

"She had also just been hit over the head, so . . . ," Katrina sighed.

Alicia shook her head. "Nothing should have happened. When a spell isn't completed, the magic dissipates. It always does. Well, it usually does." She looked away, chewing on her lip. "Although, there was that one time I was trying to—"

"Enough!" Katrina exploded. "How do we fix this?"

We were silent. This was new territory.

"Let's just lie low as much as possible for now," she finally said. "Listen, I have to go. I have a meeting with our supply chain manager to see if we can possibly keep up with demand."

She clicked away, and then it was just Alicia and me.

"I'm sorry about Joelle. She must be so scared," I said.

Alicia smiled gratefully. "Thanks. She'll be okay. How is your family?"

I thought of my children, at home, probably still asleep, Travis's seven-course breakfast feast in the kitchen.

"Weird. But I hope I can handle it," I said.

I hung up with Alicia, promising to call her later, and jumped into my car, wanting nothing more than to be home, with family, hoping that my children were still safe. And that Travis hadn't erected some kind of love tribute to me in our house.

As I pulled into my driveway, before I could open my car door, a text came through on my phone.

> Wonderful to reconnect with you this morning. I look forward to our next meeting—Scott.

Chapter 28

My house was quiet as I flung open the door from the garage. I stopped, nearly skidding on the floor, and slowly craned my neck around the laundry room. It was silent, the kids' shoes piled on top of each other in a tumble, their sports bags flung in every direction.

Okay, that's at least normal.

"Travis?" I called as I walked into the kitchen, my shoulders tense. Every muscle of my body was at attention as I waited to be hugged or wooed by my suddenly too-attentive husband.

I called my husband's name again, but the only response was the hum of the refrigerator and the sound of the ice machine dropping more cubes into the bin. The power was back on.

A flash of black appeared in my peripheral vision. I looked over and startled. There was a black cat sitting in the doorway of the kitchen, gaze fixed on me.

"Where the hell did you come from?" I said.

She looked offended, then turned and wandered off, slowly walking toward the family room.

I followed, walking past the black cat, who didn't make any

effort to speed up or get out of my way. As I approached the family room, I heard the sounds of a movie, and a few meows.

"Jesus Christ!" I called out as I stopped in the entrance to the family room. Everywhere, on every surface of the room, there were cats. The couches were covered in white, black, and tabby figures, half sleeping, licking their paws. My two white end tables were now the domain of a group of large Himalayan felines. On the coffee table was a pair of Siamese cats, standing at attention, watching the television, tails twitching back and forth.

On the rug in the center of the room was Katy Purry, surrounded by admirers, purring.

When she heard me come in, she lifted one eyelid. "Oh, hi. You're home," she said in her smoker's voice.

All of the cat heads in the room turned in unison, an unsettling vision.

"What is going on?" I hissed, stepping into the room, nearly trampling a sleeping black and white spotted feline. The cat looked up and gave me a disapproving look.

"I wanted to have some friends over to watch a movie," Katy Purry said, both eyes open now.

My gaze slid to the television and I saw they were watching *Pet Sematary*. "You're going to be in a pet cemetery if you don't get these animals out of my house."

She rolled over and sighed, and meowed out a few instructions. I heard some hisses and grumbles, but all of the cats got up and filed out of the patio screen door, where Katy Purry had clawed a hole to let her friends in.

As the last one left, I turned to her. "You are in so much trouble.

You're . . ." I tried to think of the right punishment. "Grounded," I finally said. I didn't know what else to say.

Katy Purry lifted an eyebrow and twitched her whiskers. "It's not that big of a deal. Cats clean up after themselves."

I cocked my head to the side, challenging her for a moment, before I went back into the television room. The room stunk of animal hair and kitty litter. The couches were covered in fur, a glass bowl of decorative stones had been knocked over, and I spotted a couch pillow with two long sets of scratches down the center, stuffing peeking out.

"It's like a cat keg party happened in here," I said as I frantically started picking up the spilled stones. "Shit. The kids can't see this. There's no way to explain it." Then I remembered why I had raced home in the first place. "Where are the kids?" I said.

She looked in the direction of the back door. "I think I heard them say they were going to Luke's house."

"And my husband?"

"Errands."

I sighed in relief.

"Clean," I commanded my naughty familiar.

Katy Purry grumbled but started batting around the stones, herding them into my hands.

"This is the worst possible time for you to do something like this. Do you know the morning that I've had?" I said, my voice shaking. "Something is wrong. Like, really wrong this time."

"I knew you fucked something up." She licked a paw and then looked at me.

"I don't even know what happened. But one of the spells we

did in the past—*the* spell—is all messed up now. We tried to change some things that happened that night, and it got all screwed up."

She didn't answer, and I looked up. "What?"

She stared at me, her face as serious as if she had seen us walk through the door with a new puppy. "Bad. Very bad. You tried to change the past?"

I crumpled and fell against one of the armchairs, sighing. "We wanted to make it better, fix our mistakes. We didn't even finish the spell. Alicia said it was fine."

I realized how ridiculous I sounded. Like putting a Band-Aid on a severed foot.

Katy Purry walked over and rubbed against my side. "Maybe I'm wrong. Maybe it's not that bad," she said as she nudged her body next to mine.

I nodded and put a hand on her back, spreading my fingers out and running them through her fur. I didn't know how we were going to fix it. Or if we even should try.

"I—" I started to say, when a strong smell of ammonia hit my nose. "What is that?" I turned and looked behind me and saw a pale yellow spot on the chair. The unmistakable odor of cat pee. "Really?" I said.

Katy Purry looked away. "Sorry. Butterscotch couldn't hold it."

I let my head drop to my hands.

As I stood in the kitchen after the family room was cleaned and smelling much better, I had an urge to go upstairs and hide in my closet like an injured animal tending to her wounds. To pretend that everything was just as it should have been and not have to encounter any more disasters.

Yet I wasn't a teenager anymore. I had a husband, children, a job. A home. Responsibilities. I couldn't lock myself in my closet and listen to depressing music like a high schooler who had endured a breakup during the back-to-school carnival on the Ferris wheel.

I had to face things.

I clicked over to my emails, waiting to see what was next. There was one from Marcy, a link to an article that had been posted that morning in the *North Valley Tribune*. It was about Madisyn's investigative work for the podcast. It was mostly a puff piece, designed to drum up publicity.

Yet I almost dropped my phone as I read this pull quote from her:

> I've made a lot of progress on uncovering details about the fire, and I look forward to sharing them all. I think people will be surprised by what really happened and who I believe is responsible. Stay tuned.

It shouldn't have been a shock. With everything else beginning to implode around me, I was sure Madisyn was one step closer to finding out the truth that we had kept hidden for so long. The moment when a true investigative journalist decided to delve into the source of the fire was of course the moment the magic became untenable. And that wasn't even counting whatever it was that we had done in the park.

Our window for hiding, controlling the narrative, was just about shut. And I didn't know where that left us or what options we had.

Chapter 29

The twins arrived home from Luke's house after I had cleaned up any remains from the cat party, hoping against hope that they couldn't tell, like hiding one last red Solo cup in the trash as your parents walk in the door.

My shoulders sagged with relief as they entered the kitchen, limbs intact. At least the spell hadn't gone haywire on them, too.

"Hey, Mom," Hunter said as he threw his string backpack on the ground, just next to the mudroom cabinet. He kicked off his shoes, also next to the cabinet, and walked into the kitchen.

He stopped quickly, Harper bumping into him behind.

"Walk," she said, half in, half out of the mudroom.

"What's that smell?" he said, his nose wrinkling. He frowned and looked around for the source. "Smells like a zoo."

I eyed the pumpkin spice candle dancing on the island. *Lot of help you were*, I thought. I had contemplated using magic to clean the house, but as I started to whisper the usual spell, I stopped, thinking of Scott's appearing at my listing and not taking a hint.

So my house now smelled like a feral cat colony.

Harper appeared around her brother and put a hand to her nose. "Ew. Did Katy Purry pee all over the furniture or something?"

I glanced down at the cat, who looked up at me with innocent eyes.

I looked at my daughter. "Yes. She did. No more treats for her for a while."

Katy Purry meowed in protest, and I ignored her, stepping around her toward my kids.

"How was Luke's house?" I said.

Hunter shrugged, and his long lashes lowered. He had gotten those from Travis, a win in the genetic lottery that incensed his twin. "Weird."

"Why?" I said, remembering what Taffy had told me about the scandal at Luke's dad's plastic surgery office. "I'm sorry. Is Luke okay?"

Hunter shrugged, not wanting to continue the discussion. He walked over to the fridge and pulled out a Gatorade. "I'm going to watch the game."

Which game wasn't specified, if there even was one. He just wanted to avoid any more questions.

I looked at Harper. "You good? Hungry or anything?" I then noticed her expression.

Her mouth was drawn down, like a bow with both ends pointing to the oak floor. Her eyes were troubled, and she brushed back a lock of hair in discomfort.

"Uh-oh. What's going on?" I said, gently touching her arm.

Her face crumpled, and I stepped forward, pulling her toward me. I put my arms around her shoulders, smoothing back the top of her hair. Anxiety peaked inside of me, and my hand on her head began to shake.

What if the magic really did do something to her?

"What happened?" I whispered into her hair.

She looked up, eyes red and cheeks bright. Her hair hung around her face. She shook her head.

"Here. Come sit down." I led her by the hand to the kitchen island and deposited her on a stool. I sat in the one next to her, my body facing hers, one foot on the base of her stool. "You can tell me."

"So you know Georgia's boyfriend, Zack?" she said.

I didn't, but I nodded.

"Well, we were over at Luke's today, and we were outside by the firepit. Everyone else went inside to watch some stupid ASMR video, and it was just Zack and I by the fire. And then . . . then . . . then . . ."

I put a hand on her leg. "And then?"

She shook her head, brushing back her hair and tucking it behind her ears. She exhaled. "Sorry. I'm buffering."

I smiled and squeezed her leg.

"Anyway, he said he always had a crush on me and then leaned over and kissed me. Mom, he *kissed* me." She waited for my reaction.

"And what did you do?" I said evenly.

"I shoved him away and called him a fucking loser." She looked up, eyes wide. "Sorry."

I leaned forward and squeezed her leg again. "Don't be sorry. You did the right thing. He *is* a loser to put you and Georgia in that situation. What did he do next?"

She laughed. "He got all nervous and then ran inside." She looked down and twisted her hands in her lap. "But, Mom, how do I tell Georgia? She's going to freak out."

I took a deep breath and shifted my foot on the base of her stool, considering. "Well, I suppose you don't necessarily have to tell her. Or you can make him be the one to tell her." I didn't think that sounded like perfect advice, but at that moment, I didn't feel like someone worthy of telling anyone what to do.

Her eyes widened and she dropped her hands to her sides. "Mom, are you serious? Of course I have to tell her. Even if she hates me."

I swallowed and nodded. "Of course. That's the right thing to do."

It didn't escape me that my sixteen-year-old had a clearer lens on her moral compass than I did. *Telling* wasn't exactly something I had practice doing.

"Yeah," she said. "I'll just have to deal with the consequences. But I'll have a clear conscience."

A clear conscience. Something I desperately wished for myself. But I knew the price of spilling all my secrets: police, possible charges, the loss of everything I knew, everyone I loved. It wasn't so simple.

"Well, I admire you for that. You're stronger than I ever was," I said. I lifted a hand to her chin and tapped it.

"Thanks." She looked down again and then past me, toward the television room. "Can we watch a movie?" she said.

Katy Purry's head snapped toward me; no doubt she was hoping we would put on a movie of her choosing. My on-demand bill was going to be astronomical that month, and I would have to explain to Travis why I'd watched *Puss in Boots* seventeen times.

"How about in my room? We can snuggle in bed and put something on," I said, shooting Katy Purry a glare at her perch in the doorway.

"Maybe we should watch, like, an old movie." Harper flipped through the menu on the television in my bedroom before landing on a movie that made me want to squirm in discomfort.

"Really? *The Blair Witch Project?*" I said.

Katy Purry opened one eye from her cinnamon roll position, curled on the edge of my bed.

Harper hit Play and shrugged. "Yeah. Taylor said it was good." She leaned back and waited for the movie to start, then glanced at me. "Popcorn?"

I walked into the kitchen, pulled out a bag of popcorn from the pantry, and stuck it in the microwave. As I waited for it to start popping and inflate the bag, my hand resting on the appliance's handle, I thought of the first time I'd seen that movie.

It was the summer after my freshman year of high school, and I had walked down to the local Blockbuster in town, three dollars burning a hole in my pocket. My mom worked that summer at the local Jewel-Osco, bagging groceries and checking people out at the register.

She had a long shift at the grocery store that day, and I had a blissful summer day of being alone, a day off from my babysitting job, where I spent most of my time yanking markers out of the hands of three young children and cleaning up after a small dog that peed everywhere.

I slowly walked into town, the euphoric feeling of a day on summer vacation washing over me. Most other kids my age didn't have summer jobs yet, but I had to stay busy, make money, be productive. Even on the days when I was off from my babysitting or other odd jobs, it always felt like there was some adult responsibility that I would have to manage. My mother and I were like one and a half adults trying to do the work of two.

Sophomore year was six weeks away, and I was determined to become a new person that summer. A better version of myself. It was a chance to reinvent myself, going from the introverted, shy girl who started high school, terrified of everyone and everything. I didn't want to be the awkward girl who wore weird clothes, or the girl who pretended not to notice when the birthday party invitations were passed out at school and she returned home with an empty backpack.

I wanted to fit in, find a group of friends, know who had a crush on who, and whose parents had the best basement because it had a pool table.

I wanted to finally feel normal.

I walked into Blockbuster, the employees barely looking up. They had just restocked the movies, being that it was a Tuesday and everyone had returned their weekend movies the day before. Three whole rows were dedicated to *Varsity Blues*.

On the bottom shelf, with three small boxes, was *The Blair Witch Project*. I had heard about the movie and knew it was about a group of campers who are terrorized by an evil witch in the woods. There had been a marketing campaign trying to convince people the story was real, that the movie was "found footage" of an actual event.

I walked up to the register and waited for the pimply teenager who looked like he had just rolled out of bed to come into work, and eyed the bags of microwave popcorn.

"One of those?" he said, gesturing with a pinky toward the stack of popcorn bags.

I shook my head as I handed over my Blockbuster card. I hadn't brought enough money for popcorn and a movie. "Just the movie, thanks."

At home, I huddled under a blanket with a box fan pointed straight at my face and didn't move for the entire run time.

I think, in the end, the viewer was supposed to feel bad for the campers, to feel that they had endured an undeserved fate. Instead, I felt like they had messed with something they didn't understand, and maybe the witch was just protecting her house.

Now I knew how she felt.

The microwave beeped and I startled. I lifted the bag with two fingers, shook it a few times, and poured the popcorn into a bowl, careful not to let the steam burn my face.

I walked back upstairs and climbed into bed next to Harper, who was propped up on one elbow, texting on her phone.

She didn't look up. "Did you add M&M's?"

I rolled my eyes and laughed. "Sorry, princess. I'll be right back."

She tutted at something on her phone and looked up when I stopped in the doorway.

"I'm going to tell Georgia tomorrow after practice, no matter what. Even if she ends up hating me," she said. Her face held an expression of satisfaction at having settled any debate over confessing.

In the kitchen, as I poured a handful of M&M's into the bowl of popcorn and lightly tossed them with my hands, my nose tickled with tears as I wished I could have a little bit of my daughter's agency.

Chapter 30

Your soul will be mine.

The phrase was whispered into my ear, worming its way through my eardrum and into my brain as I slept.

Come back.

Come here.

I slowly opened my eyes and froze in bed, listening.

Certain death awaits. Followed by maniacal laughter.

I exhaled as I recognized the noises. They were from the Halloween animatronic at the Redfields' next door. I'd left my window open the night before, enjoying the cool autumn breeze, and it faced their house. I wouldn't make that mistake again.

Disoriented, I felt around on my nightstand before I located my phone and checked the time.

It was 6:02 a.m.

Slightly early for Halloween animatronics to be going off, and not the most pleasant way to wake up. I made a mental note to ask Taffy to make sure they were turned off before they went to bed, even though she would probably use the friendly request to start a conversation about stockpiling medical supplies for the still-as-yet-unpredicted apocalypse.

I slowly extricated myself from Travis in bed. After the movie, Harper had fallen asleep in my bed, and I'd had to help her into her room. Travis texted that he had an emergency surgery, so I fell asleep alone in bed. I felt him climb in next to me sometime long after I had fallen asleep. He slung an arm around me and then fell asleep with his body practically attached to mine.

A couple of hours later, I woke up, sweating, and tried to scoot away from him, and nearly fell off the bed. I wound up wedging a pillow in between our bodies, just to get some air circulating near my skin. I lay there for what felt like hours, unable to fall asleep.

I tiptoed to the bathroom, not wanting to wake him. As I brushed my teeth, I turned on the radio, volume low, to get the news.

I couldn't quite hear over the brushing, but when I rinsed my mouth and turned off the tap . . .

". . . *known by her stage name as Abracadabra Alicia* . . ."

My hand frozen in the air, my feet rooted to the marble floor, cold sweat began to form on my neck.

I grabbed my phone, frantically Googling Alicia. The first hit was a picture of Alicia at one of her shows. She wore a bright pink sequined gown and a top hat. Her arms were outstretched, and a group of her serval cats surrounded her.

Reports say that an intruder broke into her home in an attempt to kidnap her, but her African serval cats were able to fight him off. Police and ambulance responded, and the suspected intruder was airlifted to the hospital.

Now to a story that's developing on the city's West
Side . . .

I tried to call both Katrina and Alicia, and when I didn't get
an answer, I sent a text that was left unread.

The fact that someone had managed to break into her house
was terrifying. The spell we had done twenty years ago had esca-
lated, transforming from the magical equivalent of a petting zoo
to Jurassic Park. The T. rex was in charge now.

I was frantically getting ready, preparing to drive to Alicia's
house to make sure she was okay, when my phone lit up with a
reminder, followed by a familiar chime.

Notification: Gala planning breakfast, 9 a.m.

Shit. I had a meeting at my in-laws' house to go over the plans
for the event. As much as I wanted to race to the city to check on
Alicia, it would have to wait until after the meeting. Travis's
whole family was supposed to attend, and he had even cleared
his schedule of patients, so I didn't think I could claim I had an
emergency real estate meeting.

I tried Katrina again, and it went straight to voicemail. I stared
at my phone, carouseling back to Messages, hoping I had missed
a text. Nothing.

My stomach began to ache as I worried something had happened to her in the middle of the night, too. I peeked out of my
bathroom and saw Travis sigh and roll over in bed. I thought of
the threat to Alicia's family and needed to be sure mine was safe.

I quickly crept down the hallway to my kids' rooms and opened Hunter's door first.

My son was a jumble of blankets on his bed, twisted around his long limbs. A pillow was over his face, an arm slung across it. I stepped over the piles of dirty clothes on the floor, ignoring for once the smell of a teenage boy's room.

My hand shaking, I rested my palm on his back, and I exhaled when I felt his chest move up and down. I bent down and peeled the edge of the pillow away from his face. His eyes were closed, long lashes nearly dusting his cheeks.

My shoulders relaxed as I watched him breathe in and out a few times, lost in a dream. Whatever my teenage son dreamed about, I probably didn't want to know.

I carefully placed the corner of the pillow back on his face and tiptoed out of the room. I closed the door behind me, and the panic revved again as I approached Harper's door, which was covered in spirit posters from the last cheer competition.

We Can. We Will. We Must! stared back at me as I opened her door.

She was facedown on her bed, hair splayed everywhere, breathing softly, one arm hanging over the side, brushing the carpet.

I went back to my bedroom, taking a few deep breaths. My family, the only thing I cared about, was safe. For now. I just wished Alicia the same comfort.

In my bathroom, I looked in the mirror, wiping under my eyes. I looked like a witch who would live in the woods, snarling at small children and terrifying young men. The Blair Witch, ready to line people up in the corners of my creepy cottage.

Somehow, I had to pull myself together and play the part formerly known as Sarah Nelson, normal mom and wife.

☾

Green Bay Road was the most direct route to my in-laws' house, and it was a twisting, dangerous road that wound through hills and past long driveways obscuring the houses behind them, which meant I had to drive slowly through the hairpin turns. I was familiar enough with the road to know when I could speed up, and when I should sit up straight and slow down.

Someone who didn't know the road quite as well had skidded into another car that morning as they tried to turn left around an oak tree that had been there for at least a century. The line of cars behind the accident stretched for at least a mile, and I could faintly see the cherry lights of squad cars up ahead, the colors bouncing off the wall of trees around me. It was a two-lane road, with no exits or entrances, so I was stuck.

Travis and I had driven separately. He had to go to the office after the meeting, and I told him driving our own cars made the most sense. He balked, feeling as though he was abandoning me, like it was a cross-country expedition and not a drive to his parents' house. I told him I didn't have to be Magellan to find my own way.

Famous last words.

And while I had always dreamed of having an attentive husband—which he always had been—this was getting out of hand.

I opened Find My Friends, and sure enough, he had clearly

checked the traffic and gone another way. At least he would arrive on time.

Unable to stop sweating, I cranked up my car's air-
conditioning, despite its being only fifty-two degrees. I put my
car in Park and leaned back, briefly closing my eyes, my anxiety
building like a tower of Legos.

When I opened my eyes and reached for my phone, my calls
to Alicia and Katrina went straight to voicemail. I sent a quick
text to both of them asking them to check in, but it remained
unanswered.

What is going on with them?

I had already decided that I was going to drive to Alicia's after
the meeting, but now I feared what I might find.

My phone did ding with a text, however, from Scott.

> Thanks again for showing me the house the other day. I
> was hoping we could meet this week to look at a few
> more listings.

I gripped the steering wheel and focused on the car in front
of me with the honor-student bumper sticker.

*You are Sarah Nelson. You live in Forest Hills. You are a Realtor,
and you're married to Travis Nelson. You have two children, Hunter
and Harper. You live a nice, somewhat boring life, and you use magic
occasionally. No one knows about it, and your past is safe. You have
nothing to fear.*

It was like looking at an old photo album. I knew too much
now, and too much had happened for me to pretend as though

the magic was under my control. That no one would ever find out. It was my magical midlife crisis.

It's a joke that men go through a (normal, human) midlife crisis and buy a sports car or start flirting with the waitresses at Tilted Kilt. Or they take it a step further and have an affair with a woman they meet at the gym, suddenly taking an interest in looking good after years of beer bellies and sedentary behavior.

And women—at least in Forest Hills—get mommy makeovers, lifting their boobs and flattening their stomachs.

It was like people woke up one day and said, *Is this it?* And then decided to turn up the dial.

My magic seemingly had done the same, but with fewer sports cars and more disaster.

Chapter 31

Nearly an hour late, I pulled up to the security gate at my in-laws' house. I waved to the camera, and the black metal gate creaked open slowly, deliberately, as though laughing at me for my tardiness. I lurched my car through and sped up the driveway to their house.

My brakes screeched as I pulled my car into the porte cochere. I wrenched open the door and flew up the stone steps, my purse catching on one of the stone lions that guarded the front, mouth open and teeth bared, one paw frozen in the air.

Not exactly a warm, welcoming greeting for guests. Which hadn't escaped Marcy, so she'd tried to have them removed. Apparently it wasn't a simple project, so she mitigated their presence by decorating them for every holiday with whimsical adornments. Bunny hats for Easter, leprechaun costumes for St. Patrick's Day, reindeer antlers for Christmas. Except it was Halloween time, and they required no trappings to spook the hell of out me.

The stone lion turned its head toward me, blinking slowly, its mouth stretching open a little wider, before returning to its frozen pose.

I took the last steps two at a time.

The Nelson estate had been in the family for two generations; it had been built by Travis's great-grandfather as a wedding present to his (second, much younger) wife. It was a stone monstrosity, more like a fortress, with pointed turrets and carved stone gargoyles on top. The entrance was a large, wide circular opening, like the mouth of a beast.

It looked like it should have been the villain's castle in a Disney movie, with Marcy as Rapunzel trapped inside.

The tall wooden front doors opened for me before I could knock. Joseph, the house manager, frowned and gave me a once-over. He opened the door wider and held an arm out toward the parlor.

I smoothed my hair back as I walked across the black marble floor, feeling as though the house was watching me, waiting for me. An anglerfish hanging around patiently on the floor of the ocean for the unsuspecting prey to swim into its mouth.

The formal living room was decorated like a medieval castle. A large oil painting of my father-in-law's father hung over the intricately carved fireplace. Three logs were neatly stacked in the large walk-in fireplace worthy of Henry VIII's lair, and a large grandfather clock ticked slowly against the wall. Again, all adornments from before my mother-in-law's tenure. Splashes of her were around the room, the most she could muster. The uncomfortable couches held pink beaded pillows. A fluffy white throw was draped across the arm of a wing-back chair. A vase full of feathers rested on the large fireplace. Scented candles were placed in silver mercury-glass votives.

Marcy and Thomas were seated in wing-back chairs in front

of the fireplace, with Travis and the event coordinator opposite. Nancy stood off to the side, her hip resting against the large onyx bar.

Their heads turned in unison as I appeared in the doorway.

As did the eyes of Travis's grandfather from his oil painting prison on the wall.

"I'm so sorry! There was an accident," I said quickly.

Marcy stood up, teetering over to me in gold heels, arms outstretched. "Oh, honey! We were wondering what happened to you." She played with the ends of my hair, affectionately bringing them to the front of my shoulders. "Do you want to sit?" She gestured to the chairs, and Travis started to stand up.

"I was so worried!" Travis said as he rose.

I waved a hand. "Just some traffic. No, no. I'll stand. Really," I added when Travis continued to stand. I made a motion telling him to sit back down. "Really."

"Want a wine spritzer or something?" she said breathily, and motioned for Joseph to come over.

I declined that as well, being that it was well before noon.

She looked disappointed. "Suit yourself," she said as she tottered back to her chair, crystal goblet of spritzer with a straw on the table next to her. She took a sip before turning back to the documents spread in front of the group, which looked to be lists of RSVPs.

I looked to Nancy, trying to discreetly see if she still had burn scars, to find out if the spell had gotten one thing right. A heavy feeling settled on my shoulders as I saw the knotted skin peeking out from her shirt collar.

She turned and mistook my gaze for an invitation to commiserate about the ridiculousness of the meeting and gave me a smirk, the corners of her mouth turned up in amusement.

The event coordinator continued talking, my arrival forgotten. I walked around the perimeter of the circle—where the people who really mattered were talking—and carefully slid in next to Nancy. She wore jeans and a denim button-down, untucked. On her feet were dark brown Timberland boots.

She shifted and crossed her arms over her chest, leaning back further onto the dark paneled bar.

"I haven't said a word since I got here," she whispered. "Do you think they would notice if I left?"

My shoulders sagged in gratitude. "Probably not," I said. "Take me with you?"

She half grunted, half laughed in response.

"Did you find a dress?" I said. I slid my eyes to her profile. She was truly beautiful, something that was easily overshadowed by her sour moods. Not that I could blame her.

She nodded. "Bought it online. Hopefully it fits." She glanced at her watch and sighed. "I have to be back at the center in a half hour, so they better wrap this up."

I smiled. "No brunch to follow?"

This time, she did laugh, and Marcy pursed her hot-pink lips in our direction, like we were two schoolchildren instead of nearly forty.

"Not if you paid me," she said.

This was the camaraderie that I had always craved from Nancy, however small. I often felt like an alien in Travis's family, an interloper who was disguised as the native species yet never quite managed to accurately imitate the behavior. The bug people in *Men in Black* trying to act like humans yet catastrophically failing at every turn. Travis was usually my shield, my guide, my unconscious model.

In the beginning of our relationship, I'd tried to build a rapport with Nancy. I would roll my eyes discreetly when Marcy tried to convince us to wear matching red, vaguely sexy Mrs. Claus dresses on Christmas. She never took the bait, stonily ignoring me and averting her gaze even though I knew she felt the same disdain for dress-up.

I'd tried and tried, like a circus clown who should have retired years ago. Sad, garish makeup running down my face, red nose displayed, flowers squirting water at children. Until finally, I let it go. She didn't have to like me or make me feel more comfortable in her own family, certainly not after what my coven had done to her, even if she didn't know the whole truth.

But how I wished she were my real sister. Wished we could have laughed our way together through the country club events, like the Fourth of July celebration with six-foot-tall cakes in the shape of American flags with sparklers on top. Wished she could validate my feelings of *What the hell is going on here?*

"How is the center?" I whispered out of the corner of my mouth, just as I saw the event planner's gaze catch on us.

Nancy turned her head, and a genuine smile spread across her face, softening its hard edges. "Very exciting. We had a mother fox come in last night who got caught in some chicken wire. Her leg was stuck for hours, but the owners were able to cut her free and bring her in. I got the emergency call at eleven o'clock last night. We bandaged her up and need to go back and check the den for the pups this morning." She pointedly lifted her arm and looked at her watch again. "Like, now."

"And the publicity interviews will begin . . . ," Marcy's sing-songy voice rose to get our attention.

We looked down and fell silent. My head still pointed toward the floor, I whispered to Nancy, "Just go. I'll cover for you. Your job is more important than all of this."

She glanced at me, eyebrows raised in surprise. "Really?"

I nodded. "Of course. Just say you have to go to the bathroom and then . . . leave. I'll create a distraction."

"Like what? Are you going to fake a seizure or something?" she said.

Something like that.

"Just go," I said again.

Nancy quickly hurried out of the room, excusing herself to the bathroom and disappearing behind one of the heavy wood doors to the living room. I picked my head up and fixed as bright a smile on my face as I could muster. I took a step forward, peering over the wing-back chairs at the papers spread on the table.

"So how's the press coming?" I said.

The event coordinator looked up and frowned at the unwelcome intrusion.

"Well, we already went over all of that. I was just saying that I invited a journalist to attend the brunch here today. She's actually due to arrive soon. It's going to be a slice-of-life piece to highlight the family's philanthropy," she said.

I nodded, my eyes darting around the room. I stepped forward and reached for the papers, Travis moving aside and beaming at my initiative.

Poor guy thought I was actually trying to be involved. I planned to pick them up and then "accidentally" drop them everywhere, giving Nancy time to slip out the front door without being stopped.

A stupid, ridiculous, childish plan. But the only one that immediately came to me in the five seconds I had to formulate it.

Two things happened as my hand closed around the papers. The first: a visitor arrived in the living room.

I heard the name "Miss Madisyn Parks" announced from the doorway, and my anxiety flared before my brain could process the words. With that, the magic activated in my body, pulsing and burning. Without my brain to calm it, bits and pieces of it escaped.

As I fumbled with the papers, I felt the magic release.

Second, a spark ignited in the large stone walk-in fireplace. It popped and crackled, and a small fire began on the logs, ashes scattering around.

A spark flew out of the fireplace, brushing the back of my hand, singeing off the hairs before dying and leaving a small black hole in the center of the press list. Then it landed on the papers.

The room activated, with Madisyn stepping back, hands on her mouth.

Marcy jumped up and started squealing, pointing at the fire like a cartoon character who had just seen a mouse, screaming that I needed medical attention.

The house manager stepped forward and placed a screen over the fireplace with startling efficiency, given the surprise blaze.

Travis grabbed me quickly, brushing off my hand and shouting for help.

"I'm fine! I'm fine!" I said as I pulled my hand back and shook it. He hugged me so tight I almost squeaked.

"Call the stonemasons and have that fireplace inspected immediately," Thomas said to Joseph. "There must be something wrong with it."

Next to Travis, I looked at Madisyn, who cautiously stepped into the room, her eyes wide. Her highlighted hair cascaded around her shoulders as she shook her head.

"What an exciting welcome. I hope that wasn't all on my account." She laughed.

Miss Madisyn Parks, it absolutely was.

Chapter 32

How is your friend Alicia doing? I saw what happened to her on the news." Madisyn held her fork above her pear and blue cheese salad. Her brows knitted together in what I knew she imagined was a concerned look, but behind it was a shark who smelled blood. Alicia's awful incident would be more fodder for *Afterburn*.

"She's doing well," I said quickly as I pushed around the arugula on my plate.

We were seated in the Nelsons' formal dining room at a long wooden rectangular table. Thomas was at the head of the table, with Marcy to his right and Travis to his left. I was next to Travis, and Madisyn was across from me. The event coordinator had frowned at Madisyn's having a more desirable placement but silently took her seat next to me.

Marcy had led Madisyn to her seat, nearly vibrating with excitement at her special guest, peppering her with follow-up questions on the Morgantown Murders and whether Peter McMichaels, the incarcerated patriarch of the family, had convinced his family to put more money in his prison commissary.

Travis had kept his hand on the small of my back as we

walked from the living to the dining room, a protective gesture after the sparks that had flown from the fire. He pulled out my chair for me.

I laughed. "Really. I'm fine. You don't have to act like I'm a damsel in distress."

He'd nodded, hurt, as we sat down, and I instantly felt awful. Maybe he really was just being extra nice.

"And Katrina? I've heard rumblings that Obsidian is going through quite the growth spurt," Madisyn said, eyes trained on me.

I shot her a warning look. *Stay away from me and my friends.*

"Yes," I said, and pressed my mouth into a thin line.

I was thankful that Nancy had made her escape; she would have picked up on the strange tension immediately. Marcy and Thomas had barely registered her prison break, more concerned with any sparks that may have singed the heavy wool carpet on the living room floor and welcoming the exalted podcaster into their home.

The event coordinator cleared her throat, setting her knife down at the edge of the gold and cream china. "Madisyn, how is the podcast coming along?"

Really? Impeccable timing.

My heart started to beat faster, and I clanked my fork down on my plate, heads whipping in my direction. I mumbled an apology as I finally lifted my eyes and looked at my nemesis.

Madisyn smiled brightly, brushing a wavy lock of hair over her shoulder. "The podcast is coming along beautifully. I still have a few more interviews to conduct, and then I'll be ready to go into the studio and start editing. I've made some interesting discoveries"—she looked over at Marcy, who squealed and put her hands in a prayer position, begging for details—"that I'm not quite ready to share, but hopefully soon." Her eyes slid to me.

"Great news. Did you interview Sarah yet?" Thomas said, clearly unaware of the gravity of the question as he lifted a piece of pear and popped it in his mouth.

All eyes at the table were fixed on me as Madisyn said, "Not yet. She's been very busy, so we've had some difficulties with finding a time."

I cleared my throat and clenched my napkin in my lap. I gave a wavering smile. "Lots going on, yes."

When no one said anything, I added, "We will have to connect soon."

Madisyn held my gaze. "What about today, after lunch? I think you'll be interested to hear what I'm uncovering," she said.

I cocked my head to the side like I was running through my schedule mentally. "Hmmm, I wish I could, but I have a client listing meeting after this. Another time."

"Well, I have a tee time at the club," Thomas said as he pushed away from the table. Marcy made a noise of protest but cocked her head so he could kiss her cheek before he left.

The rest of us began to filter out of the room as the staff cleared our plates. I felt Madisyn's eyes boring into the back of my head as she walked behind me.

"I'm supposed to go to the office, but I can stay with you if you need me," Travis said to me.

"No, go ahead. I'm good," I said quickly.

He reluctantly stood, looking torn between going into work and fawning over me for the afternoon.

"Really, go ahead," I said again, and patted his arm.

"Well, if you're sure . . ." He leaned over and passionately kissed me, in front of half of his family and Madisyn, before he jogged down the front steps. At the bottom of the stairs, he turned and put a hand over his heart, sighing as he looked up at me.

"Um, okay. Bye," I said with a wave. I wanted my husband back, not this lovesick creature who was clearly fine with PDA.

Marcy went upstairs with a "headache" (no doubt from the sweet wine), and the event coordinator excused herself. Then it was just Madisyn and me.

I smiled at her and waited until the staff was out of earshot, then dropped my expression.

"Listen, I'm going to say this again: leave me—and my family, and my friends—alone." I pointed a finger in her face, anger swelling inside me, threatening to spill out.

The magic nudged me, asking if I wanted help.

No, not again. You've done enough for one day.

Madisyn's face reeled at my change, and she took a startled step back, but quickly regained her footing. Her face went neutral.

"I apologize if you feel as though I've stepped out of bounds. But I did find something that I want to speak to you about," she said evenly, calmly.

I took a deep breath, trying to match her composure. In a conversation like this, the one who remains calm is always the winner. Not the crazed woman pointing fingers, shouting, and slamming doors.

"I doubt there is anything I'd want to hear," I said, feeling my cheeks flush despite my resolve. "I lived through it. I don't need you to stir everything back up again."

Why didn't that freezer spell work? Why?

"I traced some items at the scene back to a curiosities shop in Millville." I turned to walk away. Her words were behind me, and I refused to turn around, believing if I didn't literally face her, they would disappear.

I walked across the foyer, snatching my purse from the outstretched hands of a waiting Joseph, and walked out the front door, my eyes avoiding the scary lions guarding the entrance.

She jogged after me, her heels tapping on the stone entryway.

"The owner—Madame Serena—remembers you and your friends." My blood ran cold, even though I had known it was coming. I stopped as my hand reached for my car door. My forefinger was on the cool metal; I itched to wrench open the door and hide myself inside.

Instead, I slowly turned, my shoulders hunched forward. I had run for so long; I was tired. I just wanted it to be over.

I waited.

Madisyn lifted her brows, ready to swoop in with her discoveries. Ready to see my face when she told me she knew we had caused the fire. That it was our fault, and she was going to tell the world.

Ready to know that finally, my life would come crumbling down just as I had always feared.

"I have a theory on what happened, and it involves those around you," she said.

I closed my eyes, breathing shallow.

"And their intentions."

I slowly opened my eyes, looking at her. "What do you mean?" I whispered.

She leaned forward, close enough so that I could see she wore contacts and that her mascara had clumped under her right eye. "I think someone deliberately set the fire. Arson," she said into my ear.

My ears began to ring, and my stomach clenched. I felt the magic well up inside me, a loaded gun ready for a trigger finger.

"Really?" I said. I shook my head. "No. That doesn't make any sense."

Madisyn glanced over her shoulder to make sure no one else was around. "It's a long story, but I think you and your friends were playing around, messing with things, and everything got out of hand. But I think it was deliberate, that someone intentionally messed with the smoke detectors and sprinklers that night."

Without meaning to, I smiled and then looked down quickly. "I'm sorry, but that's a new one." A bitter laugh escaped. "Why would someone try to burn down a dorm? It was an accident, and that's the truth."

She narrowed her eyes and crossed her arms over her chest, pressing her mouth into a line.

I took a step forward. "You couldn't be more wrong." I turned back to my car and pulled open the door. I was about to slide in when I looked up at her. "Stay away from us. I mean it. There's no story here."

The woman is practically begging for a hex.

As I went to close the door, she bent down, putting her hands on her thighs. "Staying away might be a little difficult, since I'm hosting a table at Marcy's event." She stood up and smiled. "See you there."

Of course. All of us would be there. Nancy, Katrina, Alicia, Travis, my kids. The whole cast of characters for her story, all in one place. She was ready to expose us all, no matter if she was right or wrong.

Thoughts raced through my head:

You're in danger.

Something very bad will happen.

In front of everyone.

I pressed my lips together as the thoughts scrolled across my brain, a warning. A premonition.

Hope we all look good in orange jumpsuits.

Chapter 33

As soon as I walked into Butch McGuire's, an Irish-themed bar in downtown Chicago, a couple of things were obvious: the smell of old beer taps, and the fact that the fiftysomething woman by the bathrooms should not have been drinking another apple-tini.

I shoved my license back into my wallet, after I had given the bouncer a look of disbelief when he asked for my ID.

"Twenty-one and over, ma'am," he had said as he surveyed the line of suspiciously young-looking patrons behind me. I didn't point out that anyone old enough to be called "ma'am" probably didn't need to be carded.

I pushed through the sweaty throngs of people, searching for my friends.

After leaving Thomas and Marcy's, I had finally reached Alicia and Katrina. During a very convoluted and stressful call, we just agreed to meet in person that night. Alicia picked the spot: Butch McGuire's, which was about ten minutes from her house on a strip of bars known for bad decisions, police paddy wagons, and Fireball shots.

Yet I didn't see Alicia anywhere.

I saw the drunk woman leaning against a dark paneled wall, the green glow of the lights illuminating her slowly melting features. A group of twentysomething guys huddled around a television mounted in a corner, and a few tourists wore Chicago T-shirts. Butch's was a Chicago institution, known for its year-round Christmas lights, attracting people as colorful as the decorations.

I peeked my head into the back room but didn't see her. I shoved my way through the crowd gathered around the bar toward the front windows, but nothing.

I was about to pull out my phone and text when I heard my name.

"Sarah!" I squinted in the direction of Alicia's voice. "Here!"

A woman was perched at a bar table near the open windows. She wore a navy blue Windy City sweatshirt, baggy light-colored jeans, white New Balance gym shoes, and a denim baseball cap covered in rhinestones.

I took one step closer, her features coming into focus. "Alicia? Is that you?"

She nodded, pulling the baseball cap down over her makeup-free face.

"Wow. I mean, wow. You look . . . different," I said.

"I'm in disguise," she said as I sat down across from her. "Too many people are recognizing me."

I nodded and eyed the highball of whiskey in front of her. "How are you doing?"

She lowered her head, adjusting the brim of the cap again. "Awful. The news crews are asking me for interviews about what happened. And the police, too."

I reached my hand across the table and covered hers. "I'm so sorry. I've been really worried about you. I tried to call and text a million times."

A tear ran down her face and she quickly swiped it again. "I know. I saw. Thanks. My house isn't really safe anymore, so we are all staying in a hotel until everything quiets down."

"We're going to catch a disease in here." Katrina appeared at the table, frowning. She surveyed the crowd quickly, the corners of her mouth turning down even more.

"Hey, pretty lady, can I buy you a drink?" A half-drunk recent college graduate nearly fell into Katrina, spilling some beer down the front of his blue and white button-down shirt.

"You cannot," she said, and used her elbow to move him back from our table. She turned to us. "Well, we're here. How is everyone?"

I gestured to Alicia wordlessly, watching her wipe tears away.

"And you?" Katrina said as she began to fold her hands on the table, thought better of it, and placed them in the back pockets of her black jeans.

"Not as bad as Alicia, but it's not good either. I'm freaked out about Madisyn," I said. "She thinks not only that we're involved, but that we deliberately set the fire."

"That little brat," Katrina hissed. "She doesn't know who she's messing with."

Alicia sniffed and looked out the window at a group of women in a bachelorette party holding up a phone to take a video of themselves.

"I'm sorry, why did you choose here to meet, again?" Katrina said.

"Hiding in plain sight, I guess," I said as I pointed to Alicia's outfit. Katrina noticed it for the first time, having been blinded by the pints of Miller Lite and vape vapor, and slowly nodded in understanding.

Katrina's eyes flashed with determination and she could barely hide a smile. I knew what she was thinking, what she was going to say. It was what she had always wanted to do, and she thought we finally had had enough of practicing "only light."

"Well, we all know what we have to do," Katrina said confidently. She could barely hide her smile.

I shook my head. "No. Look what happened the last two times we tried something: either it didn't work or we somehow screwed up the original . . ." I didn't want to say *spell*, even though I doubted anyone could hear us. "Intention. Whatever we asked for twenty years ago somehow got supercharged overnight."

"Threefold," Alicia added with a sigh.

"Fine," Katrina said, annoyed. "Then what do you suggest?"

"Maybe"—I looked down at my hands—"we just tell Madisyn the truth. That we made a mistake."

Alicia squeaked, and Katrina stepped forward, gripping my upper arm.

"No. I'm not doing anything of the sort," she said. She gave my arm a squeeze and then let it go.

I rubbed my biceps. "Got it. Calm down. It was just a suggestion."

"Look," Katrina said as she rubbed her forehead, "we just need to see this through. Once Madisyn gets off our asses and does her podcast, she'll go away. I can handle the amplified energy, and if not, we can try and"—I gave her a warning look—"get together—and calm it down."

"So, nothing? That's our plan?" I said as I narrowly avoided the shoulder of a guy wearing a Notre Dame shirt splattered with a dark liquid.

"You don't want to do what I suggested, so what options remain?" Katrina said as she eyed the Notre Dame fan.

I turned to Alicia, tapping a finger on her hand. She looked faraway. "I thought you said nothing would happen when we aborted the mission early. So why is everything out of control?"

She nervously looked at Katrina and back to me. "I—I don't know. We didn't finish it. So something else was happening, something we don't know about. I don't know how to fix it."

My shoulders slumped forward, and I looked at Katrina, slowly nodding. "Status quo it is, I guess."

She straightened. "Great. Listen, let's get out of here. I think the guy in the college T-shirt is going to get sick again."

Chapter 34

Y ou're mine. Come here!"

I stared at the zombie, flesh hanging off his face. He shuffled along, dragging one foot behind him, as he approached a group of teenage girls huddled around a funnel cake. He came up behind them and grunted before he said, "Brains!" They turned and screamed, abandoning their funnel cake, arms waving in the air.

The zombie stood up and smiled. He rubbed his hands together before he quickly sat down at the table and started eating the funnel cake, licking powdered sugar off his fingers, quite pleased with himself. Turns out he really wanted the fried dessert, not their brains.

Hunter, Travis, and I were at Forest Hills Hospital's annual friends and family event at Six Flags. Every year, the hospital rented out the park so the employees, doctors, and nurses could bring their loved ones and enjoy all the rides. Salary increases were out of the question, but free funnel cakes and roller coasters? Game on.

The event was always held in the fall, usually around the time that the park held its annual Fright Fest, near Halloween. Fright

Fest transformed the park into an interactive Halloween display. Webs hung from the lampposts in the children's play area; actors dressed as werewolves, zombies, and vampires roamed around, scaring people as they waited for the rides. And, apparently, stealing food. Creepy Halloween music played from speakers throughout the park, too. As if it weren't unsettling enough to ride on one of the tallest wooden coasters in the world, patrons now had to be terrified even while they waited for the ride or while they had lunch.

"Ready?" Hunter said as he pointed toward the American Eagle roller coaster. Not waiting for an answer, he started jogging toward the line, confident I would follow him.

I glanced up at the large white wooden coaster, the blue cars slowly climbing the enormous first drop, and my stomach turned. But, the things we do for our kids and all that, so I followed him, hoping the ride would get shut down before we reached the platform.

Harper wasn't with us, due to an extra cheer practice, which she was perfectly fine with since she wasn't a roller coaster fan anyway. In previous years, she'd grumbled as she followed her brother onto the rides, complaining the whole time. One year she spent the entire car ride reading to us a list of accidents that had happened in the park in years past. Her personal favorite was the time when a park employee dressed as a werewolf during Fright Fest tripped on his stilts—it was unclear why he needed stilts as a werewolf—and then fell through the glass window of an ice cream parlor onto a patron. Neither was hurt, apparently.

Travis had been quickly swept up as we walked through the park's gates, a crowd of hospital administrators asking him to come take promotional photos. He was always asked to be in those photos, for everything from the hospital foundation's annual report to the marketing brochures. I heard all of the whispers about Dr. Handsome and McDreamy at every hospital function, and always pretended not to. I was proud of him and proud that others wanted him in the spotlight. I could tell he felt bad about leaving us and tried to grab my hand to keep me by his side, but I demurred.

Since Travis had been pulled away, that left me on roller coaster duty with Hunter. And he wanted to ride every big coaster in the park, possibly twice.

I stood behind him in the line for American Eagle, craning my neck to look up at the first big drop on the ancient-looking wooden coaster. The ride looked like it had been built by prospectors in the 1800s. For Fright Fest, Six Flags had hung an enormous black spider from the side of the hill, visible all the way to the highway.

"Raging Bull is next, Mom," Hunter said as he pointed to an orange coaster so twisty it looked like a pile of cooked spaghetti.

"Can't wait," I said as I rolled my eyes.

After we got off the ride, we heard, "Hunter! Yo, Hunter!"

We turned and saw Luke Tobin jogging over to us, his hair flopping on his forehead.

"Hey, Luke. I didn't realize you'd be here," I said.

I had asked Hunter how Luke was doing the week before, and he had shrugged and said things were *weird but fine*. Which I translated to mean Luke was managing, but everyone in school knew about the rumors of the affair. In our sheltered community, news of extramarital affairs apparently moved quickly.

"I sent you a Snap," Luke said, and pulled out his phone. Hunter did the same, and the two huddled together, laughing at something on Snapchat.

Over Luke's left shoulder, I saw David and Stephanie approaching. David had a too-big smile on his face, and Stephanie had her hands shoved deep in the pockets of her windbreaker.

I stepped forward and waved. "Hey there. Good to see you guys." My voice was a bit too loud, and I sounded a bit too eager, but I wanted them to know I wasn't judging them, like the many pairs of eyes looking in their direction.

"Having a nice afternoon?" David said. He put an arm around his wife, and I saw her stiffen as a few heads turned in their direction.

The hospital gossip looked to be worse than the high school's. Judgment was swift in Forest Hills, and social infractions were not taken lightly. And we had a front-row seat to all of it.

I nodded. "We just conquered the American Eagle, and now Hunter wants to try out Raging Bull." I cringed.

"Hey, Mom. Luke and I are going to go on rides together. Okay?" Hunter said, and before I could agree, he and Luke walked off. As they disappeared into the crowd, I heard Hunter excitedly telling Luke about the urban legend that one of the cast members of the show *Full House* had been decapitated on the Giant Drop.

"How is work, Sarah?" Stephanie said stiffly, her smile wavering with nerves. I knew she was grasping for something—anything—to say.

I smiled. "It's good."

"Well"—Stephanie looked up nervously at her husband—"we

wanted to talk to you soon about possibly listing our house. We . . . we think it's time." She bit her lip.

I lifted my eyebrows in surprise, so many questions filling my brain. But I knew selling a house was one way to gain a fresh start.

"Of course. I'd be happy to talk to you both whenever is convenient." I was trying to think of something to ask them, and was coming up empty, when Travis saved me.

"There you are. I've been looking everywhere for you." Travis came up to me and put an arm around my shoulder, then turned me to him and planted one of his newly famous Bewitched Travis kisses on me, dipping me down like I had returned from war.

"Okay. Okay," I said with a laugh as I lightly pushed him off. I put a hand on his chest, more as a defensive move if he should attempt another display of PDA.

Status quo it was. My husband now wanted to get frisky in a Six Flags.

Travis shook David's hand and gave Stephanie a quick hug, at which I saw more heads turn in our direction, shocked that the model doctor was associating himself with the heathen family.

A wave of anxiety moved across my chest as I saw how quickly everyone had turned against the Tobins. I couldn't fathom what they might do to me if the truth about the fire ever got out. My career would be over. My kids ostracized at school. Travis's practice would be damaged. And that would be after any marital, familial, and legal consequences.

The idea of burning at the stake suddenly became very real.

David and Stephanie looked nervously from me to Travis, so I stepped forward.

"Want to ride the carousel?" I said. I didn't want to try another looping roller coaster, and that ride seemed like the best compromise. And it would be another public show of acceptance for the Tobins.

David stepped back a little in surprise and then nodded, looking at Stephanie. She gave me a grateful smile and then nodded as well.

I saw the looks and heard the whispers still as we walked over to the ride, past a concession stand. The smell of corn dogs and funnel cakes filled my nose as I realized I was witnessing one of my greatest fears, but it was happening to someone else. They were possibly being run out of town, his business destroyed, their kid shunned, the object of never-ending whispers.

And that didn't even include the possibility of jail time.

Or the discovery of magic.

Their past had been revealed, and the world wasn't ready for it, so they were pariahs.

I didn't want to think about what they would do to me.

Chapter 35

The day after the trip to Six Flags, I drove home from a listing appointment, getting lost in the burnished tree canopies that lined Seneca Road. It looked like I was driving through a mythical forest to a witch's cottage, where she grew mandrake root. That particular plant had roots that looked like the body of a man when pulled out of the ground and was reportedly useful for curses. We had tried to find some our freshman year, but the internet had been silent on the herb, and much to Katrina's dismay, we couldn't source any.

Very good news for her economics professor.

At a stoplight, my phone dinged with a notification from Facebook. Wary, I clicked on the app. My sixth-grade boyfriend, whom I hadn't seen since middle school, had posted a picture of me and him at a school dance, tagging me with the comment, "Best date ever!"

I quickly untagged myself from the post before the light turned green, and immediately another notification popped up. He had retagged me.

I could use the magic to stop him.

Temptation bubbled up inside me, the magic stirring. It had been so long since I had used it, and I missed it. I felt like I had cut off communication with an old friend.

Maybe there's no harm in trying it out again, like an old pair of pants that still fits despite having no business doing so.

I didn't want to use the magic against someone or have it affect a person—or else sixth-grade boyfriend's Facebook would definitely be hacked by the Russians—so I thought back to a small problem I had had that morning: the shower drain.

As I'd stood in the shower that morning, water had begun to pool around my ankles. The main line must have been clogged again, something that periodically happened when tree roots grew into the pipe. We had to have it cleared by Roto-Rooter, whose technicians usually sighed, then brightened when they handed us the bill.

I closed my eyes and allowed the magic to well up inside me. I whispered a few words, asking for the drain to be cleared. Just that, nothing more.

As I pulled into the driveway, Hunter came sprinting across the front yard, arms waving in the air.

Oh no. The drain.

"Mom. Mom. Mom. Mom." His words fell out of his mouth as he skidded to a stop in front of my car. He wrenched open the driver's-side door and waved, gesturing for me to get out. "The basement. Flooded. Pipes. Water everywhere."

"What?" I heaved my body out of the car and ran inside,

following him. My blood rushed in my ears as I silently argued with myself, yelling at the magic, begging for it not to be true.

In the basement, I stopped suddenly when I was halfway down the stairs, frozen in shock. My basement now resembled a pond. Water, at least six inches deep, swirled around the basement floor, covering the plank flooring we had installed a year prior. It reached up to the sectional and the bottoms of the bar stools in the mock Irish pub in the corner, and toward the golf simulator screen hung on the wall.

Harper was perched on the bar, eyes wide and cheeks flushed. Travis was in the middle of the pond, frantically unplugging electronics so we wouldn't get electrocuted.

"What happened?" I shouted to Travis.

He grabbed at the plug for the movie projector and shouted over his shoulder, "Pipe burst in the storage room. It happened so fast that I couldn't get anything out of the way. It's fucked."

Harper's head snapped to her father when she heard him swear. That's how we knew it was serious.

I took off my shoes and stepped into the freezing-cold water, wading over to Travis. "I'll help you." I started to reach for a cord, and he turned to me, grabbed my hand, and pulled me in for a passionate kiss, wrapping his arms around my waist.

"You look beautiful," he said as he released me, his eyes shining.

"Mom! Dad!" Hunter shouted. "Hello? We have a problem."

"I don't think we have time for that," I said as I gestured at the water pooling around our legs. "Kind of a big problem here."

"Later, then," he said with a wink. "Would you call the

plumber? I didn't even have time to do that, it all happened so fast," he said as he moved to the wires connecting the surround sound system.

Even while a literal flood was happening in our house, Travis couldn't escape the effects of our spell gone wrong.

As I waded back toward the steps to get my phone, I saw a photo float by. It must have escaped from one of the albums we had stored in the utility room. It was a picture from our rehearsal dinner. We had our rehearsal at Old St. Patrick's Church and then a dinner at an Italian restaurant in the city. The photo was of Travis and me at the restaurant, making a toast to everyone there. We held champagne glasses high, true smiles on our faces as we surveyed the crowd.

"Let me know when the plumber can get here, hon," Travis shouted from across the room.

Right.

I hurried upstairs to where I had thrown my purse after running in the door and found my phone.

As my shaking hands dialed the number for the plumber, I knew what had happened: I had caused this, too.

"I'm so sorry, Mom," Harper said as she put an arm around my shoulders.

I dried off the bottom of my legs with a dish towel that I would have to throw out. The basement had a vaguely sewer-ish smell, and I didn't want to think about what was in the water.

The plumber had arrived a half hour after I called him and

was able to turn off the water to the house and patch the pipe. He said it would hold until he could come back in a couple of days to replace it.

The sounds of vacuums and fans rose up from the basement stairs, courtesy of the water mitigation company I'd called after the plumber left. They were using industrial-size shop vacs to pull out all the water and fans to dry the floor. When the crew first walked in, I saw the looks on their faces. It was pretty alarming to have a crew who cleaned up water issues for a living look like they were already tallying up our bill. They could share drinks with the Roto-Rooter guys.

"They're going to have to tear out the flooring and probably the subflooring, too," Travis said as he turned the corner into the kitchen. His jeans were soaked up to the knees, and his hiking boots were coated in the sewer water from the basement. He sighed. "At least it's all replaceable." He came over and put an arm around my shoulders.

"Yeah, except for Mom's wedding dress," Harper muttered, and then squeezed my hand. She put her head on my shoulder. "Sorry, Mom."

"That totally sucks," Hunter said as he stuffed half of a Subway turkey sub into his mouth. The disgusting smell wafting through the house had done nothing to quell his teenage appetite.

"Thanks, guys," I said.

After I had called the plumber, I had gone back downstairs to survey the damage. As I reached the edge of the pooling water, I saw a white box float by. My wedding dress, which I had carefully preserved after our honeymoon. Hermetically sealed in a white box to prevent yellowing and moth damage.

The box was warped and ripped, the water soaking through to the gown. I brought it outside and carefully opened it, the cardboard disintegrating in my hands. The dress was stained, crumpled, and waterlogged.

It was ruined.

My throat closed as I stared at the dress. I had saved up for months to buy the exact one I wanted—a Reem Acra strapless gown with gold threading on the bodice and down the train. The skirt was a ball gown style, a dress fit for Cinderella. Which was exactly who I felt like when I stepped into the dress for the first time.

I had bought it secondhand, off a popular wedding message board that had a forum where brides would sell their dresses after the wedding. Even in used condition, it still cost me a small fortune. I had to have it altered since it was four sizes too big, and it had a small wine stain on the bodice, but I didn't care. I had seen the dress in *People* magazine—it had been worn by a B-list celebrity at her wedding—and the pictures had enthralled me. They looked like snapshots of a life I wanted more than anything. With Marcy planning most everything about the wedding, the dress became my focus. An outward symbol of who I was transforming into.

The ugly duckling was finally becoming a swan, and that dress was my white feathers.

Now, years later, it was brown and gray.

Look what you have become, it seemed to say.

Did you really think you could hide forever?

I couldn't bear to throw it out, so I carefully wrapped it in a plastic tarp I found in the garage, trying to convince myself I could have it restored somewhere. Maybe damage had been done, but it wasn't past repair, was it?

If only the girl who had stood at the altar so many years ago, looking up at Travis, struggling to really believe her dream had come true, could see me now.

The Redfields had stopped by earlier to check and see if we needed any help. We declined, but Taffy leaned forward, putting a hand on my shoulder, and said, "You know, the Shelter is unable to flood. Remember what we said about protecting yourselves? You need to start thinking about that. There's always a solution." Her hand tightened around my shoulder with every word.

In the kitchen, I looked at my husband. "Do you think I could find someplace to fix my dress? Maybe it's not as far gone as I think."

In the past, I wouldn't have needed a restoration service. The magic would have fixed it for me. But now, if I tried to save it, the dress would probably spontaneously combust. Recently, there had been a price to pay, and I was afraid of the pound of flesh it would demand if I used it again.

No flashed across his face, but to his credit, he said, "Of course."

My phone buzzed, and when I saw the name of the caller, I wanted to throw my phone down into the basement, let it swirl in the sewage.

I picked it up and quickly walked out of the room and ran upstairs, nearly stepping on Katy Purry, who was observing the chaos from her perch on the top step.

"Hey!" she said.

I ignored her.

"Do you want me to come upstairs and join you?" Travis called from the kitchen.

"No. I have to take this call," I shouted back, a bit too aggressively. I closed my bedroom door and locked it, and then answered the phone.

"What?" I had half a mind to end the call, block her number, actually throw my phone into that sewage pit, but something made me stop. Maybe it was better to know what we were working against. "This isn't a good time."

I heard Katy Purry meowing and scratching to be let into the bedroom, so I cracked the door and she scurried in.

"I thought you'd want to know, I've narrowed my focus as to who I suspect was involved in setting the fire. And this might be difficult to hear, but . . ." Madisyn paused and I closed my eyes, ready for her to lower the boom. "I was wondering if I could talk to you about Nancy."

Nancy?

I was speechless.

"I'm not accusing anyone of anything, but I just have some questions about her," Madisyn said.

There was a long pause as I remained unable to form any human words or sounds. From near the bedroom door, Katy Purry saw my expression and jumped on the bed, sniffing the air.

"No," was all I managed to squeak out.

"I understand she's your sister-in-law, and like I said, I'm not making any unfounded accusations, but I do have—"

"No," I said again, more confidently.

"—some questions I'd love to find the answers to, and I think you're a missing piece to all of this," she continued.

"No," I said again, looking at Katy Purry, helpless.

I pulled my phone away from my ear, ready to hit the End Call button and scream.

Katy Purry sat up on her hind legs, and before I could end the call, she said, in her carton-of-cigarettes voice, "She said no, bitch."

Chapter 36

Boo." A paw tapped against my cheek.

Still asleep, and thinking the voice was part of my dream, I closed my eyes tighter.

"I said, 'BOO.'"

Katy Purry's voice growled in my ear, a hangry warning.

"Fine, I'm up," I said with a sigh, and slowly opened my eyes. I jumped back when I saw my cat staring at me, nose to nose. "Jesus Christ." I put a hand to my chest and tried to slow my breathing. She scampered off the bed and paused at the doorway to make sure I was moving in the general direction of her breakfast.

I was alone in the house. Travis had booked a hotel room for all of us due to the smell in the house, and the kids had quickly packed their bags. But then we remembered Katy Purry.

There was a moment of silence before I volunteered. Travis tried to argue that he would fall on the septic sword, but I insisted, nearly pushing him out the door. As much as I didn't relish the idea of spending the night in a house that vaguely smelled like a water treatment facility, a quiet space seemed inviting.

So Travis went off with the kids, after a protracted goodbye involving multiple kisses and embraces that made me feel like he was shipping off overseas, and I was left alone with the sound of the industrial fans whirring in the basement. I lay in bed for a long time, thinking of Madisyn's phone call. Twisting my options back and forth, until they began to fray. I hadn't landed on anything, so I texted Katrina and Alicia to come to discuss.

I swung my legs out of bed, ready to head downstairs and feed the little monster. She had defended me on the phone call with Madisyn, however inappropriately. Thankfully, Madisyn hadn't heard my cat's words.

As I walked down the hallway, the lingering stench from the burst pipe still hung heavy in the air. It reminded me of the gas that escaped from the sewer grates in the city on a hot day. When the kids were little, Travis and I took them downtown to the Children's Museum on Navy Pier. As we walked from the car to the museum's entrance, Hunter dropped his beloved pacifier over the side of the stroller. It bounced on the sidewalk and then arced directly into a sewer, disappearing below. Two hours of tears and screaming followed. We never returned to the museum after that, our parental PTSD too strong.

As I reached the top of the stairs, the Ring app on my phone chimed and a second later, my doorbell sounded. I peered over the railing on our open staircase and through the two-story foyer windows, past the crystal chandelier. Through the prism glass, I could see two distorted figures on my doorstep.

They were early.

"Happy Samhain! Your house is gorgeous. What a blessing," Alicia said as I swung open the front door halfway.

I had forgotten it was Halloween.

"You guys are about two hours early," I said as I wearily held the door open for them to walk through.

Alicia entered first, but Katrina paused. Her gaze flicked down to my body, and I realized I was wearing my pink flowered pajama set. Victoria's Secret spring collection circa 2007; I hadn't worn it in years but had grabbed it the night before in a desire for something old and comforting.

"Don't mention it," I said to her as I rolled my eyes.

I closed the door slowly and then turned around to follow them.

Katrina stopped halfway to the family room. "What is that god-awful smell?" She pressed a hand to her nose.

"Plumbing issue," I said with a frown. "I tried to do a spell to unclog my drain, and this was the result."

Alicia put a hand on my shoulder. "I'm so sorry."

I grunted as I wordlessly walked through the hallway, gesturing for them to follow me, and opened the French doors to the backyard. I sat down at the gray wood table off the pool deck, under the arbor we had installed the year before. Alicia sat next to me and Katrina across. I told them what Madisyn had said on the phone the night before.

"Nancy?" Alicia said with a whisper. She leaned forward and put her head in her hands, shaking it.

I looked at Katrina, who stared off into the distance. I could see she was considering something, smoothing her thoughts over an idea.

I was afraid I knew just what it was.

"Don't even think about it," I said to her, a warning tone in my voice. "We are not going to let her take the fall."

She shook her head slightly, pushing away the dark thought.

Alicia looked up in surprise, her mouth formed into an O. "No way," she added.

"Then what is our plan here?" Katrina leaned forward, her hands nestled against each other. "I might be completely screwed, you know. I might have to start laundering money, hiding assets, with all the capital that's coming into Obsidian. NBC did a news story on me last night, saying that there are questions about where the money is coming from. I'm sure you saw it on the news. My corporate headshot and everything."

I shook my head. "I'm sorry. I didn't see the news at all."

Alicia reached a hand across the table and patted Katrina on the leg. "But that picture of you is stunning. That purple scarf was really flattering."

I gave her a sideways look, and she corrected herself. "Yes, I'm so sorry."

Katrina shook her head and rolled her eyes before she fixed her gaze on me. "Did you see what happened to Elizabeth Holmes, with her startup? She's in prison right now. We're not doing anything fraudulent, but I don't have a way to explain any of this to normal, regular people without seeming shady or criminal. Orange jumpsuits aren't exactly my style, but what if it comes to that?" Her lips set in a firm line.

My shoulders slumped. "Oh, Katrina. I'm so sorry."

She looked at Alicia. "Tell her about you."

Alicia's hands flitted around the table. "This morning, I got a weird email, asking about Joelle. This guy wrote to say she looks like me. We called the police again."

My hand flew to my chest and I reached over and grabbed her

shoulders. "Oh my God. I'm sorry. That's awful. Is your family okay now?"

"Yeah. They're back at the hotel, in Naperville of all places." She made a face that clearly said Naperville, the epitome of sub-urbia, was the cherry on top of her shit sundae. Her hands were shaking as she patted my leg. "The price of fame."

"Why is this happening?" I said as I put a hand on Alicia's arm. I extended my other hand to Katrina. She carefully placed her fingers in my palm and then looked around at our triangle.

"I don't know, but I'm scared," Alicia said in a small voice. She looked like she was eighteen again.

Katrina tightened her grip on our hands, and I looked at her in surprise.

"We know what we have to do," she said. "Hex Madisyn, at the very least."

I tried to pull my hand away, but she held it.

"It's the only option." She looked pointedly from Alicia to me, daring us to come against her.

"It's only made things worse every time we've used the magic together, Katrina," I said. I shook my head and looked at Alicia for backup.

"What if something else goes wrong?" Alicia said. She tilted her head to the side, weighing the risks. "What if someone else gets hurt?"

"So what? We need to save ourselves, before things get worse," Katrina said.

This time, I did yank my hand out of hers.

My chest constricted, and I felt my face flush with anger. "Maybe you can dismiss what we did, but the person who suffered the most is in my family. I see her all the time. Every holiday, every birthday, every special occasion. You can forget, or pretend everything is fine, but I live with the reality of what we did every day." I noticed my voice rose with each syllable but didn't care. Let the neighbors hear. "Nancy is broken. *We* broke her. And then never told anyone it was us. And it was fine when no one asked questions. But now? Now someone is asking some really messed-up questions."

Katrina lifted an eyebrow, and I realized I had just made her case for her.

Alicia began to cry, long rivers of tears moving down her cheeks and dripping onto her shirt. "Why did the magic pick us?"

I didn't have an answer for that. We didn't seem different from everyone else. Alicia was a little quirkier, Katrina a little sharper, me as average as could be.

Alicia answered her own question. "Because our minds were open. We were willing to believe," she whispered, more to herself than anyone else.

Katrina leaned back in her chair, folding her arms across her chest. "She's right," she said, pointing a finger at Alicia and looking at me. "We embraced it, and we shouldn't be questioning it. It's a gift." She turned, arms still folded, and stared at the hydrangea border along the fence. The blooms had long been spent, turning to a dusty brown that I kept for winter interest. She closed her eyes, and before I could stop her, the plant wilted and died. It collapsed on the ground like a body with the bones removed, a desiccated corpse of a shrub.

"What the hell?" I said. Magic aside, I loved those bushes. I'd had them planted the year we moved into the house.

She held up a finger and closed her eyes again, and the bush rose to life like a zombie, moving up from the ground, brown blooms turning green, then white, and finally a blush pink. It stood out like a lone soldier, a glowing figure among the fall foliage. Then, slowly, it turned back to its original form, blooms brown and crispy but plant unharmed, as though it had never happened.

She turned to us and smiled.

"I just want everything to calm down. I'm the one who flooded my house by mistake. We need to fix it all. To see if we even *can* fix it. Can we do a spell that allows us to use our magic in small ways again? Can we focus on doing that?" I said.

Alicia nodded quickly and Katrina frowned but agreed.

"What do we need?" I asked, mentally taking inventory of household items we could use.

Alicia smiled. "Hang on." She leaned down and opened her purse, pulling out three small candles carved with sigils and a plastic sandwich bag full of crystals.

"You keep those in your purse?" Katrina asked.

"Of course," she said.

"Magical Mary Poppins." I shook my head slightly.

We quickly arranged the items and then held hands, and Alicia whispered a few words. I wanted more than anything to rip my hand away, look up at the sky, wait for another tree branch or debris to conk one of us out, but I kept my eyes closed, focusing on the spell.

I felt a wave of energy move through us, powerful as it zapped around like lightning. I held my breath, praying nothing would be destroyed around us.

So shall it be, we whispered at the end.

And then I felt the magic settle like water absorbing into dry dirt.

I cautiously opened my eyes and saw we were all okay and nothing had caught fire. We had done it. Finally.

"Should we test it with something really small?" I said. They nodded, and after magically coiling the garden hose around the spool without disaster, we were convinced.

I exhaled in relief, putting my forehead against the table.

"It worked!" Alicia said.

Katrina was silent, and I turned my head, still on the table, to the side to look at her. Her face wasn't full of relief or calm. Her eyes were bright, and her lips held a small smile.

She wanted more.

She cleared her throat and sat up a little straighter. "Now that that's done, let's focus on our bigger problems." Her eyes shone with power. "Madisyn. The hex."

She held out her palms, and Alicia lifted a hand but then hesitated, considering the repercussions.

My fingers itched to move forward, to grab their hands, end the questioning.

As I uncurled my fingers from my palm, ready to join in, a scratching at the sliding glass door caught my attention. Katy Purry was inside, furiously pawing at the glass. I couldn't hear her, but her mouth moved as she tapped the glass, trying to get my attention.

"Oh, hi there, little one. What's wrong?" Alicia said with a frown.

I stood up from the table, walked over to the sliding glass door, and opened it.

Katy Purry ran full speed toward the table, causing Katrina and Alicia to flinch, holding up their arms in defense. She jumped up on the table, stopped, and perched in between them, sternly looking at them.

"What the hell are you doing?" she growled.

Katrina paused in surprise, her hands still in front of her face. Alicia smiled and reached a hand forward to pet her.

"No," Katy Purry said with a hiss, and Alicia moved back, wounded. "Hands to yourself."

"I told you she could talk," I said.

"Well." Katrina regained her composure and relaxed her shoulders. "We're trying to make things right." She turned to me. "If we get rid of Madisyn, that's one problem solved." She pointed to me. "We can protect Nancy."

A strong wind blew across the backyard, taking some of the dried petals from the hydrangea bushes and scattering them on the table, bringing me back to the reality of what we were about to do.

"Bad idea," Katy Purry said.

She was right.

"No, I agree with my cat," I said as I sat back down at the table. "Whatever comes back to us could be far worse than what we put out there. Besides, it's not right." I folded my arms over my chest and surveyed my friends.

"We're taking advice from your cat now?" Katrina said with a laugh. "Ignore her. We know what we have to do."

"You idiots. What makes you think that's going to work? You guys have screwed up every big spell you've tried. Don't think I haven't noticed that your old spell has gone to shit," Katy Purry said. She nonchalantly closed her eyes and licked her paw. "There's no magical way out of this."

Katrina's eyes flared, and I knew Katy Purry was one more utterance away from getting kidnapped and taken to Animal Control.

"What about Nancy?" Alicia said. "We just let her take the blame?"

I thought of Nancy's being brought in for questioning, hearing rumors on the podcast about her involvement, the Reddit boards picking apart her life, saying she was a "likely suspect."

The idea that we—Katrina, Alicia, and I—would possibly be painted as innocent victims made my chest tighten. I couldn't let that happen, but there was only one normal, non-hex way to stop it.

"We could just come clean," I said quietly. "If we tell Madisyn it was us, she will leave Nancy alone. And we won't have to be afraid of the secret getting out anymore."

Alicia inhaled sharply and shook her head, and Katrina remained very still, a viper waiting to strike.

"I will do nothing of the sort," she said, her voice a brick wall.

I remained silent, my suggested solution hanging in the air between us, not dissipating.

"Warning shot fired," Katy Purry murmured as her head snapped between us.

I reached forward and grabbed her off the table, setting her down on the pool deck. "Go," I said, and pointed toward the door. I turned back to Katrina and Alicia, waiting.

In the long pause, another gust of wind swept through the backyard, lifting my hair off my neck, scattering more hydrangea petals on the table.

The part of me that had stayed quiet for twenty years, hidden the magical parts of me, tapped my shoulder. I didn't have to do this. We could try the hex, and maybe it would work. Maybe Nancy would be safe, and then we could use magic to clean up all of our messes, harness it better, with more practice.

But I was tired of hiding, tired of pretending. Tired of the guilt.

So I stayed silent, looking at my coven in a challenge.

Finally, Katrina stood. "Sarah, don't do anything you'll regret," she said before she turned to walk out. As she did, she stopped at the hydrangea bush and yanked off one of the dried blooms, letting the petals scatter to the wind like ashes. Then the rest of the bush crumpled to the ground, dead once more.

Alicia stood and patted my shoulder. "Please, think of us, your friends." She bent down and kissed my cheek before she left, brown petals swirling in her wake.

Chapter 37

Don't do anything you'll regret.

Katrina's words to me echoed in my mind as I answered work emails after she and Alicia left. I put the finishing touches on the Tobins' listing, sadness washing over my shoulders at their departure.

Travis and the kids came home to the water restoration crew working in the basement, ripping up the flooring and subflooring to let everything dry out. Harper frowned as she walked in the door, turned quickly, and shouted that she was going to her friend Taylor's house. Hunter followed, walking down the block to his friend Ben's house.

That left Travis and me.

I stared at him as he concentrated on sorting the mail, head down, thinking of how much I loved him. How he always remembered to turn on the coffee maker for me, even if he didn't want any. How he planned special nights out for us, even if we wound up at a dive bar. How he cared for his patients, the ever-loving doctor who calmed down even the most hysterical of children. How he loved his kids, almost never losing his cool, even when they were naughty toddlers.

Would you still love me if you knew what I did? I thought as I watched him pause on the electric bill, clearing his throat.

When he'd walked in the door earlier that evening, I saw on his face that the quieting spell had worked. He looked like a whole person again, one who had more thoughts in his head than those relating to me. He kissed me when he came inside, but it was a normal Travis kiss, not love-spell-gone-wrong Travis.

I quickly bridged the gap between us and pulled the mail out of his hands.

If you knew about the magic, would you still have fallen in love with me?

He looked up in surprise. I put my hands in his, spread his arms out, and then stepped into his body, my head against his chest, squeezing his waist.

"Everything will be okay," he said. "The basement will get fixed. We'll find someone to restore your wedding dress. I promise."

Oh, Travis. If only it were all that easy.

I nodded, rubbing my face against his shirt. I believed those things would be fine, yes. But not everything else.

I knew I had come to a crossroads, the edge of the cliff, and the army was behind me, pushing me forward.

I felt the words start to bubble up in my chest: *Travis, I have to tell you something. And you might hate me when you hear it.*

He squeezed me tighter, forcing the words to pop like soap bubbles. I couldn't tell him, not yet; I couldn't let him go.

And, besides, there was someone else who deserved to hear the truth first.

. . .

"Just one inch," I said as I shoved the blue and white beaded gown across the counter at George's Tailor, a week after Halloween. "By next week."

The woman behind the counter looked quickly from the dress up to me, shaking her head. She pointed to the curtains that sectioned off the dressing room. "You want to try it on? Expensive dress . . ." She trailed off.

I shook my head. "Nope. Just hem it by one inch, and I'll pick it up next week. Sound good?"

She hesitated, hand poised over the gown. I'm sure I was the first customer to waltz in, plop a designer gown on her counter, and walk off with a paper ticket in their pocket, without standing in front of the mirror while the seamstress meticulously pinned the hem.

The last thing I cared about was my dress for the gala. I had bought it online, a retired Rent the Runway dress that had already been worn by countless women. I would have been fine wearing a paper bag from Whole Foods, to be honest.

And honesty was something I was set on prioritizing from now on.

Before the gala, there was something I had to do. And then I would be ready to tell the world what we had done. Or, at least, Madisyn.

I didn't want to hurt Alicia and Katrina, but I couldn't stay quiet any longer. Especially not when my sister-in-law might end up being our unwilling shield. We had already hurt her enough.

I pulled up to Nancy's house, a small blue house with a gray roof and yellow shutters. Nancy lived a half hour west of us, in a small suburb that resembled Mayberry. The downtown had cobblestone streets with restaurants and boutiques and an actual general store. The town of Westmore was something of an oasis, surrounded by farmlands and nature preserves, as though it had been excavated from a rural part of the Midwest and dropped from a plane.

As I put the car in Park in her gravel driveway, my anxiety started to build. When I'd woken up, I hadn't planned on driving out to her house. I had planned on waiting until after the gala to talk to her.

Yet as I slowly got ready, and thought about my conversation with Katrina and Alicia, and the weight from the guilt of the past twenty years settled down around me, I decided it was time to do something about it.

I spotted her car parked under the carport, so I knew she was home.

Nancy opened the door before I could knock. She moved back in surprise, then looked down at my feet.

I bent down to scoop up the package on her front steps. "Sorry! I didn't mean to startle you."

She pushed open the storm door and held her hand out for the package. "What are you doing here?" She frowned. "Were we supposed to meet about the gala?" She pulled her phone out of her back pocket and began tapping at the screen, looking for a missed message.

I handed over the package and shook my head. "No. I was in the area and wanted to stop by and say hi."

She looked at me, confused. She glanced over her shoulder, trying to decide if she would shoo me away.

"I can't stay long," I said quickly. "I can go if it's not a good time." I felt my body lean toward the safety of my car, my anxiety whispering, *Go, leave, you don't have to do this.*

She pushed the door open wider and gestured for me to come inside.

I felt my escape route disappearing as I stepped through the doorway. I looked around the house and realized I hadn't been over in years. On the mantel, over the fireplace, were school pictures of Harper and Hunter from eighth grade, the last time I had given them to her. And she still kept them displayed, despite their being years old.

Taco, her Chihuahua, came scampering into the foyer, barking furiously. I turned my body in a protective gesture and lifted up one leg in defense.

Nancy laughed and let him bark at me for a split second longer than was polite before scooping him up.

"Shhhh," she murmured to the dog, who continued to shake and growl at me. She kept a hand on Taco's head and then looked up. "So what can I do for you?"

She certainly wasn't going to make this easy with any pleasantries, not that I deserved that.

I looked at the tan couch. "Can we sit for a moment?"

I felt, rather than heard, her exhale, but she agreed and I sat down in the dark tan armchair while she settled on the couch, Taco's watchful gaze on me.

"You just missed that podcaster woman," she said with a smirk.

I lifted my eyebrows. "Madisyn was here?"

She rolled her eyes. "Yes. She kept saying she had new information that she wanted to share, but Taco chased her off."

I smiled. "I would have paid to see that." The image of Madisyn, perfect red lipstick and long wavy hair, being chased down the street by a dog weighing no more than five pounds would have made my year.

"Well?" Nancy said, moment over.

It was time.

I sat up straighter and cleared my throat. "Well, what I have to say, in a way, relates back to Madisyn. Or, more accurately, the story she's covering." My voice gave out at the end of the sentence.

Nancy looked at me warily and leaned back a little on the couch. Taco looked up at her, and her hand on his back tightened.

"Is this about the gala?" she said. "Because I'm not attending. It's just not my scene."

"Oh, wow. Good for you. But no, this isn't about the gala."

Promise not to tell.

That's what Alicia and Katrina had begged after the fire, when we were reunited the next day at the hospital. They came to my hospital room, standing on either side of my bed, my arm in a sling at my chest, burn covered in gauze and bandages.

I promise.

I had kept that promise for twenty years. But it was time to break it. I *had* to break it in order to keep any semblance of my self-worth. Even if it landed me behind a defendant's table.

"I have to tell you something. It's about the fire, and what really happened," I whispered.

Nancy's jaw tightened, but she remained silent.

"The fire spread because of the faulty smoke alarms and detectors, that much is true. But I've never told anyone how it actually started," I said. My words felt like they were coming out of some other person, and I was floating above my body, listening.

"My friends Katrina and Alicia and I were in the basement that night, but we weren't watching a movie." Her eyebrows raised. "We were messing around," I finally choked out. Baby steps, I supposed. First tell her that it was our fault, and then about the magic. "We lit some candles and accidentally knocked one over." I spoke slowly. "It was our fault it started."

A whoosh went through me, a balloon I had kept inflated finally allowed to deflate. My shoulders slumped forward, and I put my forearms on my knees. I waited a beat and then looked up at Nancy.

She eyed me with a mixture of skepticism and disgust. "What do you mean?" she said.

I sat up again. "I mean that we started the fire. It was an accident. We tried to put it out but we couldn't, and by the time that we realized that, it was too late. We thought the alarms and sprinklers would go off, so we ran outside. And never told anyone because we were scared. I'm so sorry, Nancy. I should have told you. Told someone."

She kept her gaze fixed on me, the only sound the ticking of the grandfather clock on her wall.

Ticktock.

Ticktock.

"Your fault," she said. "All of that was your and your friends' fault." Her voice was even, but buttressed by anger and pain. Her hand on Taco tightened, and he yelped.

I looked down. "Yes. It was our fault. And I would give anything to change it. I wish—" I looked outside at a squirrel running along the fence line in her backyard. It stopped and sat back on its haunches, staring at me accusingly, its head cocked. "I wish I could change it. I wish I could have been the one who was hurt."

She laughed bitterly and shook her head.

"I know that's easy for me to say now. But it's the truth. I would give anything to wave a magic wand"—I paused at my unintentional word choice—"to make it all different."

I'd tried to.

Ticktock. Ticktock.

Nancy slowly took her hand off Taco and placed him on the ground. He whined and then settled at her feet, a tiny guard dog. She rolled up the sleeves of her shirt, so the silvery pink scars that crisscrossed her arms were visible.

Look at what you did.

"You should have told someone," she said. She faced me like a statue, unyielding.

My chest tightened and I swallowed hard, nodding. "I know. I'm sorry. Like I said, I would give—"

She held up a hand, closing her eyes and shaking her head. "Enough. No. Did you expect to come here and get forgiveness so you wouldn't have to feel guilty anymore?"

I shook my head furiously. "No, no. I—"

"Seems a little self-serving, no? You confess, I forgive you, and you can finally sleep at night kind of thing?"

She wasn't wrong.

"Whatever you feel about what happened, and the secrets you've kept, is between you and your friends. It doesn't change what happened to me," she said. Her gaze drifted over to the clock on the wall. "The fire changed everything. My entire life and all of the plans I had were—" She snapped her fingers.

"I know," I whispered. The memory of the pink-clad woman decked out in Juicy Couture whom I'd known so long ago jumped into my head.

"Not that you deserve to know this, but if I had the chance, I wouldn't go back and make things different," she said.

"What?" I whispered.

She stood, gaze still fixed on the ticking grandfather clock, watching the pendulum swing back and forth.

Ticktock.

"It burned down my whole life. My parents stopped expecting things from me—to marry some idiot that my mother met at the club, live in a big estate on the North Shore. After the fire, they stopped expecting me to have the life they mapped out." She turned to me. "Because I was lucky to have a life at all."

Tears pricked my eyes, and I quickly wiped them away.

She opened the front of the grandfather clock, reached in, and stopped the pendulum. The incessant ticking of the clock halted, and the room filled with silence. She slowly closed it.

"I'm not going to stand here and absolve you of any guilt, because that really isn't my job. But I will tell you this: the fire let me be who I wanted to be. And honestly"—she bent down and picked up Taco, clutching him to her chest—"you took over the place reserved for me."

Her words hit me quickly. I sat back and realized what she'd said was true. I had stepped in and become her mother's confidante, her father's doting daughter. All this time I'd felt guilty about it, but I'd never realized that Nancy might have her own perspective on what had happened.

She cleared her throat and shifted. "That's all you're going to get from me. I hope it helps you understand."

I nodded. "Thank you."

"If that's all . . ." She looked at the door.

"Yes." I quickly stood and wiped my eyes. I stopped on the front stoop and turned. "I'm so sorry, Nancy."

She frowned, then nodded. "I'm sure you are." Then she closed the door.

As I drove back home, I looked at my arm, my magically smooth skin. Nancy, it turned out, was far more healed than I was.

I had finally spoken the truth and told someone what we'd done. Something I'd never thought I would do.

It was time to keep talking.

Chapter 38

My fingers trembled as I scanned the email I had typed on my phone. My breath quickened as part of me whispered, *No. Don't do this.*

Yet I had to. I hit Send on the email to Madisyn.

It read:

> I've reconsidered your offer of an interview. I am willing
> to speak to you and tell you what happened. You're
> right; there's more to the story. But please, leave Nancy
> alone. It wasn't her fault. I will tell you everything, with
> one caveat: after the gala. I don't want to drag my
> in-laws and everyone there into this, and taint the event.

It would possibly be the last normal evening for a very long time.

I went inside the house and upstairs, to where Travis was taking a shower in our bathroom. Without hesitation, I opened the door. I stripped off my clothes and joined him in the shower. I pressed my body to his. The water ran down both of us, intertwined.

As the hot water fogged up the glass around us, I tried not to think about the gala, and what would come after.

☾

"Why is your dress like that? I thought you got it altered." Harper looked at me sideways, frowning, as I struggled to zip up my beaded dress in my bathroom on the afternoon of the gala.

I grunted and tried to reach behind me, red-faced and sweating. "Can't you help me?"

She waggled her fingers from the doorway. "Just painted. Sorry. Do you want me to find Dad?"

I shook my head, moving from side to side, trying to shove my body further into the dress. I had told the tailor to take one inch off, but instead of just hemming, they'd taken it in an inch on every seam, so it was at least two sizes too small.

I let out an exhale of frustration and she left, chuckling to herself. One day, if she had children, she would understand.

I looked down at Katy Purry, who was napping on my bathmat. Too bad she didn't have opposable thumbs. I desperately tried again, feeling like my shoulders were going to pull out of their sockets as I reached around, but the zipper wouldn't budge.

Might as well try, a voice inside me whispered.

Dress half on, half off, I crept over to the bathroom doorway, listening. Silence. Harper was back in her room, and Hunter was in his getting ready. I didn't know where Travis was, but last I'd heard, he was in the garage looking for shoe polish.

I tiptoed back to the center of the bathroom and looked in the mirror, turning so my back was visible. I closed my eyes and whispered a quick spell, and I felt the air being sucked out of me as the dress slowly zipped in one fluid motion, encasing me.

I opened my eyes, satisfied, and then my heart stopped.

Travis was in the doorway, watching me. A container of shoe polish in one hand, a brush in the other, and a terrified look on his face.

I opened my mouth, but only squeaking sounds came out. I was frozen in place, my dress fully zipped, arms poised in the air like a Barbie doll's.

He didn't say anything, and the container of shoe polish dropped out of his hands. Black shoe polish spilled onto the cream carpet.

"Mom! I said, let's go! The car is here," Hunter called from the bedroom. He appeared in the doorway next to his father. "Harper is already outside but she can't open the car door, because of her nail polish."

I waited for him to leave so I could at least attempt to explain to Travis what he'd seen—although I didn't know how—but my son didn't move. He looked from me to Travis.

"What?" he said as he jerked his head toward the door. "C'mon."

I wordlessly grabbed my purse off the vanity and stepped over the shoe polish stain on the floor. I would have to find the words another time, when I could arrange my thoughts.

"We can talk later," I said, and tried to smile, my mouth wavering at the corners.

He shook his head slightly, like he had been thwacked by an apple falling from a tree, and nodded. He smiled, although his eyebrows still held confusion and questions.

"It's showtime," he said, placing a hand on my back before a moment of hesitation.

As I carefully made my way down the stairs so as not to completely rip the dress, I swore I heard Katy Purry chuckling from the bathroom.

Chapter 39

All I wanted was a normal evening. A very unmagical one. Boring, even. Preferably one where my dress didn't split in half. One final picture of a regular family, before the chaos began.

As we walked up the stone path to Nichols Hall at the Chicago Botanic Garden, with Travis's hand on my elbow, I could feel the unasked questions about what he'd seen in the bathroom lurking in his eyes.

Not tonight. Please, not tonight.

Nichols Hall was decorated in swaths of gold and white, with strips of silk moving from the ridiculous crystal chandelier in the center to the perimeter of the room. It was dimly lit, the only illumination the lights on the tall centerpieces, plumes of white orchids stretching to the ceiling like they, too, wanted an escape route.

We stopped at a cocktail table, and a tuxedoed waiter appeared. Wordlessly, I grabbed a glass of champagne off the silver tray and quickly gulped it down.

"Whoa, Mom," Hunter said with a laugh.

I felt my cheeks flush as the champagne warmed my body, going straight to my head.

"Sorry," I said.

Travis lifted his own full glass in the air. "Cheers, I guess," he said, and took a sip, his gaze lingering on me for an extra second.

I knew he was still questioning what he had seen in the bathroom. I would have to find the words to explain it all to him, ready or not. To tell him who I really was. I just hadn't thought I would have to do so that soon.

"Mom, we're going to check out the appetizer table. We're starving," Harper said before she and Hunter disappeared into the crowd, leaving Travis and me alone.

I scanned the room. I saw a group of physicians from Travis's hospital and their wives. There were smaller groups of corporate-looking people—guests of the sponsors—and a more crowded group of people surrounding my in-laws. As promised, Nancy was nowhere to be found. I hoped she was at home with Taco, cuddled under a blanket and watching Animal Planet.

I prickled as I felt Travis shift next to me, hardening my body for his questions about what he'd seen in the bathroom.

"Your friends are here," he said instead.

I felt their presence before I saw them. My body began to tingle, and I knew Alicia and Katrina were close. I was about to turn to find them when Travis leaned toward his parents.

"I should go say hello," he said. "Do you want—" He stopped as he swiveled around. "Oh, hello, ladies. So glad you could join us," he said.

I didn't turn around, kept my gaze fixed forward as I saw a determined brunette trudging through the crowd, on a mission. Madisyn.

"Why don't you catch up and I'll meet you at the table?" Travis said.

I gave him a thin smile and a small nod before he left. I still wouldn't turn around. The seconds felt like hours as I kept my back rigid, my body prepared.

"You look stunning." Katrina appeared on my left, her voice silky, smooth. Confident. She wore a bright red dress that hugged her curves and matching red lipstick.

"Hi there," Alicia said to my right. She wore a gold-flecked empire-waist gown with her hair piled on top of her head, crystals sewn into the complicated updo, which resembled a waterfall. Her eyes were lined in gold, giving her the appearance of a Vegas showgirl.

"Have you thought about our conversation?" Katrina said.

I shook my head slightly, turned to Alicia, and said tightly, "Is Cressida here?"

She nodded, her chandelier earrings swinging back and forth. "She's at the bar, having them make her some complicated martini thing."

A gloved waiter moved past us, and Katrina swooped over and grabbed the tray from him. He stood in surprise, his hands still in front of him. She put the tray down on the table.

"Drink up, ladies," she said.

Without waiting for a response, she took a long sip of champagne, while Alicia gulped her glass.

I set mine down in front of me. I nervously glanced over to where Travis was encircled by my in-laws and their friends. Marcy looked over for longer than a quick glance, hopping up and down a little, her blond hair bouncing around her shoulders, and I turned to them.

"I really can't talk right now. This isn't a good time." I didn't want them to talk me out of what I had already decided, of what I knew I needed to do: tell Madisyn the truth. I started to move away from the table, when Katrina laid a finger on my arm.

"Please, just hear us out," Alicia said, eyes wide. She looked at Katrina for help.

Katrina gave her a measured look and then turned to me. "Listen, things the other morning got a little heated, and I apologize for my reaction."

I relaxed and folded my arms over my chest, eyes still darting around the room, seeking out any potential threats.

"But we do need to have a conversation," she continued, her voice raising.

"This is not the place," I hissed as I made a shushing motion, putting my finger to my lips.

Alicia spread her palms on the table for a moment before grabbing my champagne glass and downing the liquid. "Just give us five minutes. No magic, just talk."

Chapter 40

Down in the service corridor, accessed through a metal staircase clearly marked *No Guests*, I turned and faced them, crossing my arms over my chest, breathing heavily in my too-tight dress.

"All right, you guys got me down here. Go ahead," I said, and nodded.

"Please. I'm scared for Joelle and Cressida. I just want my old life back. Please don't say anything about what we did," Alicia said.

"You need to keep your mouth shut," Katrina added, taking a step toward me.

"You don't think I wish for the same thing? We tried to fix it with magic and things got worse. I will not let Nancy go down for this," I said, my breath coming out in short puffs. "We couldn't stop the fire then, but I can stop this now."

Katrina's eyes flared and she lifted her chin. "I could have stopped it."

My ears ringing, I took a step forward. "What?"

Her eyes slid between me and Alicia. "The fire. I could have stopped it back in college. Before we started that night, I did a spell to disable the fire alarms and sprinkler systems because I didn't want us to get caught while we were doing the spell."

Alicia gasped and moved a step back, putting a hand on the wall behind to steady herself. She fumbled around for flat space, her hand brushing the doorknob of a custodial closet. She looked up, thinking it was an escape route, then stopped when she saw the sign.

I took a step forward, feeling the hot flames of anger building in my chest. "If you hadn't done that, the alarms would have gone off, the sprinklers would have activated, and the fire would have been contained."

The magic inside me began to spark, begging to be released.

Katrina shook her head. "It wasn't like that. I didn't think that would happen. But—" Her eyes shone with determination as she righted her ship. "That's what happened. I never planned on telling either of you, but now you see. Now you see that we *can* control it . . . if we want to."

She looked at me, and I shook my head.

"I have to go find Cressida and get out of here. I've changed my mind. I don't want to be here," Alicia squeaked out, and fumbled around behind her, grabbing at the doorknob. In her panicked state, she forgot that it was a closet, not the door to the stairs, and wrenched it open, running through it.

"No! Alicia, don't!" It was a trap, not an escape route.

"Alicia, remember what we talked about," Katrina said firmly as she took a step toward Alicia, her shoulders square.

"Leave her alone," I said as I threw my body in between them. Alicia was weaker, would cave quickly if threatened. I hoped

Katrina remembered that I wouldn't. "You can't stop me. I'm going to come clean about everything."

"You will not," Katrina said as she continued to slowly walk toward us, as undeterred as a Redfield.

I took a quick step backward, putting my arms out to keep Alicia behind me. She whimpered and huddled against the rear wall of the closet. I took one more step back as I saw tiny flames appear at Katrina's fingertips.

We were now both in the closet, with Katrina blocking our exit. She stopped in the doorway and looked around the closet. Her features were contorted, mouth much wider than normal, eyes sunken in. The magic was eating her from the inside out.

"Please, stop," I said.

The magic inside me began to swell, ready to be put to use. But I was afraid Katrina would somehow be able to harness it for herself, use it against me. And I was afraid that it would be too powerful and we wouldn't be able to control it. Again.

We only had one way out, and the option was to fight her like a human.

I grabbed the closest weapon I could find—a push broom. I held the wooden handle out toward her like a sword, jerking it toward her midsection.

"Get back!" I jerked it again, thrusting it toward her stomach. It bounced off her and she laughed.

"A broom. Nice one. I get it," she said.

"Katrina, why are you doing this? We're friends!" Alicia shouted from behind me. "Remember dancing to Christina Aguilera?"

I paused and half turned to look at her. *Really?*

Katrina laughed meanly. "Christina was right about one thing: I'm a fighter." She took another step forward.

Alicia grabbed on to my shoulders from behind. "Make her stop," she said.

I knew what she meant. She wanted me to use the magic. I turned my head to the side and saw tears running down her face, creating black and purple rivulets that moved to her cheeks.

I had begun to exhale, to give in and allow the magic to flow toward Katrina, to use water to drown her out, when she beat me to it.

There was a spark and a flash, and the custodial closet illuminated for a moment. I felt the broom in my hands move on its own. It pulled out of my hands and stood in front of me, unassisted.

It was joined by four other brooms that slid across the floor from the perimeter of the closet, forming a wall. A line of magical soldiers, blocking our only escape route.

In that moment, I found the most unlikely inspiration: Taffy fucking Redfield. Her words as she tried to convince me to build my own shelter came scrolling across my consciousness.

Only you can save yourself.

I didn't need the magic in that moment to escape Katrina's makeshift bunker for us. I just needed to save myself.

I squared my shoulders. "C'mon." I grabbed Alicia's arm and yanked her toward me, pulling her near the wall of brooms.

They quivered as I barreled through them, squeezing my body in between the gaps, forcing Alicia to follow. I felt a jerk on the arm that pulled her and felt Alicia's hand slip out of mine.

"Forget her. Stay with me. Don't let her do this to us." Katrina's hands squeezed Alicia's shoulders, her eyes glittering with rage. She turned to me. "If you want to ruin our lives—'Oh, I have to tell Madisyn'"—her face contorted with mockery—"I will destroy yours."

Alicia gave a squeak and Katrina turned back to her. "Together, we can stop Sarah from saying anything." Her voice was like honey on a warm summer day, oozing out of the hive.

Alicia's shoulders relaxed, and my stomach clenched, insides roiling with fear.

But then, Alicia took a step back, raising her arms and knocking Katrina's hands from her shoulders.

"I'm not hurting anyone ever again," she said, her voice shaking.

Katrina's face contorted in rage, her eyes widening and her mouth pressing into a line. Then she went very still.

Not a great sign.

She darted forward and shoved Alicia with every molecule of latent anger and rage inside her body. Alicia flew backward, her head hitting the concrete wall of the basement with a sickening thud before she collapsed into a heap on the ground.

"Alicia!" I moved toward my friend. Her eyes were closed, and a trickle of blood escaped from her hair.

Katrina stepped in front of me, blocking my path.

"No," she said as she glanced down at Alicia. "She'll be fine." Alicia moaned and her eyes fluttered. "See? I didn't hurt her too badly. You're welcome."

"What? She's your friend, too. Why would you do this?" Panicked, I looked around the hallway for an escape route. Katrina blocked my exit to the staircase. The other end of the hallway was a dead end, and behind me was the custodial closet. The brooms clustered together and moved forward, forcing me to take a step toward her.

I could feel her power rising off her, like steam from a cup of coffee. Her rage fueled her magic, twisting it into something dark, evil.

My voice shaking, I said, "Katrina, leave. Don't force me to do something that I don't want to do. You can still walk away from this. You don't have to cause any more damage. It can all be over now."

I felt the magic spark inside me, a burning, a twisting.

She smiled. "Listen to it. Use it. You always were the most powerful out of the three of us. I don't know why. It's not like you deserve it. You're so . . . boring." She sighed deeply. "I mean, love? Really? How cliché."

"Don't do something that you can't undo. We can all stop. Go upstairs and pretend like nothing happened."

Although we might have to take Alicia to the hospital. The poor girl just kept getting hit over the head. She was about one head injury away from believing Earth was flat.

Her eyes fluttered again, and she gave a low moan as the blood continued to drip from her hair.

As I looked up, Katrina lunged at me. I twisted my body to the side as her nails caught my dress, tearing into the fabric. Beads scattered on the floor.

"Don't make me hex you," I said, my voice low.

Katrina's eyes widened and she stared at me, pupils glittering and hard. Panic ripped through my body before she reared her head back and screamed, a guttural sound that reverberated through the hallway. I slapped my hands over my ears but felt the scream worming its way into my brain, searching for a source to feed on.

She snapped her head back like it was on a hinge, and I saw that a small fire had started behind her. A manifestation of her rage. It quickly spread, framing her body like a backdrop. It illuminated her hair and figure, making her look as though she was on fire herself. It licked around her, flames reaching toward me.

I heard a voice behind her, coming from the service staircase.

"Hello? Oh my God, fire!"

"Help!" I screeched as Katrina threw herself toward me, grabbing on to the other side of my dress.

She had truly lost any sense of right and wrong. She was ready to hurt both of us, stop at nothing to silence us, without thinking of the consequences.

The voice coughed a few times, and then a figure appeared through a gap in the flames. Madisyn.

Of course it was Madisyn.

Chapter 41

In a navy blue satin floor-length shift, Madisyn waved a hand around in front of her face and coughed again, and then took in the scene for a moment.

"Help!" I said again.

Madisyn didn't hesitate before she reached for Katrina, trying to grab her arm to move her away from us. Katrina's nails grew two inches, sharpened at the end like tiny daggers. Before I could cry out, she slashed forward, cutting through Madisyn's satin dress and sinking the claws into her thigh.

Madisyn yelped in pain and collapsed on the ground next to Alicia. Katrina stood above her, smiling, her features contorted like a Halloween mask. A circle of fire appeared around Madisyn, trapping her.

"I hated your podcast," Katrina said. "Why couldn't you just keep your mouth shut? Now I have to help you with that."

The world moved in slow motion. I had few choices. And there was only one way to help Madisyn. I would have to go through the flames that surrounded her.

I thrust my right arm forward, through the circle of flames, toward Madisyn. I didn't feel the pain, just saw my sleeve turn black and peel away. My hand groped for Madisyn, and my body shielded her as I pulled her away, toward me, onto the floor outside the fire.

I wrapped my arms around her, hugging her head to my chest, my reddened arm protesting in pain. The skin on my right forearm looked like a rare steak that had been thrown on a grill.

I would have a scar on that arm once again. And this time, I wouldn't even attempt to erase it.

The sounds of the roaring fire and Katrina's screams punctuated the air in the corridor, the smell of burning flesh and smoke filling my lungs. Ash rained down on my face as I closed my eyes, finding my power within.

The magic was there, waiting, like a horse behind a starting gate.

Now?

Yes. I'm ready now.

As it burns, so shall it be. Only for good.

I imagined the reservoir of magic that lay deep inside me, brought forth and opened up by our spells two decades ago. Our coven had widened the pathway, poked holes in the dam that held back my true power, letting it come rushing through as something that I couldn't control.

When our coven had reunited, the water had found a weak spot to erode to come through again. Water always finds a way through, wanted or not.

But I had found a way to guide it, to dam it.

I had to believe in my own power for good, to know that I had a light inside me that could direct the magic to illuminate those dark places.

As Madisyn screamed in my arms, I pictured dipping my fingers deep into that sparkling well, pulling my hand out, and painting my body with it. I felt it hum through me, moving from my center, down to my limbs, and then out my fingers and toes.

I called the water forth, to come and extinguish the flames.

There was a hiss, and I felt drops begin to move down over me, pelting my body. I opened my eyes and water dripped down from the ceiling, where I had activated the building's sprinkler system.

It sprinkled down, fighting the flames, but it wasn't enough. The water only slightly quelled it, and Katrina smiled from across a wall of fire, her fingernail daggers illuminated in the orange glow.

She took a step toward us, over Alicia's crumpled body, hand raised in the air. Madisyn began to scream, clawing at my burned arm, sending waves of pain through my body that ricocheted up into my skull, whispering that I was going to pass out before I could stop Katrina.

Above us, I heard screaming and running, doors being thrown open from the ballroom, people scattering toward the exits, and shouts calling out *Smoke!* The flames swiftly moved toward the steps, stronger than before. It would be a matter of seconds before they reached the upstairs and made their way through the gala.

I imagined satin dresses being reduced to tattered, burned shreds. Flower arrangements igniting.

So much destruction. And for what?

Katrina was only a few feet from me, and as Madisyn continued to scream in my arms, I closed my eyes again.

So shall it be. So shall it be.

An ocean of water, effortlessly moving across the flames, waves sparkling in the sunlight. A waterfall, crashing down on everything below. A tsunami pulling sand from the beach back into the sea.

Unleash your power. Do not be afraid.

I exhaled and let go of everything I had held back, everything I was afraid of. For there was nothing to be afraid of; I was a witch, and always would be.

And soon the world would know.

I called the water forth, unleashing the dam that held it back in the arena of explainable events, releasing its power to flood the system and overtake the fire.

A scream echoed through the corridor, bouncing across the walls. Katrina stood underneath a sprinkler, which was now gushing water, the sprinkler head shooting off and bouncing down the hallway. The ceiling was raining down water, beating back the flames below.

"No!" Madisyn screamed as Katrina reached us. She brought her hand above me, water dripping down her blackened face.

Her fire may have been extinguished, but she was going to take me with her. It didn't matter that she would have no way to explain what had happened to us, no "electrical fire" excuses to tell the police.

We were snowdrifts, and she was the plow.

Logic, reason, a sense of right and wrong, had all been burned away from her decisions.

She took another step toward me, ready to tear into my skin. Yet just as she did, an object moved across the floor, and she stumbled forward. Her legs went out from under her, and she landed on the floor with a sickening thud. I looked over and saw that Alicia had slid herself across the floor and thrust her leg out to trip Katrina.

She lifted her head weakly and reached out a dark hand. I saw her face was dotted with dirt. Around her was scattered mud, a pathway through the corridor. She had called the magic forward to make her a path to stop Katrina from killing Madisyn and me.

Earth.

I pulled myself to a standing position, propping Madisyn up against the wall. Her leg was covered in blood from where Katrina had stabbed her. The water around us was taking care of the fire, and I held my burned arm against my body, my throat constricting with the pain.

I used my good arm to pull Alicia across the floor and saw tiny plants sprouting from the trail of dirt in the corridor. The botanic gardens would have some new residents.

"We have to stop her," I said to Alicia.

She wiped her forearm across her face, smearing her lips with mud. "Get outside," she sputtered.

I nodded, but before we could do anything, a loud roar came from Katrina's body on the floor. She began to army-crawl toward us, flames erupting on her back despite the sheets of water falling down on her.

I knew we only had a few moments before she regained her strength, the dark magic fueling her where nature couldn't anymore.

"C'mon," I said to Madisyn as I reached for her with my good arm. She grabbed on to it, limping, and we both pulled Alicia to standing, blood escaping from the back of her head.

We made it up the stairs by sheer force, one step at a time, pushing and pulling each other closer and closer to the safety of outside.

The last thing we heard as we reached the door was another scream from Katrina.

Come back.

Come here.

Chapter 42

Outside the ballroom was chaos, with party guests shouting and the wails of fire trucks in the distance. The building was still on fire, although the water had bought people time to escape.

The three of us collapsed on a grassy area near the entrance, next to a lone red satin shoe that someone had discarded as they ran from what was supposed to be a lovely evening instead of a horror movie.

We heard a growl come from the building, the ground beneath us shaking. Katrina was getting stronger.

Alicia said, "We have to hex her. It's the only way."

I looked at her, at the angry rivers of blood soaking her hair, and at my arm, chunks of skin hanging off.

"What about the Rule of Three?" I said.

"If we stop evil—true evil—not"—her eyes slid to Madisyn—"just do something self-serving, we should be safe."

That may have been true, but I knew we weren't strong enough to hex her. Her powers were stronger than ours now, that much was clear.

It would be like David fighting Goliath with both hands tied behind his back.

"We don't have enough power," I said.

"Air," Madisyn gasped next to me. "Earth, fire, water. You're missing air," she said, her face turning a shade of gray.

"What?" I said.

She began to pant. "I know who you guys are. I've always known. Because I'm air."

"Are you being serious? You're a witch?" I said.

Her grim expression told me she very much was.

"How did you know we . . . ?" Alicia said as her head snapped back from Madisyn to the building.

"I felt the underground magic at that site, as I'm sure you all did. That, coupled with the magical items—and what my father told me about the fire—made me realize there was more than just a natural explanation. After I started digging, it really wasn't that hard to connect it all back to you guys," she said.

"But why did you want to expose us?" Alicia said. "If you're a witch, too?"

"I just wanted you to tell me the truth," she said.

"So, you were trying to blackmail us?" My voice rose with every word.

Madisyn's face crumpled. "I guess you could say that. But really, I never thought it would have these consequences."

"'Consequences' is an understatement," I said, scanning the crowd for Travis and my children, for my in-laws, but I couldn't see anything through the haze of smoke.

"I figured you guys might try a freezing or binding spell on me, so I preempted you and did a protection spell to ward it off," she said.

Now things began to make sense.

"And the playground. I stopped you with the wind because I was afraid you were calling dark magic," she said. "I thought you might try something during the full moon, so that afternoon I scryed and saw your plans. I was watching from the trees near the playground that night."

So I hadn't hallucinated Madisyn's brown hair in the trees—she really had been there. She thought we were doing something nefarious. And yet her good intentions had led to dark outcomes. Her interference, however pure her expected consequences, had sent us all down this dark path.

"If you knew that, why were you going after Nancy?" I said, palm in the air.

She shook her head. "I wasn't really. I figured it would flush out the truth, though," she said.

I wanted to strangle her, grab her by the shoulders and throw her to the ground, just like Katrina had done to Alicia.

But I wasn't Katrina.

Despite my anger, a thought occurred to me. "If you're a witch, too, then the three of us might be strong enough to stop Katrina," I said.

There was a scream as the windows inside the building began to explode, the power of water only holding back Katrina for so long. Broken glass rained down on the crowd below as people ran and trampled each other. On the outskirts of the crowd, I saw Travis with one arm around each of our children's backs, guiding them away from the glass.

We had to stop her.

Alicia held out her hands, her palms bloody. Madisyn winced as she took Alicia's hand and reached for mine.

I swallowed hard as I first put my left hand into Alicia's and then slowly lifted my burned arm toward Madisyn, my body screaming in pain. She lightly touched my fingers, but it still sent sparks of agony through my body. I gritted my teeth as I closed my eyes and began to speak.

"We call forth the magic inside of us, to the power of air, earth, and water, to hex Katrina. We hex you, Katrina, from this day forward. You will stay away from us, lest misfortune befall you"— I felt Alicia shift at my unnatural, improvised words but continued—"and you be unable to use your magic from this day forward."

"We hex you, Katrina," Alicia whispered.

"We hex you, Katrina," Madisyn said, her voice shaking.

"We hex you," we said together.

I felt the magic rise up in my body, pulsing in my center, extending like a balloon until it burst forward into the middle of our circle. I kept my eyes closed, feeling the pull as my magic met theirs, all three melting together.

"We hex you," we said again.

I turned to Madisyn. "This is how we close out the casting: *By the power of us three, so shall it be.*"

She laughed at the corny turn of phrase but joined in.

"By the power of us three, so shall it be," we said in unison.

The heat from the fire was reaching us, and I felt the ash raining down on my arms, along with small pinpricks of shattered glass.

We continued to whisper the words through the cacophony of fire truck sirens and people shouting for loved ones. Through the sound of fire hoses drenching the building. Through the shouts for EMS workers to come help us.

I finally opened my eyes when I heard my children.

"Mom?" Harper said. "Oh my God, Mom! Your arm!"

I lifted my hands from Alicia and Madisyn's and turned toward her voice. She stood behind me with her brother and Travis behind her. From the look on her face, I knew there would be a lot of therapy in the future for her.

Travis knelt down and looked at my arm and shouted for a paramedic to come over. Alicia waved off Harper and Hunter, who went to her side. Her head wound had stopped bleeding.

I felt the weight of the magic in the circle departing our space, leaving me like a rag doll without stuffing. My vision tunneled, and my spine turned to dust. I knew I was going to pass out just before I did, and before my eyes closed and my head rested on the grass outside the circle, I looked up at the building.

The flames were gone. It was quiet.

Finally.

Chapter 43

"You're going to feel a pinch when I put the IV in, okay? Do you want me to count down?" The nurse in the emergency room looked at me, his face full of concern, gloved hands poised above my arm.

I shook my head and laughed. "After the night I've had, nothing could rattle me. Go ahead." I winced as he put the needle in, securing the line.

"Nice work, Jake," Travis said as he walked into the room, two cups of coffee in his hands. He nodded at Jake, who beamed.

"Thanks, Dr. Nelson," Jake said as he stood. He looked down at me. "Do you need anything? Someone should be in shortly."

I accepted the coffee cup procured from the cafeteria by Travis and lifted it in the air. "Just this. Thanks."

I shifted on the bed, the seams of my dress digging into my sides. I'd woken up in the ambulance, Travis at my side. I'd tried to protest that they should have saved it for someone else, but thankfully they told us that there weren't any other injuries.

Minus Alicia's head injury and Madisyn's clawed leg.

It was just the witches who were hurt this time.

"You doing okay?" Travis said as he pecked at the room's computer, looking up my chart. We were at Forest Hills Hospital, so I was getting the royal treatment from the staff. Which really only meant that I was offered a few extra cups of water while waiting to be seen.

I nodded and carefully shifted my arm, gently moving the plastic tubing of the IV up on the bed so it didn't pull.

He looked over and down at the bandage on my burn. "Does it hurt?"

"A little, but not bad."

Physically, I would be fine. Emotionally and mentally, it would take a while to process everything. The fact that Katrina had turned on us out of desperation to keep our secrets was something I would be thinking about for a long, long time. And the fact that Madisyn had known all along, and had powers herself.

I didn't know what any of it meant, or should mean, but I knew that for now, I was safe, and my family was safe. Marcy and Thomas had taken Harper and Hunter back to their house while Travis came with me to the hospital. He told me that Marcy had screamed for "medical personnel," even though an EMS worker was already helping. Travis had finally sent her away with his dad and our kids, whispering to give her a stiff drink when they got home.

I set the paper coffee cup down on the table next to the bed and looked at the bandage. "I'm going to have a scar again," I said quietly. I looked up and saw that Travis was gazing at me strangely. He got up from the stool at the desk and slowly walked over. He sat down in the chair at the edge of the bed and took my good hand.

He ran his thumb over the back of my hand before he looked

up. "Do you think you'll heal this one, too?" His voice was barely above a whisper.

My hand stiffened as he held it. "What do you mean?" The room suddenly felt overbearingly hot, and I started to kick off the blankets that covered my legs.

He smiled and reached down to move the blankets off the bed. "Heal this one. Like you did the other one?"

He stared at me, and I looked right back. A silent conversation between us passed. I studied the face of the person from whom I had desperately tried to hide the darkest part of myself. A face that I had been terrified would reject me if he found out I was a witch. Yet it had all been for naught.

He knew. I didn't know how, but he knew.

He shifted, placing my hand on the bed and clasping his together in front of his legs. "Look, Sarah, you can trust me. I know about all of it."

My vision started to tunnel and sweat pricked my scalp.

"How?" I croaked out.

He looked down and smiled. "I've known for a long time. Years, in fact. I saw you clean the kitchen countertops, the sponge moving on its own one day. I thought I was seeing things, but I heard you whispering. I figured I had imagined it, but then I saw things just like that a few other times." He laughed. "The turkey in the basement, for one. Plus, I've overheard Katy Purry talking, of course."

And here I thought I had been so sneaky, so smart in my secret magic. All those years. And he knew.

"You . . . knew?" was all I managed to say. He nodded. "Then why didn't you ever ask me about it?"

He sat back and ran a hand through his hair. "I figured you'd tell me when you were ready." He cracked a lopsided smile.

I slumped forward and forgot about my injury, lifting my hands to my face. Pain shot through my arm and I winced. I looked at the bandage again.

"So now you know," I said, my eyes still on the wound.

But he didn't know all of it.

"There's something else," I said steadily, unable to look him in the eye.

"More than you being a witch?" he whispered, laughing. "Oh wait, you're serious?"

I looked up and nodded. I needed to say it before I lost my nerve.

So I did. I told him about the night of the fire in college, how I cast a spell for love. How Alicia, Katrina, and I were the ones responsible—accidental or not, although Katrina's culpability had been greater than I thought—for Nancy's being hurt, and that we had been trying to cover our tracks for two decades.

He didn't say anything for a long time, just sat back and stared at a fixed point on the wall above my head.

"Please don't hate me." My voice was very small, weak.

Travis finally met my eyes. He leaned forward and slowly took my good hand and exhaled. "Never." Then he brought my hand to his lips and kissed it. "It's not the magic that made me fall in love with you, Sarah. Maybe it turned my head at first. But I stayed in love with you. *Despite* it."

Relief flooded through my body, and I leaned toward him. Twenty years of secrets and denials and hiding had finally been released, at least with the person who mattered the most.

"Travis, I—" I started to say, tears welling up, when a doctor in a white coat walked through the door.

"Nelsons! Good to see you! Well, not good considering the circumstances, but you know what I mean." It was Dr. Parsons, a seventysomething emergency room doctor with an obscene golf handicap and twenty-seven-year-old third wife.

Travis stood and shook his hand, and they exchanged a few doctor-speak notes.

"Not to worry. We'll get her fixed up just right. Like it never happened," Dr. Parsons said. He looked at me and smiled. "Just like magic."

There was a pause, and Travis and I looked at each other and couldn't help but laugh.

Magic, indeed.

Epilogue

FIVE WEEKS LATER

Snow blanketed my front lawn, the crystalline surface smooth and sparkling in the moonlight. It was one sheet of white with specks of silver in it, unbroken by footsteps. We were only supposed to get three inches, but the snowfall had turned into a foot over the course of the day. Mounds of snow covered the bushes filled with Christmas lights outside, making them look like ice cream cones. Evergreen garlands decorated the front porch of my house, red bows at each point. In my family room, the lights were turned off, only the multicolored lights from the Christmas tree illuminating the room.

There was magic in the air, but this time, it didn't come from me.

Travis tucked an arm around my shoulders on the couch, and I settled back into the cozy nook between his neck and chest.

Katy Purry was curled up on the rug at our feet, occasionally opening one eye and whispering, "Temptations?"

It had taken Travis a few beats to get used to the cat openly talking in front of him, but to his credit, he had.

I thought, after our hex on Katrina, everything would go back to the way it had been before I reunited with her and Alicia.

It hadn't. So Katy Purry still had a voice, although she didn't, thankfully, use it around Harper or Hunter or the Amazon delivery driver.

I still felt the magic every day and used it when appropriate. Like that morning when I couldn't find my car keys. (In the kitchen cabinet, of all places.) What mattered was the fact that I embraced it and didn't feel like it was my dirty little secret anymore.

The week before, I had heard Katy Purry and Travis in the bedroom, discussing how tired I looked and whether I should be getting more rest.

And here I thought she was *my* familiar.

I rolled my eyes but obediently bent down and gave her a scritch between her ears.

"What do you want to watch?" Travis said as he absentmindedly flipped through the guide on the television.

"A bad Hallmark holiday movie, please," I said as I took a sip from the wine in my hand.

He laughed and rolled his eyes but obliged. "*The Christmas Kitty*," he said. "'A woman finds the love of her life with the help of a stray cat that appears out of nowhere, harboring the spirit of Christmas.'" He shook his head. "Sounds believable. What do you think, Katy Purry?"

Her head popped up in interest; she was ready to watch.

I'd spent time in the burn ward, wrapped in gauze and medical tape, skin being grafted from my leg to cover my arm. My right thigh had shiny marks where they had taken skin—an almost literal pound of flesh. But my arm had been saved. It was still there, but different.

This scar was much larger than the first one, wrapping around my forearm in angry red streaks. Every morning, my arm throbbed and burned to the point where I felt like it was still on fire. But it was just skin, just a scar. I hadn't lost anything—anyone—that I truly cared about.

I don't think any of us had really bothered to try to explain it all, make sense of what happened, although Madisyn and Alicia were certainly trying. They'd FaceTimed me two weeks ago, giddy with excitement. The call popped up as I was wrestling with the evergreen wreath on the front door, the bow refusing to stay flat until I used a little magic to make it stand at attention.

"You'll never guess what we're doing," Alicia had said, screen too close to her flushed face. "You won't."

Madisyn nodded furiously, seated in her bedroom. "What do you think when I say *podcast*?"

My eyes went wide and I shook my head. "I think: *Please, God, no.*"

They both laughed. "Ha. Sorry, had to. But seriously, another podcast. We are going to start one together, the two of us. Tentatively titled *Spell the Tea*, about real-world occult and magic things," she said.

Alicia smiled wistfully, the screen still too close to her face so her eyes were cut off. "After that night, I want some time out of the spotlight, to be in control of my own destiny. Behind the scenes, I think, can be just as fun."

"Oh, Alicia, that's wonderful. I'm so happy for you," I said. My chest tightened with joy for her. My eyes flicked to Madisyn. "And you'll get to tell some new, juicy stories."

She twisted her mouth to the side. "I do have a knack for flushing out the good ones."

Despite what had happened at the gala, my in-laws still moved forward with the scholarship. In a rare moment of clarity, Marcy had declared the money should benefit an animal science student in honor of Nancy.

The fire that night, and the mirroring of the inciting event at Hawthorne Hall, did not go unnoticed by the media. In fact, the "strange timing" received widespread, national media coverage, and donors came out of the woodwork to give money to the fund. It was like something out of *Stranger Things*, where mysterious events were happening all around people, and no one was questioning it. I guessed the bonus was that three college kids would get full rides next year, portal to another world aside.

Nancy had just adopted another Chihuahua, Brutus, and he hated every other human more than Taco, which I didn't even know was possible.

She'd sent me a text the day before with a picture of Brutus and Taco snuggled together on the couch. It didn't have a caption or follow-up text, nor did she respond to my reply. But it made me cry. It was her way of reaching out, letting me know that there might be a reason to have hope we could someday be friends.

She was also gearing up for a capital campaign to expand the wildlife center, and I was on the committee. I had already secured a hefty donation from the Johnstons for the enclosure for the raccoons, who were more than pleased with their new home.

The Redfields had also already made a significant pledge, but only after I sat through a PowerPoint presentation on solar lanterns. Their donation would be put toward a new turtle habitat: the TNT Turtle Sanctuary. Marcy and Thomas had the rabbits— after Nancy declined Marcy's request to name their habitat the Bunny Ranch. Travis and I were funding a new enclosure for Tom and Jerry, the unstable blue jays, with the hope that a new environment would help them chill a bit.

"Another glass?" Travis pointed to my empty wineglass in my hand, snapping me back into my yuletide family room.

I nodded and handed him my glass, and he extricated himself from beneath me on the couch. *The Christmas Kitty* went to a commercial, something about a Medicare Part B plan, so I grabbed the remote and absentmindedly flipped to a local news station.

My eyes landed on the fireplace across the room. A roaring fire would be the perfect complement to this snowy evening. I sighed happily as I stood to turn on the fireplace.

I stopped to soak in the moment. I had faced the past, and I hadn't broken. The people I loved the most had stood with me.

As my finger flipped the fireplace switch, a breaking news alert came on the television. Before I heard the newscaster speak, my body was at full attention, the hair on my neck standing up. Like a magnet drawn to metal. Involuntary.

"Entrepreneur Katrina Andrews, founder of medical device startup Obsidian, will be taking her company public next week. The announcement comes after whispers of an offering, with an influx of orders this fall," the newscaster said.

My finger still on the switch, my body turned cold as I watched the footage of Katrina standing in front of a podium, the

Obsidian logo behind her. She wore a black suit, red heels, and red lipstick, her hair pulled back in a twist.

We'd never told anyone about what she had done that night, figuring the hex was punishment enough.

My body began to shake as she looked directly into the camera. My breath quickened, and the new burn scar on my arm ached again.

Katrina's pupils dilated. "We always knew this day would come for Obsidian. I could not be more proud of those who have stood beside me through this journey, and my apologies and condolences to those who didn't." She laughed, as did the room around her.

As she said the words, the flames in my fireplace began to reach outward, like fiery hands grasping for my body.

I snapped out of the trance and scrambled back, away from the fire. Katy Purry was at my feet, back arched, a low growl emanating from her terrified throat.

I squared my shoulders and brought forth the magic, narrowing my eyes and commanding the flames to stand down, go away, get out of the house. Katy Purry hissed, an exclamation point at the end of the magical order.

The flames receded as quickly as if I'd turned the burner down on the stove.

As I slowly sat, my attention was drawn to the front bay window. I saw the headlights of a car, stopped in front of my house. Harper got out of the car, being dropped home after a late cheer practice. She was bundled in her winter coat, the hood up to keep the snow out of her hair. Her cheer duffel bag was slung across her shoulder.

She waved to her friend and then shut the car door before trudging up the walkway, head down. I smiled and began to stand up to greet her at the front door.

Yet I stopped, half crouched, when I saw her halt abruptly on the walkway, which we hadn't shoveled yet, as the snow was still coming down. She glanced over her shoulder to make sure her ride had left. Then she removed the hood from her head, so I could see her face. She closed her eyes for a moment and squared her shoulders before taking a deep breath and exhaling from her mouth. She then looked down at the snow-covered path.

Small sparks of light appeared on the pathway, turning into tiny flames and melting away the snow. I saw the layer of snow become smaller and smaller, moving down toward the ground. The flames fizzled out once the snow was gone from the pavers, a perfectly cleared walkway up to the house.

She smiled proudly and began walking toward the door again, nearly skipping with glee at what she had done.

My body felt like it was frozen in time, like I was watching myself twenty years ago, using the magic to assist me, smile on my face, not knowing the consequences of what I was doing. My legs shaking, I stood up straight, my feet rooted to the floor, as she opened the door. My burned arm started throbbing, and I put my hand on the scar, pressing down, to stop the pain.

"Oh hi, Mom!" she said as she shook some snow off her pony-tail. Her smile faded when she saw my expression. "What?"

My mouth was open but words escaped me.

She stared at me for a moment, confused, before her face changed. She stood up straighter and pressed her lips together.

Then she nodded slightly. She understood that I had seen what she'd done.

She, too, had the magic.

Then she winked and laughed. "Don't look like that. I'll be careful," she said before she turned and walked into the kitchen to say hi to her father. I heard her greeting him, her voice coming out like soap bubbles popping, telling him about the new stunt they'd learned in cheer practice. I heard her bound up the stairs to her room, taking the steps two at a time.

I walked into the foyer and looked up the stairs, staring at her closed door.

It was time to tell her the truth. I wanted to protect everyone from the magic, and I'd always thought the best way to do that was not to tell my family, or anyone, and keep it a secret.

I was wrong.

And if Katrina decided to enact revenge for the hex, we would need as much power as possible. Madisyn, Alicia, and I were strong, but we didn't have the power of fire. Harper, it seemed, did. How she had harnessed it, or why, I didn't know. She could have been the strongest out of all of us. The rest of us had cultivated our magic, found shortcuts to access the powers. But if she had been born with the magic, she was already far ahead of us.

I heard Travis still puttering around in the kitchen, muttering to himself about a broken wine opener.

I slowly walked up the steps to my daughter's door, knocking on it lightly. When she told me to come in, I opened it carefully and stepped into her room.

It was time. Now that I had reconciled my past, it was time to look to the future, and to pass down my lessons to my daughter.

I would show her how to embrace her power and be who she wanted to be, to work for the greater good and to never hide who she really was.

She would be a Bad Ass Witch, as we all were, talking cat included.

Our time was now.

Acknowledgments

Growing up, books, movies, and TV shows featuring witches and witchcraft enthralled me. I was fortunate to come of age in the era of movies like *The Craft* and shows such as *Charmed*, showcasing the power and magical potential when women come together. So when the opportunity arose to write a book about witches, it didn't take a spell to start drafting. Despite that, I can't say I didn't at times wish I had a few magical words to write a chapter or two. I had the best time bringing this story to the page and exploring the concept of wish fulfillment as a suburban mom. (As opposed to *Suburban Hell*—no wishes for a demon in my neighborhood, unless it's me and I just haven't figured that out yet.)

That said, there are so many people I need to thank for their guidance, love, and support while I was writing this book.

To Ryan, Paige, and Jake—thank you for dealing with a mom whose brain is in another world half of the time. You guys inspire me every day to be a better human. Please keep saying and doing hilarious, amazing things every day.

And to Kevin—thank you for not calling the authorities when you saw the huge stack of black magic research books on my desk as I brainstormed this book. I'm glad the love spell I did on you more than twenty years ago worked.

Thank you to Holly Root, agent extraordinaire. Over the past decade plus, you've weathered many ups and downs in my career with me, and I'm so lucky to have a (calm, cool, collected) agent in my literary lifeboat. I think we qualify for a common-law literary agent marriage at this point.

To my editor, Kate Dresser—I am forever grateful for your wise words and editorial guidance. Working with you is such a joy, and I'm continuously amazed at your ability to make me laugh while giving tough edits. Go Fighting Irish! And thank you to Tarini Sipahimalani for your detail-oriented editorial support, which has saved me more times than you know—you are a gem! Elora Weil, Shina Patel, Alexis Welby, Sally Kim, and Ashley McClay, thank you for all that you did and continue to do for my books, and for helping connect readers with my work. Everyone at Putnam is such a joy to work with, and I'm beyond grateful to have landed at such an amazing place. You guys are what's right and good with this industry.

The KL crew and extended families—thank you for always making me laugh, and for the memories I will continue to exploit in my books. Sorry/not sorry. Love you guys!

The Leurck family—thank you for all of your love and support throughout the years. I'm so fortunate to have such an amazing bonus family.

To my friends—thank you for your unwavering support, and for always giving me new material to shamelessly exploit for my books. And thank you for not murdering me when I had to cancel last-minute plans due to being on deadline for this book. I want all of you in my Bad Ass Witches coven. Next girls' night? And thank you to my author friends, especially Jillian Cantor, who have supported me (usually involving panicked emails and/or texts) and told me over and over not to stress or worry. No way would I have lasted more than a minute in this world without your friendship.

To all the readers, reviewers, booksellers, and Bookstagrammers who have supported me—it's been such a wild, fun ride to enter horrorlandia, and thank you all for being the most gracious welcoming crew into this wonderful genre. I am forever grateful for every note, message, word of encouragement, and post. I hope to keep making books that both scare you and make you laugh for a long, long time.

Discussion Guide

1. During the night of the dormitory fire, Katrina, Alicia, and Sarah make three distinct wishes. What is so tempting about each of their desires? Which one did you relate to most?

2. As witches, Katrina, Alicia, and Sarah have access to power that's inaccessible to others. Still, they must blend in with those with less power. What would you use magic for, if you had the ability? Name three chores you'd never do yourself again and compare to see which chores are most loathed in your group.

3. Discuss the role of fire in the story, as well as the other elements, and how each contributes to the magic.

4. College often signals a pivotal life inflection point—discovering who you are and who you want to be, and figuring out the steps to get there. In what ways do the three witches' paths dictated by the ritual-gone-wrong depict or defy this? How much of their lives reflect the idea behind self-fulfilling prophecies?

5. Katy Purry steals the show with some great catitude. How would you react if your pet suddenly started talking to you? What would *their* initial reaction be? Share your favorite Katy Purry moment.

6. Given Sarah's desire to keep her magic a secret, to what extent can we think of secret keeping as self-sacrifice versus self-preservation?

7. Ask and you shall receive, at least if you're Sarah, whose greatest desire was realized with her sweet and loyal husband, Travis. Still, he too is kept in the dark for most of the book. What role does honesty play in Sarah's character arc?

8. Seated around a cluster of candles, adorned with select crystals, the witches call out to the elements in perfect synchronicity. If you could create your own spell, what would its purpose be? In groups of three, brainstorm your concoction of ingredients and recite your incantation.

9. How did the scandal surrounding the Tobin family affect Sarah's willingness to come clean about what happened in the fire and her magical abilities?

10. Nancy's presence looms large for Sarah throughout the book. How did Nancy rise from the tragedy? To what extent is the strength of her presence a result of her association with the tragedy versus who she is at her core?

About the Author

Photograph of the author © Meagan Shuptar 2021

Maureen Kilmer graduated from Miami University in Oxford, Ohio, and lives in the Chicago suburbs with her husband and three children. She thankfully has not had to battle the forces of darkness (unless going to Costco on a Saturday counts). She is also the author of *Suburban Hell*, her horror debut.

MaureenKilmer.com
🐦 MaureenKilmer
📷 AuthorMaureen